THE UNFORTUNATE GIFT

KENT SMITH

ISBN: 978-0-578-89789-9 (paperback)
Library of Congress Control Number: 2021906761

Published by KSmithBooks.com
290 E John Carpenter Frwy, #2700
Irving, TX 75062

Edited by Magnifico Manuscripts, LLC
www.magnificomanuscripts.com

Cover and InteriorDesign/Layout by MINDtheMARGINS, LLC
www.mindthemargins.com

Printed in the United States.

*To my mother, who forged the way by being
an author and a voracious reader.*

To my wife, the ultimate instrument of encouragement.

*To my four daughters, Amber, Makenzie, Madison
and Danielle, my unwavering cheerleaders.*

PROLOGUE

Off the Fajardian Coast of Puerto Rico, 1774

Omelia was going down for her fourth and last dive of the day, but something . . . someone . . . was telling her not to go. Was it the tug of her father's admonitions or her underwater caretaker, Vastriel, beseeching her to go home? Or were her ancestors, the Taíno free divers, warning her of danger? Whoever or whatever it was, she was Omelia, dive queen of San Juan Bay, and she felt no fear. She took a deep breath, brought her arms up in a swoosh to propel herself downward, then flipped and swam to the bottom, thirty-five feet below the surface.

Hiding behind a staghorn coral was the most beautiful starfish she had ever seen. *I knew this would be my best dive.* She carefully lifted the elegant but bewitching echinoderm and headed toward the surface. She did not see the Portuguese Man-O-War floating above as she raced to the surface. Its tentacles enveloped her as she ascended.

Holding tight to her prize, she fought her way out and surfaced, taking lusty gulps of air as her chest screamed for relief from the pressure. Not until her heart rate had calmed and her respirations had normalized did she feel the sting on her wrist. She held it out of the water to see it in the sunlight and shivered in the warm Caribbean water. The sting left the shape of a star-fish on her wrist.

CHAPTER 1

1886

Harlan Bell arrived at the front door of BMP International. Making sure his boots would not bring traces of dirt into the establishment, he wiped the bottoms of both feet with a handkerchief and entered. He approached a welcome desk and was blocked by a large man, towering about a meter above him.

"May I ask what business you have with BMP?"

"Yes, I have a telegraph from Captain Baird." He pulled the paper from his pocket, realizing it had torn, then held it out for the large man with *Nuñez* sewn into his jacket. "He asked me to pick up the package for the *Widower's* voyage to the Caribbean Islands in a fortnight."

"Baird sent you?" Nuñez asked, disgustedly.

"I am his boatswain, and he has a bad case of winter fever. We're hoping he recovers in time for the trip."

At this, the large man pivoted and walked toward an ornate door, opened it, ducked, entered, and closed the door. Soon, a matronly but well-dressed woman with white hair pulled back in a bun walked through the door, holding an unimpressive wooden box.

"Mr. Bell, I am entrusting this to your care, but you must sign this affidavit stating you are who you say you are and that your intention is to transport it to Señor Baird." Not knowing what an affidavit was, he took the board on which the paper rested and signed "HB."

"That's your signature?"

"Yes ma'am. I can't write my whole name." He looked the part. Predictably unshaven, he had leathery skin from years in the sun and a set of linear scars that traversed both cheeks in a pattern that left him with a permanent half-moon grin.

"I also need the address where we can reach you if needed." She extended the board again.

"Uh, I can't write, but I'm sure you can. I'm at the Alcon Apartamentos on Adolpho and Mierno in Gijon."

"Very well." She wrote the address down. "I will be following up with Señor Baird in one day's time to ensure the contents have reached him safely. If not, we know where to find you. Señor Nuñez here is quite capable."

Harlan headed to the villa owned by Baird, and on his way, he inspected the box. It had a seal over the latch with the BMP symbol impressed into wax. Frustrated with not being able to see the contents, he wondered aloud, "Not heavy enough to be gold. Could it be a gold crown or a treasure map? He flipped it over to find a painted picture of a uniquely designed gold chest. His sainted mother had a chest that closely resembled the one in the painting.

Harlan's chance materialized. He assumed the painting depicted what was inside the box. Its destination was the commanding general's palace in the capital of Chan Santa Cruz. He crossed his fingers, hoping Baird would break the seal to inspect the contents. Harlan lifted the chest to his nose and farted for good luck.

The high decibel snoring from the room was so rhythmic that he knew the timing had to be right. Harlan's hunt for a vial of belladonna proved unfruitful until the night before they set sail and slipping the solution into the guard's rum keg when he relieved himself in the head proved easier than expected. The door was not locked, but he found the door key on a shelf in the cabin and slid it into his pocket.

With the sudden onset of the storm, navigation through the ship was not easy. Holding on to some unevenly canted planks in the floor, he crawled to his own cabin, lifted the mattress, and extricated his mother's small gold chest. The ship tilted and heaved in tortuous patterns.

With difficulty, he was able to edge through the unlocked door and slide a wood chip under the door to prevent it from slamming back and forth.

He managed to replace the mysterious coffer with his mother's chest, hide the real chest in his breeches, and crawl out of the cabin without the guard waking. He threw on a waterproof trench coat hanging by the ladder to help conceal the bulge.

"This was too easy," he muttered, stumbling to the ladder. Harlan tentatively navigated his way up to the deck, just as a river of water sloshed across his torso. The sky had blackened by now, broken apart by a few stars peeking through unseen clouds and a hazy, marginless moon. Harlan managed to slide upright across the deck to a spot where he knew Baird would see him.

"Bell, what the hell are you doing?" Baird bellowed. "Get portside and see that the squalls aren't tearing up the mainsail and try not to show your incompetence!"

Without a response, Harlan headed toward the back of the boat as he held on to the railing to steady himself. The sea was angry, and he wanted no part of its wrath. When he rounded the wheelhouse and angled toward the mainsail, he felt a smashing blow to the side of his head and tumbled toward his left, momentarily losing his bearings. Reaching for what he thought was the side of the boat, his hands grasped the sail boom and with a sudden wind shift, he was catapulted headlong into the torrid sea.

He tried yelling for help, but the saltwater rushed into his mouth, choking his words. "I can't swim! I can't die now!" But the ocean did not have ears.

A shroud of frigid water enveloped his body and thoughts, the cold shocking the blood in his veins. He took one final look at the *Widower*, praying someone would notice his disappearance. His ability to stay afloat waned with each effort, and the saltwater slowly filled his lungs. As Harlan drew his last breath, he had no consideration for what sank with him.

CHAPTER 2

2019

"Wake up, Reagan. I can see the shore and we'll be landing soon."

"OK, Mom." Reagan stretched and rummaged for her cell phone, an opened mystery novel by Baldacci slipping to the floor. "Hey, it's not weird that I was dreaming about Shane, right?"

"Well, it depends on the dream."

Twenty-one-year-old Reagan Prefontaine had recently broken up with her boyfriend of ten weeks, and a relaxing vacation in Tulum would be the synapse between Shane and the next chapter of her life. A recent graduate of Texas A&M, she considered taking a year off to travel and find out who Reagan really was, out from underneath the membrane of parental oversight. This trip would provide her an opportunity to judge that option, even with her parents joining her.

"When did you say Dad would be coming?" She located her phone between the seats and powered it on.

"I made his flight for one week from today, so he'd better make it. Honestly, I'm going to enjoy this week for more reasons than being with you and seeing your brother. Your father started snoring more lately, and I'm going to enjoy the quiet."

"What's this sabbatical backpacking trip all about . . . a mid-life crisis?"

"Nope. Just wanted to go off the grid . . . no phones, no computers, no people walking into his office unannounced. He misses the early years of backpacking in the Weminuche Wilderness. With us gone for two weeks, it was the best chance to get away from the Pentagon and just think . . . or not think. Trust me. He needs it."

Reagan stretched. "Well, I hope he comes home safe. The bear habitat in that wilderness has grown by two percent each year for the last seven years and attacks have increased by forty-five percent in the last five years."

Reagan's recall—hyperthymesia—troubled her mother because Reagan never forgot a single parental misstep or an unpleasant event in her past. She needed to stay active to prevent neuroses, but that presented no problem.

"Your father will be fine. Once an Eagle Scout, always an Eagle Scout."

"I'll still worry. Hey, when do we get cell service here?"

"I paid a monthly fee for us to have free roaming, so as soon as we land, you can text Shane."

Reagan rolled her eyes, then pointed out the window. "Those hues of turquoise and blue. They're so beautiful. We have to go to the dive shop after we check into our villa. I don't want to miss the chance of diving in the morning."

Reagan prioritized her list of things to do. First: Scuba dive every day. Second: See the ruins. Third: Watch her brother play baseball. Fourth: Read fiction novels. These would help erase Shane from her life. Shane had become possessive of her . . . something unacceptable.

After a lengthy delay, blamed on the step assembly not being placed close enough to the plane on the first effort, Reagan and Shelly grabbed their matching carry-ons and hurried down the steps into the bright and unforgiving sunshine of Mexico. Reagan hastily pulled back her shoulder-length hair into a high ponytail and switched out her glasses for sunglasses.

"I'm pretending I'm the First Lady visiting Mexico for the first time." She waved to imaginary admirers on both sides, drawing stares from the soldiers who looked like they were ready for an insurrection.

Shelly waved and smiled. "I'll be the president. Not sure my oxford shoes, baggy capri pants, and Hawaiian shirt impresses anyone."

Although Shelly could have, and often had, shown off a figure that belied her age, on this trip, she was not out to impress anyone. Her career for twenty years had been in nursing, and she learned early on that if she didn't disguise her figure, the physicians on staff, married or not, would not appreciate her brain as much as her shape.

Entering the customs area, Reagan said, "You'd think they'd let the First Family skip to the front." Finding the shortest immigration line, they got the stamp of approval from the smiling and toothless officer and headed for their baggage at Carousel Four. A smiling man wearing a Mariano name tag helped them get their bags from the "luggage nursery," as Reagan called it, and they headed for the exit, wading through a few salespeople attempting to draw them to their booth.

"Are you the Prefontaines?"

"Yes, we are."

"Great. Follow me. I am Hector." He took their bags and headed up the crowded platform to a van parked among many other similar transportation vehicles.

They navigated between the crowds of people. The smell of palm trees mixed with the grill close by gave Reagan goosebumps. "It's going to be an amazing two weeks!"

"It will take about ninety minutes to get to the Villa Sueno del Mar. Would you like some water?"

"Thank you," replied Shelly, reaching for two bottles with a Bonafont label. "I'd rather have a margarita, but this will do for now."

"Very soon, madam, very soon. There will be one waiting for you at the villa."

On their way to Tulum, Reagan noticed cars parked along the road, usually in front of an establishment with some derivative of the name Gonzo adorning the sign. "Hector, what's with all the names with Gonzo in them, like La Gonzo Restaurante and Banca Gonzo? Is he someone important?"

"That depends on your definition. He strong-arms owners into changing the name of their business. My cousin told me his men came by last year and said they would keep him safe if he changed the name of his clothing store from Juanita's Threads to Gonzo's Threads." Hector spit into the floorboard to telegraph his opinion. "That store has been in the family for eighty years."

"Mafia, I guess?" Shelly asked.

"Si. Hetacalín cartel. Are you ladies here to meet the cartel?" Hector grinned into the rearview mirror.

"Not this time around," replied Shelly. "My son plays baseball for the Tigers . . . they call them the Tigres here—"

"Si! I am a Tigres fan, but they're playing out of town today in Campeche."

"Yes, he told us . . . might be late tonight before they get in, but we'll be scuba diving this week. Gives us time to get that set up."

"Hetacalín runs most of the scuba dive outfits here, but I hear they treat everyone well . . . not to worry, ladies!"

Knowing this conversation made her mother uneasy, Reagan changed the subject. "Mom, do you know what Tulum stands for?"

"No, tell me. I love having you along as a travel guide."

"It's the Mayan word for 'wall.' It was built in the tenth century, but it took a few hundred years for the Mayans to fully appreciate what they had. Once the Spanish started occupying Mexico, it was completely abandoned within seventy years. So sad. The ruins are close to our villa, so let's see them for sure."

"Sounds great." Shelly's great-great-grandmother married a Mayan following a missionary stint in El Salvador, and she planned to see a small piece of her heritage.

Hector took a U-turn and maneuvered onto a road headed toward the sea. After a few minutes, they went through a security gate and drove to Villa Sueno del Mar.

"I love the name of our villa," Reagan said. "Dream of the Sea."

The palm tree-guarded Villa Sueno del Mar stood before them. Curving stone staircases flanked both sides, winding their way to the second floor. The pristinely manicured landscaping included ivy climbing the walls. The adobe exterior was painted a sunglow yellow, and the roof had more than a dozen levels. A man dressed in white clutched a white clipboard and came out to greet them.

"Hola, Prefontaines! I am Eduardo, and I am here to make sure everything goes right for you." Eduardo's short-sleeved shirt had LaCaste Villas stitched in green above his left pocket.

"You have AC in your bedrooms and in the living room and kitchen. We have two golf cars for you to use. You can get to most places on these, which should be helpful since you did not rent a car. As you can see, there is a pool, a jacuzzi, and a beautiful beach. The barbeque grill is electric."

Shelly hurried to the glass door at the rear of the villa, slid it open, and walked to the edge of the pool. "People have free access to our beach, I see. Do we need to keep all doors locked?"

"You can if you wish, madam, but you noticed the security gate you went through?"

"Yes."

"The area is heavily patrolled. I have not heard of any evil here in many years. I've been here eight years and manage several other properties in this bay."

Shelly and Carlisle had spent thirty years together and he taught her to be prepared for anything and to remain vigilant. His years of work in the Bureau of Labor Statistics and later as the chief statistician for the FBI earned him a level of paranoia. He knew the real numbers relating to corruption, transgressions, and overall lawlessness. Shelly decided she would lock her doors.

"Mom, let's unpack later. I want to get to the dive shop."

Shelly glanced at the bar. "OK, margarita, you'll have to wait."

Reagan rolled her eyes and picked up a map of Tulum from the bar. "Thanks, Eduardo! We'll let you know if we need you."

"The keys to the house, the front gate, and the golf cars are on this." He reached into a small black plastic bowl on the kitchen counter and withdrew a keychain with a miniature coconut attached. "My phone number is on this sheet, along with a list of restaurants in this area. A maid will be by each morning, and if you would like any meals cooked for you, the number of our chef is also here."

"I am sure we'll be calling the chef," Shelly grinned. She also wanted to find some Mayan ingredients and cook some dishes from the cookbook given to her by her grandmother.

Reagan put on her prescription sunglasses and they walked out the front door, dive bags in hand. She attempted to start the golf car several times before it finally came alive. On their way out, they drove by a large iguana lounging in the villa parking area. It had faded horizontal stripes and the end of its tail was shorn off. It seemed to say, "This is my domain. You can stay for a minute, but don't stretch it."

"I'm calling her Michelle," said Reagan. "She def looks like a Michelle."

"Your Aunt Michelle would not appreciate that, but now that you mention it . . ." They laughed together and moved on.

With the slower pace of a golf car, it was easier to enjoy their surroundings. The bright blue sky with trade winds blowing through the foliage brought the salty air tinged with chamomile and an occasional whiff of road dust. Reagan ducked under some zapote foliage that canopied over the edge of the road and told her mom it was used to make chewing gum. After fifteen minutes of bumpy terrain had sufficiently numbed their hands and butt, they arrived at AAK Diving.

A gray-bearded man with a weathered face and an AAK Diving ball cap removed his reading glasses and looked up. "How may I help you ladies?"

Shelly placed their equipment bags on a worn wooden bench containing pools of water in small divots.

"I'm Reagan Prefontaine and I have been—"

"Ah yes! Miss Prefontaine! I am Armando. And this must be your sister?" He smiled warmly at Shelly.

Shelly shook his hand, grinning with effort. "Thank you for the compliment, but I'm her mother."

"Where would you both like to dive? I assume you would also like to dive the cenotes?"

Reagan said, "Let's hold off on those right now. We want to see the reefs more than anything." The underground inland freshwater cenotes were void of much life and bored her.

"You really must dive the cenotes. They are so important to the area with a rich history. It was the way the—"

"Yes, I know. It's the only way the Mayans have survived to this day after the Spanish drove them out of Tulum into the forests."

"I am impressed! You have been studying Tulum?"

Shelly rolled her eyes. "Don't get her started. Let's get the paperwork done. I have a margarita waiting for me back at the villa."

"But of course." Armando tore two sheets off a pad and two more sheets off another pad and handed one of each to Reagan and Shelly. "What kind of certification do you have?"

Reagan responded. "We're both open water divers with PADI. No extra certifications."

Reagan started diving at age eleven the first time Shelly had taken her to the local dive shop. They offered certifications through both of the top associations, but she was told she could get certified faster with PADI. That is all she needed to know. Since she had been watching her parents dive for years, peering down from the boat above while they explored the depths, she wanted to get her underwater certification in the least amount of time.

"And when was your last dive?"

"I went with some friends to Turks and Caicos over Christmas break. Mom?"

"I'm afraid it's been a long time. Pretty sure it was the summer of 2018 when we went as a family to Fiji."

"Do you think you'll need a refresher?" asked Armando.

"I don't think so. I've been diving for thirty years and have logged over a thousand dives. I'll be fine, but thanks for asking." She didn't mention that she co-owned a dive shop in Roatan in the '90s, knowing that could lead to an unwanted and protracted discussion.

They continued to answer questions about any health issues that could cause a problem while underwater, signing away the customary recourse including if the boat sank or the divemaster forgot to turn on their air.

A man filling tanks in the corner glanced their way every few minutes, and Reagan wondered about his interest.

"You ladies staying in the Hotel Maricabe next door?" Armando asked.

Shelly stalled a few seconds while she decided if this was a time to be careful. She knew Reagan would allow her to make this call.

"We are not staying at the Maricabe. We have a villa down the beach, but we will drive to the shop every day to dive. No need to pick us up." Shelly felt better about her decision to rent a villa, recalling how Carlisle always said hotels in foreign countries were notorious for theft. "What time should we be here tomorrow for the morning dive?"

"Since you have already finished the paperwork, just be here by eight-thirty. Boat leaves at nine. Will you need any gear?" Armando's eyebrow lifted in anticipation.

"We brought everything. We're good. Can we put it in a locker?"

"Just give me the bags, and I will have them put away for you."

Reagan pointed to the bench. "Those are ours."

"Your equipment is in good hands. See you in the morning!"

Shelly stepped carefully over some water hoses in the wash bay area, and Reagan dodged a laconic older man pulling a cart full of tanks. Donning their sunglasses simultaneously, they strolled to the golf car like detectives in a cop show after they had solved a big case.

Reagan swept her windblown hair away from her shamrock-green eyes and drove the golf car back toward the villa. The western sun made her auburn hair appear crimson.

"Mom, I need to tell you about the loggerhead turtles that come to the beach by our villa during this time of the year. I checked and the villa has flashlights with red cellophane over the lenses."

"I thought this was about loggerback turtles."

"It's loggerhead." Reagan smirked.

"Is that what you were reading about during dinner last night? Turtles?"

"Yes, but I've been fascinated with them since watching a special on the Travel Channel. It's another reason I wanted to come this time of year. From May to October, they and the green turtles come out of the sea at night to lay about a hundred eggs each in the sand. They use their flippers to dig holes about two feet deep, then lay their eggs into the nest. When the mama is done, she covers them all up with sand."

"Watch out!" Shelly screamed. A white cargo van with blacked-out windows barreled through a stop sign just as Reagan jammed her right foot against the brake, throwing Shelly forward and into the dashboard. Reagan felt the draft of the van as it whizzed by without slowing. The back wheels of the car lifted off the ground and for a short second, Reagan thought the car might flip over. She regained control, and as Shelly climbed back into her seat from the floor, she held her right shoulder and massaged it.

"You OK, Mom?" A horn blared, and a taxi swerved around them.

"Yes, but now I get to live with a bruise on my arm for the next few weeks. Who do you think that was?"

"Someone not paying attention, maybe texting. I should have paid better attention myself. I could have prevented that." Reagan tried to convince herself it was an accident. She cautiously merged onto the road, checking for oncoming traffic.

"Back to the turtles. We can watch them burying their eggs if we're careful and use flashlights that shine red light. They aren't bothered by red light."

"Why do they do this at night?"

"Predators. Mainly birds. They love to eat eggs, so they do this under the cover of darkness. Then after about two months, the baby turtles hatch and crawl out of the sand, also at night."

"Wait, how do they know to come out at night?"

"I'm pretty sure that Mama Turtle whispers through the eggshells," Reagan cupped a hand next to her mouth. "Be sure to wait and crawl to the ocean when it's dark so the mean birds don't eat you."

Shelly smiled. "Maybe you don't know everything about turtles."

Reagan negotiated a tricky Z-shape in the road, alternating between leaning into and away from Shelly. "I'm sure it has to do with circadian rhythms, but what's even more amazing is that these guys migrate thousands of miles away over many years after they're born but come back to the same area to lay their own eggs. Each coastline has its own magnetic signature, and turtles—and many other animals—use the magnetic fields to navigate their way back home."

"That is amazing. I have a newfound respect for turtles. I would love to see them tonight." She continued to rub her aching shoulder.

Reagan turned right onto a dirt road. "Here we are. Michelle is waiting for us." The large lizard glanced at them as Reagan skidded to a stop at a wooden fence that had seen better days. A few crumpled slats told the story of some miscalculated or perhaps inebriated applications of golf car brakes.

Shelly inserted the key into the entry gate lock, relocking the gate behind them. They climbed the eight steps to the front door, and although the dual entry seemed like overkill, it would not take much to breach the barriers.

Better not mention that to Mom.

"Time for my margarita!" Shelly headed to the mini-fridge for two chilled glasses and rubbed the rims into a sugar-lime-salt mixture. She then filled the shaker with ice, added some Patron tequila, lime juice, simple sugar, and orange liqueur from the bar, then shook it for thirty seconds. Reagan watched with scant interest, wondering how she could see some night life before their turtle run tonight.

Shelly handed a glass to Reagan. "Here's to an awesome week." They clinked glasses and sipped the salty cocktail.

"Time for some reconnaissance on the property," Reagan suggested, heading up the spiral stairs.

Shelly lacked the nimbleness of her athletic daughter but managed to keep up, careful not to spill her drink.

"Nice. All three rooms have a view of the ocean, and they all have central air. Which one do you want? Hey, since Dad's coming later, you guys take this one." There was a tub in the middle of the room.

"Not much privacy."

"Never knew you to be a prude, Mom, but how about this?" She pressed a "Down" button located on the wall just left of the bed and a thin TV monitor slowly descended from the ceiling. "I don't know if you guys will ever watch TV here, but that's pretty cool."

"I think I'll take it easy until our turtle hunt," Shelly said as she held her shoulder and winced. "This is getting worse. I may sit out by the pool. The jacuzzi sounds like the ticket right now. I may read my book or just come in here and see what they're showing on TV here in Mexico. I know you want to check out the city, so you go ahead. I'll be fine. Please be careful, though. You still have the mace in your purse?"

"Not taking my purse. They don't check ID here. I'll be fine. I can defend myself, but I'll avoid any unsafe situations." Reagan knew this was the right thing to say to Shelly. Her mother had been raped as a teenager when she attended a frat party. It was never spoken of, but the tragedy often underscored dialogue between them.

"Sorry to be channeling your dad, but where are you going? We need to know each other's whereabouts all the time."

"I was researching interesting bars and found something called the Sweaty Old Cigar downtown. Think I'll head there."

"Why don't you call and make sure they're open?"

"Mom— "

"Please?" Shelly pleaded.

"All right." Reagan found the number and called.

"SOC."

"Hello, how late are you open?"

"We close at one in the morning."

"Great, thank you very—"

"May I have your name so we can expect you?"

"It's Reagan."

"Are you staying at one of the hotels nearby?"

"No, we're at a villa. I'll be there in about ten minutes."

"We'll keep the lights on for you, Ms. Reagan."

Shoving her phone in the front pocket of her yellow capris, Reagan said, "Satisfied? I won't be in late. Love ya!"

"Love ya, sweetie. Oh, if you're coming home after dark, you might take your other glasses with you."

"Mom," she said. "It's time to stop 'momming' me."

"I'm sorry. Have fun."

CHAPTER 3

"Watch the kid in center tonight," Bobby said to no one in particular. He thought Silva was nearby, but he had retired to the nacho bar and was pouring himself a tequila, straight up. Gonzalo Silva was the owner of the Tigres, and his loosely termed "friends" called him Gonzo. A stout, fifty-eight-year-old ex-boxer with a dagger tattooed on his neck, he had financial interests throughout the region. His right ear was cauliflowered, and his slate-gray fedora with thin black stripes usually canted to that side.

"Gonzo, I want you to come outside and see this kid. Never seen anyone with his speed."

"Damn, Bobby, it's fucking hot out there." Gesturing toward the large screen in the corner, he said, "Can't we just watch him on that?"

"Trust me, it's not the same. Just come out on the balcony for one inning."

"Shit. OK, one inning."

They weaved their way through the crowd, managing to slosh more than a few drinks and nestled down into the closest seats. Silva crossed his legs over the seats in front and his stingray cowboy boots sparkled in the early evening sun.

"There he is. Number seventeen. He's in center tonight and batting second. I guarantee, if a ball gets hit over Valentine at second, Baxter won't miss it."

"I need another drink. I was right. It's fucking hot out here."

"Barbara, can you get *el Jefe* a cold Amstel?" In the sun, the J-shaped scar Silva earned in a knife fight at fifteen glistened proudly on his right cheek. Most committed to address him as el Jefe or the boss as the penalty of insolence could be swift and painful.

"*Pleibol!*" screamed a five-year old boy into the microphone. "Play ball!"

"Shit!" Silva blurted after the kid stole third base without contention. "Where did we get this guy? He's the fastest player I've seen since I bought this team."

"We traded Wingate for him. He came from the Frisco Roughriders."

"You know where we can use him, right, Bobby?"

Bobby Delvecchio was Silva's administrative assistant, but that job landed in his lap recently when Prunes was caught with his hand in the till. The cartel's accountant, Nibilo, reported some missing cash and they traced it to Prunes, whose hand was stuffed into a food processor by Silva and shoved up his nether regions with a hot branding iron. No one would know for sure, but those in the room felt he appreciated his throat being slit shortly thereafter.

"No, Gonzo, he has a bright future ahead of him. Baseball is where he needs to be."

"Did you see him at bat? The guy won't hit above the Mendoza line in our league, much less in the bigs. He's a wasted talent here. He's got much more potential."

"He comes from important stock, Jefe. His dad is a statistician with the Feds, and he works closely with the FBI. I don't think we should take any chances."

Bobby was born in Stuttgart, Germany, to an Italian father and Swedish mother who met when she was running a high-class culinary school. He was an attaché at the Italian Embassy and neither of them wanted a child that would hamper their careers. An abortion was out of the question for the two Catholics, but the life Bobby led in his early years was another type—an emotional abortion. He left at the age of sixteen and his parents did not flinch. He took a job in a dive shop in Providenciales and developed a love of the sea where he could dive and feel clean . . . feel reborn.

The young man who spoke English with a German tilt had bleach-blond hair from his mother and the nose and cheekbones of his father. One of Silva's confidantes noticed him during a drug run to Malaysia, and he was recruited to come to Tulum. His devotion and intelligence moved him up the ranks of the cartel, and this new family who took him in was something he never wanted to lose. Even so, his heart would often reach out to those he could relate to—those who took him back to his early years of unrest and innocence.

"Bobby, I get paid to take chances. You know what our investors pay for and you know how much they pay. There will be no more discussion and you will make the arrangements, am I clear?"

"Yes, sir," he quickly answered, mentally imagining a branding iron in unpleasant places.

The next morning, Silva's brain trust assembled at his request, assuming their usual seats. A large print of Silva shaking hands with Pablo Escobar hung at the twelve o'clock position, where Silva sat. His Harvard-educated Jamaican bodyguard, Winston, sat to his right. The Hawaiian floral shirt he wore ensured no one would miss his presence, and Silva gave his muscle man a gold chain for every cartel he helped overthrow. Twelve gold chains impressively draped over his expansive torso. His head was shaved, and his white cargo pants were special ordered from a Big & Tall Men's Store in the states. To many, he resembled a black Bluto from Popeye. The Machiavellian Silva only cared that he kept him alive.

"Steffen, what's the status on the Matisse painting?" Silva had become obsessed with collecting antiquities and famous paintings over the past twelve years, tying up a large majority of his wealth in collectables. He did not have cash buried across the country like his mentor, Escobar. Steffen was hired to seek out opportunities, report to Silva, then obtain the piece if he showed an interest, which happened often. A slender and unassuming man, he peered over his wiry spectacles and spoke to Gonzo in German-influenced English, the least fluent of the seven he spoke.

"You vill be relieved to hear that it vas one of the POK members who had some insight into this, heir Gonzo."

"Splendid! After our meeting here, get with me in the library and fill me in."

"Of course. The piece vill be available on the market at the Hamin Tower in Lima on the twenty-third. It vill be, shall ve say, a silent auction? Shall I procure it?"

"I think you know the answer, so just let me know when it's in our hands."

Kara Wilder served as Gonzo's personal assistant in public and his not-so-secret lover in private. "Kara, how is the theater panning out for our event on the thirteenth?"

Kara's tan business suit accentuated her slender waist, and her unbuttoned jacket revealed a taut white shirt. "We have the usual suspects, plus two Danes and a Saudi joining us for the first time. You're still offering fifty percent off for first attendees, right?"

"Yes, but did you tell that to the Saudi?"

"He mentioned it to me . . . the Danes did not."

Silva groused visibly. Although he made good money from the Arab, he did not have to like it. "Have they all wired the money?"

"Of course. No seats are saved until that happens."

"OK. Keep the discount you offered to the Danes but refuse the Saudi entrance until he pays the million in full."

"As you wish, *cariño.*"

Kara's realty firm, Mayan Holdings, served as a front for laundering the cash Silva brought in from the cocaine business. Although clever enough to sift a sizable amount to some of her personal offshore accounts, she understood he could turn on her at any moment if he ever discovered her peccadillos. Their relationship, although passionate, was volatile.

She left Silva to call one of the Danes. "Henrik, he's going to the city this evening. Meet at the usual place?"

CHAPTER 4

Dim lights blinked, and whispers of cigarette smoke hung in unseen places, providing the Sweaty Old Cigar with all the charm of a whoreless brothel. Reagan slid onto an empty seat at the bar, hooked her heels over the seat ring, and picked up a wrinkled drink menu.

"What are you having, lady?" The bartender spoke with a southern accent, reminding her of a friend on her archery team. The charm stopped there. He wore an SOC apron, and his bulging stomach indicated he spent hours after closing drinking the rest of the beer on tap. His name tag read, "Austin," but his demeanor said, "New Jersey." He inspected glasses, waved at a patron walking in, and rang up another customer while she pondered the question.

"I've been wanting to try a mai tai." He left without a word and headed down the bar lane to gather the ingredients. As Reagan waited, she pretended to scan the food menu but surveyed the room, honoring her mom's wishes to be hypervigilant. A raucous group of young teens were at a corner table, their volume knob ratcheting up since her arrival.

Several patrons dined alone: a sixtyish man with plaid shorts and a zipped-up black windbreaker; a tall, muscular young man with his back to her, his bald head shining; a girl with air pods to block out her surroundings; and an unshaven man with pretzels and a Corona. A few couples shared intimate gazes over drinks, ready for a good time. Lynyrd Skynyrd played through the speakers. Three female college-age girls, each with cropped blond hair, arrived on the dance floor and begged their dates to join them. The familiar aroma of THC wafted through Reagan's senses, reminding her of an after-prom party in the distant past.

Her mind wandered to the reefs. She floated effortlessly, perfectly trimmed, mesmerized by the interplay of the sea life. Starfish edged toward safety. Blue damsels frenetically scoured their surroundings. Honeycomb cowfish minded their own business. Barracuda patrolled their domain. Lionfish nestled into their protective overhangs, doing their best to avoid the angry spears of the environmental hunters. She loved it all and could barely wait until they hit the water tomorrow morning.

"Here you go, ma'am."

"Thank you."

He glanced at her tanned wrist. "Mind me asking what that tattoo is? I haven't seen anything like it." Austin was sounding more like Austin now.

Reagan was used to this question. "No, it's just a birthmark."

"It's a starfish."

"That's what most people say, but I don't know what God had in mind for this birthmark."

Reagan enjoyed her mai tai and was about to ask for another when a heavyset mustachioed man with rum breath, a sallowish complexion, and a leather necklace plopped down next to her. With eyes in dire need of toothpicks, he slurred, "Let me get you a second one."

Reagan winced visibly. He had been part of one of the couples. "How did you know that was just my first?"

"Ah, ya caught me. Yes, I been starin' at ya from that table over there."

"I'm OK, thanks. I was just leaving anyway. Have to drive home."

"I saw a taxi drop you off," he said, just before a belch.

"You're making me too uncomfortable. Where is your lady friend?" She stalled while she considered a way out.

"I don't have no lady friend. That's why I came over here. Just let me buy you one, and I'll go back to my table."

"Hey buddy, I think the lady would like you to leave her alone." A man about the age of her big brother walked up, and Reagan felt he could handle himself with this intruder.

"I was just leavin', dude." Although unsteady on his feet, he managed to get back to the table, his chair creaking unsteadily beneath his weight.

"Thank you . . ."

"Chris. Chris Tucker, and you are?"

"I'm Reagan. Thank you for rescuing me."

"For the record, I also saw a taxi drop you off." He grinned. "What are you doing here? I come here most evenings with some friends, but I've never seen you."

Reagan thought he was cute and realized he was the bald young man with his back to her. She stared at his captivating and intriguing smile.

"I just flew in with my mom today. We're here to do some diving and see the Mayan ruins. My brother plays baseball here, and we want to see him in his 'element.'" She mimicked quote signs for emphasis.

"You're kidding. I play on the Tigres team here."

"The team is already back from Campeche? And Jaden hasn't called me yet?"

"Your brother's name is Jaden?"

"Yes. Jaden Prefontaine."

"Hmm . . . we have a new center fielder named Jaden Baxter but no Prefontaine. Maybe he plays on another team in the area."

"Someone taking my name in vain?"

"J! Great to see you!" Reagan wrapped her arms around her slender brother and squeezed tightly, not realizing how much she had missed him. She ruffled his bleached-blond hair. "No one would know we're related, but I've never seen your hair this blond."

Jaden was at least fifty pounds lighter than Chris, but his build fooled everyone. The rumor was he could outrun a cheetah. No one had actually *seen* him race a cheetah, but since he had one tattooed on his forearm, many believed. As he had the same Hungarian ancestry as Reagan and played ball in the sun most days, he was even darker than she was. He wore jeans and a V-necked turquoise pullover. His hazel eyes sparkled as he looked at Reagan.

Chris was puzzled. "All right, what's with the name change, J?"

Jaden placed his index finger against his lips and said with a whisper, "Reagan, Dad probably never mentioned this, but he asked if I would go by a different name until I reached the big leagues or at least got out of the Latin American countries. Players who're related to rich or influential people over here get kidnapped and ransomed all the time. It's really not safe, considering Dad's influence in Washington."

In a hushed voice, Reagan said, "Hey, I'm OK with that, of course, but jeez, you could at least tell me!"

It was so good to see Jaden. He was her idol growing up in Argyle, Texas, always the best athlete on the field but never having an athlete's ego. He let her be a part of his sports, regularly inviting her to sit on the bench at games and track meets. He excelled in the sprint races, baseball, ultimate disc, swimming, and as a wide receiver on their football team, but his love was baseball. When he was drafted in the sixteenth round out of high school, he started the long climb to the major leagues, leaving the other sports behind. He was the reason Reagan wanted to excel at everything she did.

"Now that you and Chris know, you have to keep this on the down low. We can't risk Dad's job or my life . . . in that order."

"I get your point, but you don't have to be so dramatic. I'll have to warn Mom."

Jaden raised his hands palm up. "Where is Mom?"

"We had a close call in the golf car today, and she's a little sore. She's enjoying the jacuzzi and exploring the bar at the villa. She really just wants to relax this week, so I won't be pressuring her to go with me on these little excursions."

Jaden nodded. "That sounds good. I know she needs some getaway time. Dad still coming up next week?"

"That's the plan, but he can't be reached where he is. He wanted it that way."

Jaden motioned to the seating area. "Let's sit down and catch up. Are you at our usual table, Chris, or did you just get here?"

"I was, but let's get one that's a little more private."

They found a booth along the wall closest to the restrooms, and Chris slid in by Reagan. The waitress appeared immediately.

"My name is Heather, and I'll be serving you. Would you like to start with a drink?" Heather wasn't wearing a name tag, but Reagan decided not to probe.

"I'll take a mai tai. Can I see a food menu, also?"

Heather leaned around the booth partition and grabbed a menu from another table's caddy.

"I'll be right back with your drinks and pretzels."

"Mexican adults drink eighteen gallons of beer a year. How about you guys?"

"I'd say we get there by midyear." Chris showed his serious dimples when he smiled. "Here, they drink beer to celebrate but also to treat depression. They drink at weddings, funerals, sports events, and every party. It's their water."

Jaden asked Chris, "Have you ever seen Heather in here?"

"I was about to ask you the same question. She must be new." Somehow, the teens in the corner had managed to ramp up the conversation to another level.

"So, what's your story, Chris? Is that *your* real name?"

"All right, Reagan, I said I was sorry," Jaden said.

"Yes, my name is really Chris."

"So, I know how Baxter got here," Reagan smirked at her brother, "but tell me your story."

"I wasn't as good as Jaden coming out of high school, but I grew up on a working ranch in Nebraska. I didn't get any serious consideration and wasn't drafted, so I went to college at Clemson and spent three years there until I was drafted after my junior year."

"It was his bat that got him drafted," said Jaden. "He's a beast."

"What was your major?" asked Reagan, not believing she asked the trite question.

"I always had an interest in psychology. I lived with my grandparents on the ranch and my Grandpa Willett was my inspiration. He was a big-animal veterinarian, and I'm quite sure he was one of the first animal behaviorists. People used to call him Dr. Doolittle because he talked to his animals and tried to teach them good manners. He claimed the more we learned about animal behavior, the more we would discover about human behavior.

"He used to show me how to hypnotize rabbits. He could make them do some funny things. Every time I was with him, he would talk about how powerful the mind was. He taught me that it was more powerful than the body, and even though I wanted to play baseball, I always thought I could fall back on psychology to make a living if I couldn't make it in baseball. I've used what I learned in that field to help both *my* game as well as other players I've met over the years. I don't think I could've made it to this level without his training. My grandpa took me to a hypnotist when I was eleven, and I never forgot that experience. My ill-spent youth was in the form of playing with hypnosis, but it could have been worse, I suppose."

"Reagan was shooting rabbits when you were hypnotizing them. She's a toxophilist, by the way."

"A what?" Chris asked.

Reagan rolled her eyes. "Just a fancy word for archer. I was on the team in college, and I didn't shoot rabbits."

Heather approached with a tray holding the drinks and pretzels. "Have you decided on food?"

After ordering, Heather moved off to the kitchen and Reagan said, "By the way, I noticed several establishments on my taxi ride here from the airport with the name Gonzo. Who is this Gonzo?"

Chris laughed. "He pretty much runs this area, and he also owns the Tigres that Jaden and I play for. We don't say this in his presence, but we call him Uncle Guano."

Reagan struggled with her attraction to Chris, determined to have a few weeks unencumbered with any love interests. "Let's get a selfie for Dad, Jaden. Chris, we want you in it, too."

They eased out of the booth and stood with their backs to the bar. Chris had the longest arms, so he volunteered to take the photo. They grinned appropriately, then Reagan had to approve the photo before the photo session was declared done. "Did you guys know that more people die from selfies than shark attacks?"

"Where do you get this information?" Chris asked.

"She reads," Jaden said humorously. "Oh, and she freakin' remembers everything. She's one of those."

"OK, so how do you die taking a selfie?"

"People take lots of chances," said Reagan. "I'm sure you can imagine some dangerous situations where people are trying to document the danger and aren't paying attention. But I also say this to convince you guys not to be scared to get in the ocean. It's very rare to die from a shark attack. You have to really insult them. Call them a guppy or something."

"Ha. This is all fascinating, but I'll be right back," said Chris. "Those beers went right through me." He weaved his way through the dancers who now had their partners on the floor and disappeared through the bathroom door. The tallest of the teenage boys put a quarter in the jukebox and pushed the button for "Karma Chameleon" by Boy George.

"I can't wait to see Dad next week," Reagan stated. "Did you know he was in the wilderness, going off the grid this week?"

"I sure didn't. We haven't talked much lately. He wanted me to be an attorney, remember? Unless I get to the big leagues, he'll always see me as a failure."

"That's not true, J. I hear him bragging about you all the time. I'm sending him our pic, even though he won't see it for another week."

"Hey, where did the teenagers—"

An ear-piercing sound burst preceded a table that flew toward her. A flash of light surrounded it like an eclipsed sun straining to be seen. She heard screams and then saw blackness.

CHAPTER 5

Reagan slowly opened her eyes to see Shelly in the corner chair reading. She tried to yell but managed only a whisper. "Mom! What happened?"

"Oh, it's so good to see you awake. Do you know your name?"

"Of course. It's Reagan."

"Your brother's?"

"Jaden. Why are you asking me?"

"We were worried that you had a concussion, but they've done some scans and there's no damage."

"The last thing I remember is a loud explosion and a table, but that's it. Not sure why I remember a table. Hey, where are my glasses?"

"They were broken when that table hit you, but you had another pair back at the villa that I brought you. There's a bad cut on your face and your cheek is turning black and blue, but there's a bandage on it right now so you can't see it. You also have some cuts around your eyes from your broken glasses. How sore are you?"

Reagan attempted to shift in the bed. "Wow. How long have I been here?"

"They sedated you at the bar because they saw your facial injury and assumed you were concussed."

"Who sedated me?"

"We aren't sure. That's what's so unusual about this. The explosion was yesterday and you're just now coming out of it, so the sedative was very strong. I'm so ready to get you out of here."

"It really was an explosion? Do you know anything?"

"Two Federales have been here a few times. We're supposed to contact them when you're awake, but I want to wait a while to let you get your bearings. Jaden has a concussion, and they wouldn't let him play for two days. He's been at his place since then. His friend Chris was in the bathroom when it happened, so he's fine, but he's also been by a few times to check—"

A nurse opened the door. "Welcome back to reality. How are you feeling? You took quite a blow." The nurse had the requisite white smock with white socks and shoes, her hair frizzed back into a tight bun. A second chin leapt forward to avoid being crushed by a twenty-pound head.

"Just a little sore," Reagan painfully responded as she tilted her head toward the door.

"My name is Estella and I need to check your vital signs. Then we'll get you something to eat."

"Good, because I'm hungry." An IV tube fed her the vital fluids she needed, Demerol included, but she needed something solid for her empty stomach. The nurse removed the sphygmomanometer from around her neck and gently raised Reagan's left arm off the bed.

"Ow!"

"I know you're sore, but I'll be finished shortly."

The pressure of the cuff wasn't as bad as she had expected. She released her arm, being careful to lay it down slowly, then put her two fingers on her wrist and glanced at her watch. "You must be a healthy girl because you experienced some trauma that would have had most people in here for weeks, but other than some soreness and a facial abrasion, you seem to be fine. All X-rays were negative. Of course, we would like to keep you here for observation for a few days, but we can't keep you if you would like to get on with your vacation. Your mother and I have had some interesting conversations. Your birthmark is fascinating. She said you get asked about it all the time."

Reagan glanced anxiously at her mother, checking for any breach of confidence in her eyes. "Yes, I do, but I don't mind. And yes, I would like to leave this afternoon, if possible. I've been flexing my limbs and moving around to see if anything hurts, but my left arm, a sore neck, and of course my face are all I can find that seem out of sorts."

Estella walked over to the bed. "Let me get this IV out for you. Don't think we'll need this anymore." She deftly removed it, placed a small circular band-aid with a Tigres logo over the puncture wound in the back of her hand, and dropped the materials in the red medical container labeled *AFILADOS*.

"Mom, I don't want to take the bandage off my cheek yet, but how bad is it?"

"Not bad at all. The doctor said it will heal up well and not leave a scar. I've seen it a few times when they changed your bandage, and it's mostly just discolored. They've been great here, by the way, and Estella has been here most of the time, taking good care of you."

"Gracias, Estella."

"De nada. It has been my pleasure. Your mom brought some fresh clothes from your villa."

While Reagan dressed, she said, "The police wanted to interview me, and I want to interview them. Did they leave a number to call?"

"Yes, I have their card and we can call them from the villa when we get you settled in. I have your things put away, but you might want to hit the jacuzzi to work out the soreness in your neck. It worked great for my sore shoulder." Shelly hesitated. "You . . . do remember the golf car incident?"

"Yes. But how is Jaden back at his place? He's not in the hospital, is he?" Reagan felt guilty for not asking about her brother earlier.

"No," Shelly replied. "He stayed one night, but a concussion takes time, so he's hanging at the condo he rented for the season. We'll go see him when you're up to it or maybe he can stop by."

Leaving the hospital, Shelly waved at a taxi on the curb. "I took a taxi here because I didn't think you would be comfortable in the golf car. Chris and I brought the golf car from the bar to the villa. He's a genuinely nice young man." Although being upbeat with her daughter, she hid her reservations about Chris's fortuitous timing in avoiding the bomb that could have killed her children.

Reagan's head throbbed from a Demerol rebound, the bright sunshine, and poor suspension in the taxi. She squeezed her eyes shut to stop the mean little man shoving an icepick into her temple. Shelly tapped her taut shoulder, holding a tablet in her outstretched hand. "Take it. It's Vicodin."

"You know I hate to take anything," she said through gritted teeth.

"I know, but the doctor told me you would need these for a day or two only as you come off the barbiturates. I promise it will only be for a few days at most."

Reagan swallowed and hoped the onset of pain relief would be faster than the onset of pain. Shelly wrapped her right arm around her and said nothing. By the time they reached Orchid Lane, Reagan felt better.

Michelle, the iguana, silently greeted them. *Where you been, Reagan?*

Once inside, Reagan quickly changed into her pink bikini and eased herself into the jacuzzi. "Ahh . . . just what I needed."

Shelly pulled up a chair while Reagan relaxed. The stiffness in her neck was subsiding, and she let the jet stream massage her left forearm. The steam moistened the bandage on her cheek. "Can you hand me a mirror?"

"Are you sure? It's not your best look." Shelly tried to make light of it, but her face told a different story.

Reagan tensed. "I have to see it sooner or later."

Shelly retreated to her bathroom and returned with a hand mirror. "You asked for it."

Spinning the mirror, Reagan frowned and nonchalantly said, "Ah, it's a little swollen, but nothing a little makeup can't hide. Besides, the saltwater tomorrow will help it heal faster."

"You sure you feel like getting out tomorrow?"

"Yes. We need to let AAK know we're coming. Did you let them know what happened?"

"Yes, but the dive shop was not my first concern. I didn't call them until this morning. They heard of the explosion and were sorry to hear you were in the bar. They also said they had some spots all week and we can just show up when you're up to it."

"Great. I am up to it, so tomorrow, we dive."

Shelly looked toward the water. "That's odd. There's two men walking on the beach in suits." Reagan didn't bother moving. The jets felt too good. She kept her eyes closed.

"They're headed this way." Reagan sat up. She couldn't decide which was less acceptable: the men seeing her purple swollen cheek or her pink bikini. She maxed out the speed on the jets to produce a swirl of waves and froth.

"Ms. Prefontaine?" The taller Hispanic man spoke with only a trace of an accent. "It's our understanding you were at the SOC on Tuesday night when a bomb went off." The shorter and younger partner said nothing.

The taller man's glossy-black shoes bore none of the sand he had waded through. His eyes stayed professionally on Reagan's. They were confident but not intimidating. "I am Inspector Raul Isuega. This is my partner, Timothy Garvey. We are with the Policía Federal Ministerial and are investigating what happened on Tuesday night. We think organized crime is involved. Some of my men visited you in the hospital, but you were not in a position to discuss this. What do you remember of that night? Don't think anything is unimportant. Many times, it's the little thing that solves the big thing."

Reagan said, "Let's go inside. You guys aren't dressed for the heat, and I want to hear what you know as well."

"Thank you," Timothy replied, perspiration dripping off his left brow.

Shelly picked up a folded floral beach towel and unfurled it. Holding it up as a shield, she wrapped Reagan in it. They headed through the glass door and found seats in the spacious living area on some matching backless sofas heavily decorated with palm trees and hairy coconuts.

Sensing Raul waited for her to start, Reagan settled into the seat across from him. "I made the decision to go into town that evening and decided on the SOC. I drove one of our golf cars that are out by the front door." She motioned over her right shoulder.

Raul scribbled in an unfolded leather notepad. "How did it get back here?"

Shelly spoke up. "Chris and I brought it back here the next day when Reagan was still incapacitated.

Raul's head jerked up from the pad. "Who is Chris?"

"He's a friend of my brother, Jaden. Did you not talk to him at the SOC? I was told he was in the bathroom and wasn't hurt. I do remember him going in there, but it's about the last thing I remember."

"This is the first time I have heard that name. Please continue."

"When I walked into the SOC, I talked to the bartender, Austin, and then a guy started bothering me."

"Never mind that guy. We have already spoken with the bartender, Mr. Austin Strainwater. He was in the kitchen when the explosion occurred, so he was not hurt. He offered little help but mentioned some young teenagers that were there, although we did not see them in the wreckage. We do have eight bodies, but they have all been identified."

Reagan flinched, covering her mouth with both hands. Shelly quickly interceded. "Reagan, I wasn't going to tell you until you had time to recover fully." Some rainfall pattered on the patio, then acted like it was sorry for the intrusion and stopped quickly.

Raul said, "Yes, we have eight dead and two are still in intensive care at the hospital where you were. If you're up to it, can you tell us what else you saw or if there were others you could describe?"

Reagan's mind reeled from the death of so many people, but she kept it together until she could process it all later. "Can you tell me the descriptions of the deceased, so I don't include any of them in my details?"

"Of course," Raul consented. "Sadly, seven of the eight and one in critical condition were other older teenagers on the dance floor. Another was the wife of a couple, and the husband is the other one in the hospital. Everyone else has been released."

"I know what couple you're referring to because they were seated nearest the dance floor. They seemed like a nice couple from the states. He had a Yankees cap on."

"You're right," Raul nodded. "They were from New York, and I was able to speak to the husband this morning after he was moved out of intensive care. He and his wife were in the west side of the Pentagon on 9/11 and survived. He will lose an eye and a leg, more than likely. This is the largest death toll we have seen in Tulum in one day in our history. I'm sorry you had to be a witness to it. Again, if we can go on, what else do you remember?"

"Most of what I remember about the others comes from my time at the bar because after Chris rescued me from Butt-Crack—sorry, but I don't know his name—and my brother got there, I talked with them until the explosion happened.

"There was an older man, perhaps mid-sixties, by himself. He was working a *New York Times* Sunday crossword, but it was from the year 2015. Working it would be a stretch. I saw about three scattered words filled in. You said no detail was unimportant, right, Inspector?"

"That's right, Ms. Prefontaine," he replied as he scribbled some more.

"He also had plaid Bahama shorts and a black windbreaker that was zipped up. I wondered if he might be sick. There was also a girl, about my age, sitting in the corner by herself. She had mahogany-colored, short-cropped hair and wore jeans. She was Filipino or maybe Malaysian. She had a white T-shirt with a big "G" on the front. She was listening to music on her Apple pods."

"How do you know it was music?" Timothy asked.

"Have you ever watched younger people with earphones?"

He grinned. "OK, I guess you can just tell."

Raul continued the questioning. "What about the younger teens that Mr. Strainwater mentioned?"

"There were six of them," Reagan said. "Three boys and three girls. They were very into themselves, and as they drank, they became more obnoxious. The leader had a rattail and was about six-two and thin. He was at least five inches taller than the others. They spoke Japanese, so I have no idea what they were saying."

"How did you know they were speaking Japanese?" Raul asked.

"Chris told me. He played baseball there for a year and got to know the language pretty well."

Raul said, "Did he mention what they were talking about?"

Reagan thought about a response before offering hers. "Well, we were pretty involved in our own conversation, so I don't think he paid any attention, but you can ask him." Reagan had some questions as well to ask Chris and Jaden.

"Is there anything else you can tell us about that evening?" Raul closed his notepad and stuffed it into the inner pocket of his coat.

"Yes, there was one more man sitting under the window. Alone. He reminded me of a bear hunter for some reason, the kind of guy you would find living off the land, deep in the woods."

Raul once again extracted the notepad.

"I tried placing where he might be from, but really, he could have been Russian, Hungarian, or even French. His white slacks and Tommy Bahama shirt did not seem to match. And he was drinking a Corona and eating pretzels."

"Anything else?" Raul asked as he rose from his chair.

"Oh!" Reagan suddenly remembered the waitress. "There was a waitress who Jaden and Chris had never seen there before. Her name was Heather."

Raul face said he was puzzled. "Are you sure that was her name?" He rifled through his notepad.

"Well, all I can tell you is that she told us her name was Heather. I didn't ask for an ID."

"Then can you describe her for me? I don't have a Heather we have talked to and no one else has mentioned her." Raul continued flipping the pages. Timothy got up and paced.

"Of course," Reagan responded, "but I won't be much help. She was about five-six, wore a taupe SOC uniform, had short brown hair, and no distinguishing features. I think she was Hispanic, but lighter skinned than most. Her fingernails were short and unpolished, but that's about it."

Raul produced a final closure of his notepad and rose. "You have been extremely helpful, Ms. Prefontaine. Don't be surprised if we contact you again. In the meantime, here is my card." He wrote his cell number down and handed it to her. "Please call me if you think of anything else."

Timothy stepped forward, handing Reagan a card. "And here's mine if you can't reach Inspector Isuega."

"Thank you, Inspector Garvey, but before you leave, I have a question. What do you know about the bomb? Where was it located and what caused it to go off? Did it have a timer?"

Hercule Poirot was one of her favorite characters and she had learned to ask questions. Any question unasked is a question unanswered.

Raul smiled, approvingly. "I expected that question from you. Unfortunately, I can't disclose—"

"I think we need some quid pro quo," Reagan said.

"All right, there are a few details I can offer since they're part of the public record already. The bomb had been dropped into a spittoon at the corner of the bar. It had a timer on it but not a clock. We do not know when it was placed there."

"That would make sense. The explosion would leave only traces of the timing mechanism." Reagan was pleased to have gotten this much information.

"Exactamente, Ms. Prefontaine. There is little else—"

"Wait." Reagan held up her left hand, palm forward. "Do you have any suspects?"

"That is something I can't comment on."

"I feel like my life could be in danger. A van almost ran us over, I have had several people who seem bothered by my birthmark, and a bomb that could have been meant for me exploded in the first bar I went to on the first night of my vacation. No one has luck like that, so I deserve to know if I am being paranoid or if there is some other force at play that should have me hunkered down or leaving Mexico."

"Ms. Prefontaine, I do believe you had some bad luck on your first day in our fine city. I am quite sure that no one is after you. As you know, there were others much less fortunate than you in the SOC."

Reagan pestered, "So, do you have any suspects?"

Raul sighed. Timothy was making his own notes in a spiral notebook. "Nothing solid, Ms. Prefontaine. It is not professional nor ethical to divulge any information that is speculative in this game we play. I am sure you understand."

"Of course," Reagan said. "Thanks, anyway."

"By the way," Raul said. "The birthmark you mentioned. What makes it so disruptive?"

Reagan reached down and pulled up her left sleeve, revealing her birthmark shaped like a starfish. Raul and Timothy stared for a second, Timothy with interest, Raul with concern. "That is interesting, Ms. Prefontaine. I can see why some have asked questions about it. It's not the typical birthmark. Please stay safe. Pretty girls like you and your mom can't be too careful. Stick together." They headed toward the front door.

"Thanks for the advice, Inspector. Aren't you going to leave the way you came—from the beach?" Shelly asked, pointing seaward.

"We're parked out front, but it's hard to get anyone's attention when there's a locked gate, so we walked around. Have a nice day, ladies!"

Once they were gone, Reagan said, "I still haven't talked to Jaden. I need to call him. By the way, did you know he was going by a different last name here?"

Shelly smiled, "Yes, when he was in the hospital, he had to use his real name, and when another player came to check on him—Jaden called him C-Ham—the front desk had no idea who Jaden Baxter was, so I heard the whole story. We both told C-Ham he had to keep quiet about this. We have to protect your father."

"I don't remember a C-Ham from my talks with Jaden. Does he have another name?"

"Yes. I asked the same thing. His real name is Cunningham. I didn't ask his first name, but he kinda creeped me out. Had shifty eyes. Never trusted shifty eyes."

"If he's a friend of Jaden's, I'm sure he's fine, Mom. I'm glad you're good with Jaden using a different name. I was worried you might be upset. I'm gonna call him. Maybe we can meet for dinner. I'm starving."

"Your cell phone is on the charger in the kitchen, but it's been off. You were getting lots of texts when you were in the hospital. Your dad is still out of touch, but it's likely best he doesn't know any of this yet. I do wish he were here, though."

The phone came to life and a string of texts came through.

"Ugh. Sixty-three text messages. I'll get to those later." She punched Jaden's name and it started to ring. It didn't take long.

"I'm so glad to hear your voice." His tone revealed a deep sense of relief. "When they told me you were unconscious, I couldn't stand thinking of you like that. I should have known better. No bomb could knock you out of commission for long."

Reagan laughed. "Well, I'm a bit sore. The jacuzzi helped for sure. Are you up for dinner with Mom and me?"

"You sure you want to get back out? I can pick up some dinner and bring it over to the villa. Mom gave me the address."

"That would be great, J. Whatever you get will be fine."

"I know just the place.I know you like good sushi and the best place on the island is on the way to your villa—"

"Sushi? I got sick the last time I had it." Just thinking about eating it again roiled her stomach.

"OK, you said anything, so I guess you mean anything but sushi?"

"All right," Reagan said. "Is there a pizza place on the way? I could eat a whole one by myself."

"Yes, Gonzo's Pizzeria is also on the way. I know the owner, so it'll be no problem getting you enough to eat."

"Oh, that's right! He owns your baseball team. I hope he makes good pizza."

"I'll see you in about forty minutes." The connection ended. Reagan sat, holding her phone for a few seconds. Something wasn't right. She felt uneasy and rubbed her birthmark.

CHAPTER 6

"Hey, let me in!" Jaden pleaded over the cell phone.

"Oh, sorry, J! I'll be right there." Reagan sprinted to the gate and let him in. "I would hug you, but I'd rather hug the pizza."

"Very funny." She kissed him on the cheek, and they walked back through the door. "Gonzo was at his pizza place. I'm not sure how he knew about you, but he said to give you his regrets for how rudely Tulum has treated you already. He also said he would be using his influence to find the damn criminal that blew up the SOC." He laid the three pizzas on the bar counter and opened each. "One pizza for each of us. Compliments of Gonzo."

Reagan had that uneasy feeling again. "Let him know I appreciate it the next time you see him. But with your concussion, when will you get to play for the Tigres next? I really want to see you in a game here." They each had a piece of pizza in their hands and were talking in between bites.

"They cleared me today, so tomorrow night, I'm back out in center field and you better be there!"

"We'll both be there, Jaden," Shelly said. "Do you want a beer?" Shelly opened the mini-fridge and pulled out a Modelo Especial.

"Reagan?"

"Same." Shelly already had a margarita in hand.

Reagan had eaten half her pizza by the time she opened her Modelo. When she slowed down, her mind returned to Tuesday night. "Two inspectors came by today. Have you met Raul and Timothy?"

Jaden said, "I don't think so. I had a pretty good headache and don't remember much, but I don't think it was them."

"Anyway, they said the bomb came from a spittoon by the bar. Do you remember anything about a spittoon?"

"Of course. It's been there forever . . . well since I've been going there." Jaden shook his head. "The deaths were senseless. I heard they were all seniors from Clemson. One was a wide receiver on their championship team. By the way, they raised the threat level to three for the Tulum area. Not even sure Dad can come next week after this. I doubt the Pentagon will let him."

Shelly bravely massaged her eyes and wiped away some of the moisture. Carlisle was her rock and brought stability to their family when all seemed so unstable. She was sure that when he found out Reagan was almost killed, no Pentagon dictum would keep him away. "Do you really think Silva has enough influence to find out who did it?"

"If anyone can, he can. I sure don't trust the police force here."

Trying to shift the subject, Reagan said, "Hey, Mom and I are diving in the morning. Want to join?"

"Wish I could, but I have to meet with the general manager of the Tigres tomorrow. They like my speed and want to talk about another opportunity."

"Sounds mysterious," Reagan said teasingly. "I'll see you at the game. I need to go to sleep so I can be rested to dive tomorrow. Mom, I'll be up at seven and will make us some eggs and bacon. Night!" She headed up the stairs as Jaden threw away the pizza boxes.

Shelly held Jaden's arm. "Wish you could go with us tomorrow. We haven't dived together since Fiji."

"We'll get more chances. You're here for another ten days, right?"

"True. I sure hope your dad can get here."

"Me, too," said Jaden. "He hasn't seen me play in Mexico." He headed to the door. "You guys have fun tomorrow. Who are you diving with?"

"AAK Diving. We checked in with them when we got here, and they seemed nice."

"I've heard good things about them but have only dived a few times since I've been here. They frown on any risky activities when you get paid to play baseball."

"We'll have to sneak you onto a dive boat at least once."

"Deal!" He hugged Shelly and kissed her on the cheek. As he walked out the gate, he waved to her and was gone.

"We're back!" Reagan and Shelly parked their golf car and stood in front of the counter where Armando sat, disheveled and mildly distracted.

"I am happy to see you. Your mother told me what happened, and I did not think you would be diving this week, but here you are! You must be superwoman."

"No, just super-excited to dive. Where is our gear?"

"On the boat, of course. Full service here! Carlos will be your divemaster." He craned his tattooed neck around the corner. "Carlos! *Sus buceadores están aquí!*"

A moment later, Carlos rounded the corner. "*Hola, chicas!* We are diving Tankah Deep today. The visibility is good, and the current is acceptable. Have you dived with us before?"

Shelly replied, "I dived Tulum many years ago, but it was not with AAK. How long have you been with them?"

"About nine months. I was in Roatan for a few years before coming here. Let's make sure we have everything you need. You don't need nitrox, do you?"

"No, we're good," Reagan said. She considered getting nitrox-certified years ago to give her more time to spend underwater, but she was usually with others who weren't, so she never took the course.

"I see you both have integrated BCDs. How much weight?"

Shelly's buoyancy control device was new, and she was anxious to see how comfortable the vest was. Reagan had used the same one for the last few years. To keep from having to use the weight belts from dive operators, they both had BCDs with pockets they could use to hold the weights. Reagan did not need much extra weight to help her descend.

"I need four pounds."

"Eight for me," said Shelly.

"Ladies, please follow me. Your other gear is already on the boat." Carlos hoisted the BCDs over each shoulder, and they waded through sand down to the dock.

Reagan negotiated the uneven topography of the litter-strewn beach and hoped the effects of the SOC explosion would not create any side effects underwater. She had been quick to recover from past athletic injuries, but this was not athletics. She found herself second-guessing her acceptance of this dive.

Following Carlos down the dock, they stopped at a boat that had a middle-aged couple straining to slide inside wetsuits clearly bought when they were twenty pounds lighter. Shelly had her 3 ml suit on for protection rather than for warmth. Reagan never wore a suit in the Caribbean unless the temperature edged below eighty degrees.

"Shelly and Reagan, this is Tom and Eleanor."

"Hey guys," Reagan said as she held out her hand. Eleanor had finished the suit negotiation and grasped Reagan's hand.

"Nice to meet you both. Is this your first day to dive here?"

"Yes, it is." She knew they were both trying not to stare at her uniquely colored cheek. Pointing to it, she said "I got this from the explosion at the SOC."

Tom finished zipping up his suit. "Was the SOC the name of the bar that blew up?"

"Yes, it was."

"I'm sorry to hear you were there. Does that still hurt?"

"Nope, and I'm expecting this saltwater will help heal it." Tom and Eleanor both nodded in agreement.

Four teenaged boys climbed into the boat. "Put your shoes into the bucket on the dock, boys," Carlos said. They retreated to do so, then hopped on. "You must be Tucker, Taylor, Will, and Carson."

"Yes sir," said the taller one.

"OK, your tanks are these four." He pointed behind Shelly and Reagan.

Shelly asked, "Where are you boys from?"

"Oklahoma," said the one with curly hair. "We're on the baseball team—this is our precollege trip."

"Oh, are you playing baseball at Oklahoma?"

"Nah," said another curly-headed guy who closely resembled the first one. "And yes, we're twins."

"I thought so," Shelly said. "It's nice to meet you boys."

"Listen up, divers! This is my captain today. Jargo." Carlos placed his right hand on the young man's shoulder. "Let me tell you a little about our boat."

The divers listened intently.

"In front of me is a water jug for those who didn't bring any, but you can also fill your bottles with it. The black bucket here is for cameras only, and that doesn't mean your iPhones. I'm talking about real cameras. I don't see anyone with those, but the rule stands. There are showers right here," he said, pointing to the two spigots above him, "for washing yourself down after a dive. Bathing suits optional, ladies." Jargo rolled his eyes at the joke he had heard Carlos tell many times. "Be sure to aim the sprayer away from your fellow divers, or at least warn them it's coming.

"The weight belts are right here for those without integrated BCDs and if you're using one of ours, they aren't integrated. There are two buckets down there. The left has four- and five-pound weights and the right has two- and three-pound weights. If you need help adding numbers together to get the weight you need, ask your buddy. I flunked math. Be sure and check your weight in the water, especially if this is your first dive in Tulum, so we can give you some more from the boat if needed. We have a cooler on board if you want to put any food or drinks in it, but if you leave beer, it might be gone when you get back on the boat.

"Down there toward the front of the boat is a marine toilet. There's a little silver button for flushing and everything will disappear into our holding tanks. Only rule we have is no paper or plastic. No metal, wood, goldfish, or small children go in the toilet. The general rule is that if it went through you, it can go into the toilet. Everything else goes into the trash can. We don't throw anything overboard because it's a marine park and that includes food. We don't feed the fish here.

"We're very safe on this boat, so there's life jackets ahead, a first aid kit, and a life raft just above me. If the boat goes down, the raft goes up. We also have two man-overboard rings, so if someone falls overboard, you can toss them one of those.

"It won't take long to get there. Maybe fifteen minutes, so go ahead and get suited up. Be sure you have everything for diving before we leave the dock: fins, mask, snorkel, hot dogs." He asked for and received nods from everyone. "There's a bottle of defog hanging on the rail, and no, it doesn't work on brains, just masks." This drew some groans.

"Any questions?" The portly third baseman from Oklahoma raised his hand. "Yes, Will?"

"Are there sharks on this dive?"

"You never know! I'll give you the dive briefing while we're headed out. The name is Tankah Deep for a reason. The reef is about one hundred feet down, so this will be a short dive. Expect to see turtles, maybe some eagle rays, grouper, yes, some reef sharks," he said, "and some barracuda hanging out around the boat on the way down." He made the hand motion for each animal as he mentioned them.

Shelly appreciated the refresher course, as she never could remember how to make the turtle sign. Carlos continued. "Everyone has a buddy. Jargo is mine, but he stays on the boat. We will be doing a back roll at the site. Everyone comfortable with that?"

They all nodded, continuing to engage their BCDs, rinse their masks, check their air, and slip on their fins.

Pulling up to the site, Carlos pulled out a piece of paper and began drawing the site anatomy. "The boat is being tied to a mooring right now. Underneath the boat is about fifty feet to the sandy bottom, and we will have a maximum depth of one hundred feet. If I see you go below that, I will be motioning you to rise. If you stay shallower, you get a longer dive. If you spend much time below one hundred feet, it will shorten the dive for everyone, and you don't want that, right?"

All but Eleanor nodded. She fidgeted with her mask.

"You all have computers, so essentially, you'll be doing your own dives. Pay attention to yours. Do you all know how computers work?"

No one answered, so he said, "It turns on when you hit the water, but I'll turn it on with this button right now to show you. The upper right number is your dive time. That's zero right now. Lower left is temperature. The water will be a nice eighty-two today. The middle box is your decompression box. This number tells you how long you can stay at whatever depth you are at that instant. You need to keep your deco time at a healthy number, preferably above ten. If it gets below, just go shallower and the number will rise. If it gets to zero, you just bought yourself a six-minute safety stop and no diving for forty-eight hours. No one wants that, and don't act like you're smarter than your computer because you're not.

"I'll have a bright yellow shirt on down there so you can easily find me. I would prefer for you all to follow me, but I will be going slow, so if you take off ahead of me, I may just do a dive by myself. If you decide to do that, just make sure you have your buddy with you. The dive is over when you reach seven hundred PSI or after fifty-five minutes, whichever comes first. If you are not with me, please start your return to the boat at two thousand PSI." He placed two fingers on his forearm and received confirmation from each diver. "Everyone know what PSI means?"

Two of the baseball players pointed at each other shaking their heads. "I shouldn't have asked," said Carlos. "PSI stands for pounds of air per square inch in your tank. We put about thirty-one hundred in your tanks to start with and like I said, I want you back on this boat with at least five hundred to spare. Got it?" They all nodded.

"We have a hang bar at fifteen feet for your three-minute safety stop if you would like to use it." He drew the hang bar on the paper as he talked. "Once there, your computer will show a three, then a two, then a one, then at zero, you're good to come up to the boat. Off the side of the hang bar is an emergency regulator. It's for emergencies and not to extend your dive. At the back of the boat is a buoy with a line to the boat. Use it to grab onto if the current is working against you. Just pull yourself to the boat, and we'll help you in.

"There could be other boats that come to this site, so make sure you get back on the right one. It's tradition, by the way, to buy everyone on the boat a beer if you come up on the wrong one. Also remember that we don't touch, caress, ride, kiss, or molest any of the marine life down there. We're the visitors, so be nice to our hosts.

"The ocean's open! Let's meet at the buoy, and if anyone needs to use the rope to descend, we will head toward the anchor anyway. Wait for me. We will all descend together."

Reagan was in first, unable to contain her enthusiasm, and Shelly soon followed. Tom said he had an air leak, so Carlos attended to him on the boat. As they hung out waiting, Reagan said, "Hey Mom, did you know this is the second largest reef in the world?"

"Let me guess. The Great Barrier Reef is the largest?"

"Yep. This one is part of the Mesoamerican Barrier Reef System that runs from Cancun to Honduras, and it's in better shape than the one in Australia."

"Wait, you said largest. What about longest?"

"Good catch. The Great Barrier is also the longest, but this one is only the fourth longest."

The others swam up.

"Everyone good?" Carlos held up his thumb.

Each diver put their thumb up. She did not know why, but this exercise reminded Reagan of the groundhogs that popped up in Grandma Jenkin's backyard.

"Max depth of one hundred feet. See you on the bottom!" Carlos released his air and disappeared below the surface. Reagan and the others followed, although Eleanor cleared her ears four times before starting her trip to the bottom.

The initial descent on the first dive of a new trip was always Reagan's favorite part. The visibility was ninety feet, and the thrill of the moment gave her goosebumps. She could already see the colorful reef below her, and she made out a Caribbean stingray as it shook loose some silt and glided away.

Reagan felt more comfortable in the water than she did on land. She had learned to swim when she was six months old and lifeguarded a few summers. She thought back on her childhood as she descended on the reef. She did not see anyone but Shelly, so she glanced toward the surface and Carlos was working with Eleanor, who apparently still had some clearing issues.

Reagan proceeded, circling the reef, watching the blue damsels darting for cover, a pair of spotfin butterflyfish, some black durgons suspended above the reef, a lionfish hanging out under a ledge, several conchs, a trumpetfish hiding in ambush amongst some sea rods, and a trunkfish moseying past her.

Soon, the other three descended and Carlos motioned for all to follow. Reagan trailed for a moment to pee, another favorite moment of a dive, and then caught up as Carlos showed Bob a Caribbean lobster's antennae poking out from a cave. In the distance, she could see garden eels as they teased anyone to get close. This would bring a quick retreat into a hole that was no hole at all. She had played the game enough to know it was fruitless.

After twenty-eight minutes of reef inspection, Tom motioned that he was at 1,000 PSI and Carlos pointed toward the surface. They slowly ascended to twenty feet and began their three-minute safety stop. A shiny silver barracuda with a chunk missing from his tail swam past Reagan, and she congratulated herself for removing her jewelry before the dive. She amused herself by thinking these skinny fish with underbites had to be fairly stupid to mistake jewelry for a fish.

Back on the boat, she and Shelly compared notes. Shelly had seen a loggerhead, apparently when Reagan was relieving herself, but Shelly had not seen the royal starfish. They wrapped themselves in towels after their showers, then took their seats. Jargo handed them some pineapple slices and a bottle of water.

Reagan looked toward the south and did not like what she saw. "That looks bad," she said to Shelly.

CHAPTER 7

Jaden's emotions vacillated between excitement and worry. It was a quarter to noon, and a few players stretched on the field while others took batting practice, but most of the team had already left for lunch. The manager, Nieto Fregas, had requested that he come to the owner's box for a special meeting at noon. It involved a unique opportunity that did not involve baseball. It was a sweltering day, and the heat bounced unflinchingly off the concrete.

He knocked on the door. It abruptly opened and Silva's administrative assistant, Bobby, said "Jaden Prefontaine! Oh, I mean Baxter." His amused grin threatened to dampen Jaden's mood. He canvassed the room, seeing only the outline of the unmistakable Silva as the light from the field-side window cast a black shadow across his face.

"Hello, sir," Jaden said, hesitantly.

"Jaden, good to see you again. Did you enjoy my pizza?" He walked toward him and now was standing with his right hand outstretched. Jaden shook it.

"Best pizza I've ever had, Mr. Silva."

"Most people call me Gonzo or el Jefe or even Guano behind my back. I'm impressed that you even know my last name."

"I'm from Texas, sir. We show respect for our elders by saying 'Mr.' I hope I didn't offend."

"On the contrary." Silva wrapped his right arm around Jaden's shoulder. His grip was authoritative but comforting. Leading him to a set of couches in the center of the room, he said, "You must come from good stock."

"Thank you, sir."

"Let me get straight to the point, Jaden. Would you like to make $100,000?"

Jaden swallowed uncontrollably. "That sounds good to me, but I would need some details. Is it legal?"

"Of course! We would never ask you to do anything illegal. And before you ask why we would choose you over someone else, the answer is speed."

Feeling more confident now, Jaden asked, "So what is this all about?"

Silva turned toward Bobby. "Can you get the lights and start the video?"

Bobby, who had been standing in the corner during the exchange, pushed a button under the bar counter and an LED screen dropped out of the ceiling while the curtains closed over the windows on the ballpark side and the room lights went out.

A video opened of two men facing each other at opposite ends of a large grass field, wearing only a loincloth. A thick forest rose behind each player. To Jaden, this looked like no game he had ever seen. Concrete walls rose three stories high on each side and each of the two walls had a hoop near the top.

Both men had a large bat in their hands and a rubber ball about the size of a soccer ball at their feet. Jaden noticed that the concrete walls were slanted at forty-five degrees away from the field and assumed this would make it easier for the players to run up each one without using ropes and get closer to the hoop.

When a horn blew, each man kicked the ball down the field in the direction of the hoop on their right. As they neared the center of the field, one man picked up his ball and attempted to bat it through the hoop on the slanted concrete wall but missed. He raced to retrieve the ball.

The other man used a different technique. As he neared center field, he kicked the ball up the concrete slope toward the hoop, precariously maneuvering the ball as he worked to maintain his balance on the sloped wall. As he neared the circle, he kicked the ball through and raised his hands in victory.

The video went to a commercial for PokBall. It talked about twelve leagues being formed and multiple sponsors including Grupo Televisa, Arca Continental, and Bimbo. There were photos of betting windows with long lines, packed crowds at either end of the stadium, and players being wined and dined. As the video appeared to be reaching its conclusion, Bobby stopped it, and the lights came back on.

"So, what do you think?" Silva asked, grinning like he had won the lottery.

"Well, I'm not sure what to think right now," said Jaden. "Is that all there is to it? Just one game? One score? Do I have to win to make the $100,000?"

"All good questions," said Silva. "It's a team game, much like baseball, but there are eight contestants per team. Each contestant competes against an opposing team member, and it's a double elimination tournament. Seeding is done by each team manager, and they are reseeded after each round. Each contest is a best three out of five decision, and the tournament is not over until only members of one team remain."

Jaden asked, "So, if one team has five players left and the

other has only one, what happens?"

"The one player plays each one in turn until only one team has any players left. That team then moves on to play the next team in a tournament that lasts eight days. This is scheduled during the off week for our baseball team next week, so there would be no conflict. You are paid the $100,000 just to play next week's tournament for my team. Are you in?"

Jaden hesitated, then asked, "Are any other players from our team involved?"

"Only Chris Tucker," Bobby said.

"He hasn't mentioned that to me."

"That's because it is forbidden to discuss this with anyone who is not on our PokBall team, and you have not yet signed with us."

"Am I free to discuss this with Chris now?"

"Once you have signed the contract."

"Just to be clear, I will receive $100,000 to spend eight days playing this Pok game?"

"That is correct, Jaden," Silva replied quickly. "You get a $50,000 signing bonus and another $50,000 when the tournament is over."

"Where do I sign?" He knew Chris rarely made poor decisions, and he hoped his dad would think better of him if he went a few years without having to ask for money.

Bobby withdrew a one-page document from the mahogany rolltop desk. After Jaden read the sparsely worded contract, he felt confident and signed it.

"Welcome to the team, Jaden!" Silva smiled. "As you know, tonight's Tigres game is the last game of this series, so the start of the PokBall tournament has been set for tomorrow night. Meet us here at six in the morning, and we will get you and Chris to the stadium."

"So, this will be played at night?"

"Yes, but there will be lights."

"When do I get the $50,000?"

"When you get here tomorrow."

"But I thought it was a signing bonus."

"We have to make sure you show up," said Silva.

"Oh, I'll be here, but first, we have to win this game tonight."

"Exactly what I wanted to hear from my center fielder."

"My mom and sister will finally get to see me play here. I'll be sure to introduce you to them."

Bobby shot a quick glance at Silva, who held onto the grin. "I look forward to meeting your family," said Silva. "Now get out of here. We have to work on our strategy for the game."

Jaden wondered which game but did not think too long. He relished the prospect of adding $100,000 to the paltry $500 per week salary he received for being the Tigres center fielder.

CHAPTER 8

"Bad news, divers," Carlos started, doing his best to appear contrite. "We just got word of a storm headed this way. Not just any storm but a bad storm. They aren't saying hurricane yet, but it sounds like it and this is never, and I mean never, seen this time of year. They're saying it's severe and will come and go quickly, but we must get out of the water fast. I know you were expecting more dives today, but it's safety first, and after our surface interval, the storm would hit while you are on the next dive. I'm afraid we must return to the dock. The ocean is closed."

Reagan and Shelly looked at each other and shrugged. "I'm getting hungry anyway," Reagan said, holding her stomach for emphasis. "I was reading in Conde Nast Traveler about a great restaurant called the Blue Conch, and they make great mai tais."

"Not today," said Shelly. "I've lived through a few tropical storms, and even if this isn't a tropical storm, we need to hunker down. I hope it doesn't wash out Jaden's game tonight, but I'd be shocked if they play. It's a shame because it's the last one for over a week."

After arriving at the dock, noting the threatening premature darkness, they quickly climbed into their golf car at the dive shop and headed home. The skies were sending a message. "We may get dumped on, so gun it!" Shelly said.

Halfway home, the skies emptied, and gale-force winds drove blinding rain into the right side of the golf car, heavy winds threatening to topple it. Reagan found an abandoned gas station and navigated the car up against the wall to protect them. Debris flew over the station, away from the angry sea. Rocks, shells, sand, and fragmented reef pelted the establishments on the other side of the street.

"Wow! The fish are flying!" Bar jacks and blue striped grunts were expectorated by the ocean. The concrete walls of the gas station quivered next to them but not enough to force them to another spot.

Twenty minutes later, it stopped. They cautiously edged away from their shield, worried a reprise was on the way, but calmness remained. They were just a few blocks from home, but the devastation was catastrophic. Debris covered their patio and the beach behind the villa, and the pool and jacuzzi were seas of mud. "I doubt we need to alert Eduardo about this. I'm sure he'll be checking on us," said Shelly.

"Hey, let's just wear swimming suits to the restaurant. Whatever we wear will get wet from driving through puddles anyway. I hope the Conch is still standing."

"I sure hope that storm doesn't have a second act."

"Mom, the skies are clear now. It'll be fine."

"I am not going in this bikini, and neither are you, and why do you think it will be open?"

"Well, if it isn't, we just come back to see what this storm did. It's an adventure, Mom!" After drying off and changing, Reagan deposited the bag in the rear compartment, and they headed to town.

Debris made the trip an obstacle race for Reagan. Shelly hung on to the rail with both hands, being sloshed by rainwater every few yards. When they arrived at the restaurant, Shelly said, "I can't even tell the storm came through here." They put on some baseball caps, then waded through dirty water to the front door where an awning was ripped away from its home.

"Are you guys open?" she yelled through the screen door. A young lady with a white apron boasting a caricature of a blue conch shell taking a bite of a taco showed up and waved them in. Reagan cleaned the droplets off her glasses.

"How do you like our weather?" She led them to a nearby booth.

"Kept us from diving this afternoon," said Shelly. "Did the storm just kiss you on the cheek here?"

"It's the strangest thing. It's like it went down the bay in front of the restaurant and took a turn left to create most of the havoc north of us."

"That's good news for you," said Reagan. "I'm worried about the visibility tomorrow, but we're diving anyway." The concierge was already walking away toward the next customers.

"I'm worried about the game tonight," Reagan lamented.

A middle-aged woman, heavily decorated with tattoos and slightly bent where bending did not seem possible, suddenly showed up at their booth. "Welcome to the Blue Conch! Is this your first time here?"

"Yes, it is," said Shelly.

"Well, I'm the owner. Blessy's my name. This restaurant has been in my family for many years."

"This is my daughter, Reagan, and I'm Shelly. We're sorry to be dripping on your seats."

"Oh, no worries. It's just water, and we have quite a mess on the ocean side. Katie will be right with you. Enjoy your meal." With that, she disappeared as fast as she had appeared.

"Have you heard from Chris?" Shelly snuck the question in nonchalantly after they had ordered conch salads and mai tais.

"You've been with me, Mom. You know I haven't, but honestly, I'm not here for romance, so I will not be pursuing that relationship. He is cute, though."

"Jaden seems to really like him, and he's always been a good judge of character."

"Was that a dig at me?"

"No, of course not. You might have had a few lapses, but in general, you're a good judge."

"Gee, thanks."

"Well, anyway, I enjoy spending time with you, so you won't see me trying to foist any new alliances on you."

"I appreciate that—"

Katie set the drinks and food on the table. "Anything else?"

"Not unless you have towels for us to sit on." Showing a severe absence of humor, Katie picked up the menus and went to the next booth.

"By the way, Mom, do you happen to know if the stadium is close enough to drive to in our golf car?"

"No, but let's ask someone here. Maybe they'll know."

As they were surveying the room, Blessy came over to the table with a shorter Hispanic woman with necklaces heavy enough to bend her forward, a gummy smile, and eyebrows an inch higher than Blessy's.

"Ladies, this is Sabbi. She owns the Villa Sueño del Mar."

"We love your villa, Sabbi. Nice to meet you," said Shelly.

"I am so glad to hear that. I trust that Eduardo has taken care of you?"

"No complaints, but this storm has wreaked havoc on the pool and patio. We just came from there."

"Already on it. I have a crew there right now. You must have just missed them."

"Now that is service. The pool and jacuzzi will needs lots of love. That beach may take a week to get cleaned up."

"We may surprise you."

"The natives here seem restless from the storm, Sabbi," observed Reagan. "We're not regulars, but I bet this one was not expected and certainly not normal for this time of year."

"No, this was most unusual. I've lived here most of my life and haven't seen anything like this . . . the timing, the pattern . . . nothing was normal. Some are saying it's a sign of some kind, but I don't engage in tilting at windmills like so many here in the Yucatan do on a regular basis. Back to the villa . . . Are you going there after your lunch?"

"Yes, we are. I may take a nap. Naps seem like a requirement in the Caribbean." Shelly smiled warmly.

"Let me follow you out there to show you a few more things about the villa. Sometimes Eddie doesn't communicate all the fine points. Plus, I haven't seen it in a few months. I've been traveling and would like to see the damage from the storm."

"I appreciate it. Do you know where Estadio de Beisbol Beto Avila is?"

"It's in Cancun," said Sabbi.

"Oh, we thought it was closer."

"You could drive, take a bus, or even take a boat. A car is the quickest way. Do you need a rental?"

"We hadn't planned on needing one, but that sounds like a good idea," said Shelly. "How could we get one soon?"

"I can have one brought to the villa. I know people." She grinned. "The paperwork will be minimal. The car will get there when I am there so I can take the driver back."

"Thank you so much. We'll see you at the house."

Sabbi and Blessy smiled and walked away.

"Well, you didn't say much, Reagan. What were you thinking?"

"How did Blessy know where we were staying?"

"Hmm. Maybe Sabbi was given a picture of us by Eduardo and she told Blessy she recognized us here?"

"If he took a photo of us, I wasn't aware. Did you see him with a camera or cell phone?"

"No, but maybe he researched us, or maybe Sabbi did after we booked the villa. Was your picture in the paper from the explosion?"

"I don't know. Just makes me uneasy."

"I know the events of the last few days have been upsetting. I can't see the bomb being meant for you, or it would have been planted closer to your table, and that van was not paying attention."

"I'm not so sure. I was sitting at the bar, right by the spittoon. I would've been sitting there when the bomb went off if Chris and Jaden hadn't come in. I only left that area to sit at a table with them. If I had been sitting there, I would have been killed . . . just like those poor teenagers on the dance floor."

"But you don't know when the bomb was placed there. It could have been after you were at the table or even days before it exploded."

"Thanks, Mom. I hope you're right."

They enjoyed their salads in silence, thinking about their bad luck with diving and absentmindedly hearing the murmurings and silverware harmonics of the other diners . . . and "Red, Red Wine" by UB40 on the jukebox.

The jukebox! Reagan remembered one of the boys played a song on the jukebox just before the explosion. Boy George. "Karma Chameleon." Then his group disappeared. Maybe the song set off the bomb in some way. Reagan stored this information away.

"Hang in there, Gigi," implored Blessy. "Chaz will be home tonight, and he wants to see you." Blessy's grandmother, Gerene Stephens, had raised Blessy since she was three after Blessy's parents died in a prop plane explosion off Puerto Rico's coast.

"I will do as I please. Chaz hasn't been to see me in three years and now that I'm waiting to see my Jesus, he wants me to wait around for him to escort me?"

"Now, Gigi, you know he's been busy. He really cares." Blessy rearranged her grandmother's frosty gray topknot. "You're trembling. Let me tuck you in good." Blessy wrestled with Gigi's favorite twill blanket.

"I wish you'd quit fussin' over me. If you're gonna fuss, get me a glass of brandy."

"I'll be right back." Blessy straightened as much as possible, but years of waiting tables and bending down to pick up stray utensils had contorted her frame. She wanted her grandmother to stay alive until Gigi's brother arrived from Manila, but her restaurant needed her, too. They were down two waiters this week, so she needed to get back soon. Giving Gigi the glass of brandy, she said, "Gigi, tell us again the story of the girl with the starfish necklace." That was all the prodding she needed.

Her voice sounded like a car battery that wouldn't start. "I learned about young Omelia from my grandmother, who heard about her from her grandmother and so on. I don't recall how many generations, but it was in 1744. I know that's right because I still have a copper half penny for that year from my grandmother Lesia. She said it had been passed down to help us remember Omelia. You don't see many half pennies anymore, given the rate of inflation and—"

"Gigi, get to the necklace part."

Gigi bristled at the interruption but continued her story, laced with frequent painful expressions indicating the physical discomfort she experienced.

"Anyway, Omelia was living with her daddy in Fajardo, Puerto Rico, by the water, and she learned to free dive at a young age to grab conch during the day and octopus at night. They said she was the best diver around because she had six toes on one foot and the other was webbed between several toes. She also dove for starfish, which was her favorite. She kept a collection of the starfish skeletons around their home beside the beach and loved making necklaces from them for friends.

"One starfish she pulled out was a species she had never seen in those waters. It was an iridescent sapphire green with yellow circles ringed in a magenta color, evenly spaced down each arm. She decided this was a necklace she would keep herself, but when she brought it to the surface, a man-of-war stung her, leaving a mark on her wrist that looked like the green starfish . . . only it wasn't green.

"Over the years, stories were told of Omelia forecasting the future when she wore the necklace. She would predict a hurricane, a bad year for sugar cane, and even how many fish her father would bring back from fishing each day."

"Did she predict how you would fall on hard times, Gigi?" Blessy's twenty-six-year-old niece had walked in a few moments before.

"That comment doesn't surprise me, Barbra, but if I could predict your future, it wouldn't be rosy."

Gigi disliked Barbra because she came and went when she pleased, brought questionable men to family events, and always got so drunk she would hit on other guests. Barbra had aspirations of leaving Tepich to make it big as a professional photographer. Gigi wished she could see Barbra's face when Gigi's living will was read.

Glancing at her watch, Blessy stood quickly. "I've got to rush over to the restaurant, but I'll be back later tonight to check on you."

The floor manager handed her a message when she arrived.

"He can kiss my Blarney Stone!" Blessy didn't cower to any-one, especially a creditor from Wolf & Sons. Business had picked up after the seasonal lull, and she knew the creditor would wait. This happened every year.

"Just hang up the next time he calls. No, on second thought, give me the phone next time. He'll be sorry he called." The Blue Conch was a well-known locale for vacationers, particularly after Blessy's travel-agent cousin recommended the Conch to every client for the best food in Tulum.

Situated in a prime area on the beach side of the highway, it was tucked in between a mall and the Manju Hotel.

Her state of inflammation had risen after the outburst, and her recent tattoo of a snowflake throbbed. She was a frequent customer of Alpheus Blizzard, known as the "painless tattooist." His shop, located between the bank and the pharmacy, allowed people to start at the bank and hit each shop in succession.

Alpheus, a successful artist, also knew where the secrets were buried in Tulum. He knew the right time in the tattooing pro-cess to begin the interrogation, and all secrets he uncovered were sold to the appropriate bidders. The Hetacalín cartel, run by Gonzalo Silva, was his best customer.

Blessy had seventeen pieces of Alpheus's art on her body, and she didn't feel like she was done. Her husband and five-year-old son Simon had died in an avalanche on a trip to Peru, and her tattoos were a tribute to them.

"Blessy? Are the bad people going to take our restaurant away?" Rose, Blessy's special-needs sister appeared worried. Rose had been born three months premature twenty-eight years ago and had been by Blessy's side since then.

"No, sweetie. It's just a tactic they use to try and scare us. No reason to get worried." She knew that might not be true.

Back at the villa, Reagan and Shelly were shocked to find a clear pool with the jacuzzi bubbling and a clean beach.

Reagan settled down in a hammock on the newly renovated beach to read *11.22.63* by Stephen King, and Shelly sent a long email to Carlisle, knowing it would be waiting for him when he returned to civilization. She warned him of the alert level and Reagan's involvement. Shortly after she hit "Send," there was a voice at the door.

"It's Sabbi. May I come in?"

"Of course," said Shelly as she hurried to the door. "It's your villa, after all."

"Thank you, Ms. Prefontaine. Your car is here. May I have him come in with the paperwork?"

"Yes, please." A thin Hispanic man entered through the door and a husky vibrato delivered, "I brought you a 2019 Lexus SUV. Will that be OK? I was told you might use it to also transport some scuba gear?"

"That sounds perfect." He laid the paperwork on the bar counter and Shelly completed it in a few minutes. "How will I return it at the end of our trip?"

"You needn't worry about that, Ms. Prefontaine. We will pick it up here. Enjoy your stay!"

Shelly said, "Sabbi. Your people cleaned up the place so fast! I expected this to take a week or longer."

Sabbi's expression was unexpectedly coy. " I might expect a little quid pro quo in the future."

Shelly considered a follow-up question but chose to ignore it.

"Did Eduardo help you with the WiFi and the safes?" Sabbi broke the extended period of silence.

"The WiFi password was on the laminated sheet, so it was no big deal, but we couldn't find the safes."

Shelly followed Sabbi up the stairs. At Shelly's room, she pointed to the closet. "It's in there. Instructions for locking it are on the safe door. It's easy to program. There's one in both of your rooms, by the way."

"Thank you."

"All right, now for the fun stuff." Sabbi led her back downstairs and out the back door. "The combination is 11-22-63. I see your daughter has found the book. She should be able to remember it." In the shed were several bikes, a rowboat, a canoe, a jet ski, and two kayaks.

"This is great. How far out can we kayak?"

"The reef is about one hundred yards out. I wouldn't go past that, since you may get so fatigued that you couldn't row back. Please be careful. The current can also take you down the beach, so row toward the reef at about forty-five degrees to your right to account for that."

"Thanks, Sabbi."

"Oh, I almost forgot. We have some weights and scuba tanks behind the bikes on some shelves that are filled if you want to kick off from the beach here or row out and get in near the reef. There are some buoys out there you can tie up to, but there is also an anchor in the boat if you can find a sandy bottom. That should not be a problem out there, but just don't damage the reefs by dropping anchor into them, OK?"

"Thanks, but we do have arrangements with AAK. We prefer to go with a divemaster when we can."

"Of course. I just wanted you to know in case you decide to go it on your own. Reagan told me you had over a thousand dives, so I wouldn't even be telling you about the tanks if you didn't have the experience. Also, feel free to use the barbeque. It's electric. The best place to get good meat is at Gonzo's Supermarket, but we also have our chefs to shop and cook for you if you wish."

"Thank you. You've been so helpful."

"It's my pleasure. I'll be flying to Boston to see my wife tomorrow, but my number is also on the sheet if you need to reach me. However, Eduardo should be able to solve any problem you may have. Enjoy your stay!"

At that, she left Shelly, wandered around the property for a few minutes, then walked out the front door without another word.

Shelly crossed the back patio under a cloudless sky, navigating around the scuba equipment that had been originally but pointlessly laid out to dry. She then edged down the stone path to the set of hammocks shielded from the Caribbean sun with a bamboo pergola.

Reagan, engrossed in King's back-to-the-future thriller, looked up at Shelly. "Come join me?"

Shelly did her best to make it appear as if hammocks and she were best friends as she climbed in but failed miserably. After a few miscalculations, she rocked gently in the hammock. "Yes, but we need to talk."

"This sounds serious."

"Not really. I just wanted to see what you remember about

our visit with Dr. Brancaccio when you were five or anything else since then about our return visits to see him in Dallas."

"I remember everything, unless there is something you haven't told me."

"No, the main thing was the Puerto Rico Liveaboard when you were three and got stung by the Man-O-War."

"Yes, I know, I know. My DNA was altered after the sting, and that could be one reason for my ability to recall the past so well."

"Right. We haven't mentioned it, but Dr. Brancaccio has been researching to give us more insight into how this has affected you. Your dad and I wanted to wait until he found something significant to tell you, but I received notice that the doctor passed last week."

"Oh no, was it expected?"

"No, it was rather bizarre. I did some quick investigations and read that his car was found in a ravine. No suicide note, and it was vague about any suspicions of foul play, but it did hint at it."

"That's so sad."

"It also mentioned that he had discovered something new about DNA changes with certain Man-O-War stings."

"Surely they found something in his car? On his computer?"

"I couldn't find anything online about that, and his office phone isn't a working number anymore. I was hoping to speak with his administrative assistant."

"Do you know his or her name?"

"All I ever knew was Sharon. Never even knew her last name, and you know how many Sharons there are in Boston?"

"Sounds like a dead end."

"I also did some digging on my own."

Reagan put her book down, feeling like this might go on for a while.

"It seemed like there were a lot of people in this area who were staring at your mark in a different way."

"I agree that there's a different vibe here when they see it."

"Here on the island, there is an old wives' tale about a witch who had a starfish birthmark centuries ago. She was eventually burned at the stake after she showed up in the Yucatan. She escaped Puerto Rico after a tsunami was blamed on her and moving to this area upset the population. There is no written history of this area in the eighteenth century, but it's believed she was burned by the Spanish because several ships off the coast sank within days of her arrival."

"You really did your research."

"I'm worried about you. Maybe you should hide the mark when we're out. It's not safe."

"I can't wear long sleeves, so maybe a wristband. I brought some for working out, so I'll save one for going out."

"Thanks, honey." Shelly closed her eyes, enjoying the sway of the hammock, the rhythmic white-noise waves, and the oceanic breeze. She drifted into a restful sleep. Reagan drifted in and out herself for a while.

Thirty minutes later, Reagan yelled, "Mom! Wake up! We have to get ready for Jaden's game."

Shelly had been dreaming of Reagan being burned at the stake, so she was happy to be woken. "What time is it?"

"It's four-thirty and the game starts at seven. It takes ninety minutes to get there, but we don't know our way around. We should leave here at five. I'm driving anyway, so I make the rules," she said playfully. "Besides, I'd like to get there early. Maybe we can talk to him."

"Did you make sure they're still playing after the storm?"

"Yes, I texted him. They took the team bus and were leaving

at three. I'm sure they get in some batting practice before the game. Are you up for a turtle watch tonight after the game?"

"Looking forward to it."

The trip to Cancun was free of obstacles, as the road crews had cleared the major freeways. There were still many downed trees, signs blown off storefronts, and a general raking of the landscape. Radio stations declared the storm an anomaly.

Today's storm has meteorologists baffled and scrambling to find answers. They have scoured the almanacs and found no evidence of anything like this in recorded history. Local authorities did report finding one tropical storm that threatened to elevate to hurricane magnitude in 1979 in the month of July but nothing else at this time of year. Our reporter who braved the torrential onslaught talked to business owner Sebastian Hybal.

"I've lived here since I was seven years old and I've never seen anything like this. My real estate business had every window smashed. We had no warning! Our office is flooded, and we may not be able to recover."

Experts are also researching how or why the tropical storm was so compact, tore through Quintana Roo in less than twenty minutes, and why it took a ninety-degree turn when it was finished destroying much of the reef system just off our coast. Crews around the city continue to clean . . .

"I wonder if the stadium was damaged," said Reagan.

"I hope not. Thanks for bringing towels, by the way. Good call."

"A wet spot on the back of my shorts would not be sexy."

"Ah, I didn't think about Chris playing tonight."

"That comment had nothing to do with him, Mom."

The GPS system got them to the stadium by 6:15 p.m. At the ticket window labeled Taquilla, Reagan asked, "What are the best seats on the Tigres bench side?"

The attendant showed her the map and pointed to two seats on the end of the third row behind the bench. "We'll take those." After they were handed to her, Reagan said, "Let's go see if we can find Jaden."

They weaved their way around vendors selling hats, T-shirts and other merchandise to their seats. Tejano music played over the speaker system and their mascot was fighting with a big parrot, the mascot for the visiting Pericos de Puebla. The pristine sandy infield had been covered during the storms, with little evidence of damage. "I hope there isn't too much water in the outfield. Jaden will have a hard time wading through a flood to catch a flyball," said Reagan. "Look! There's Jaden's name!"

"Ugh. Baxter?"

"I know, but at least it's him."

"I'm gonna text Jaden to let him know we're here. I don't know if they let them have their cell phones this close to game time, but I can try." After about twenty seconds, she put the phone back in her pocket. "Guess we'll talk to him after the game. Want to get something to eat?" asked Reagan.

"Sounds like a plan."

They both ordered a Nathan's hot dog, got some nachos to share, and a couple of Modelos. While enjoying their food, the music abated and the announcer began his banter, welcoming all to the final game before the All-Star break between the Quintana Roo Tigres and the Pericos de Puebla, mentioning the sponsors and then introducing the teams. When they got to the Tigres and the announcer said, "Playing center field and hitting third, Jadennnnnnnn Baxter! Baxter, hitting third!"

Reagan's attempt at verbally expressing joy and excitement resulted in portions of a mustard-laden hot dog in the lap of an elderly woman in the second row.

CHAPTER 9

Curtains closed, seemingly oblivious to the announcer or the impending game. Silva's water team and special foreign attaché sat on two couches separated by a map of the ocean on the coffee table. Silva was two suites down, enjoying some time with a whore Bobby helped arrange.

Iggy began the meeting. "First of all, as you know, el Jefe has been in search of antiquities for many years, but the Witch's Necklace has held a special interest for him. We do not know if it truly holds the power to tell the future, but he will not rest until we know. Our intel led us to believe that Dr. Brancaccio connected the dots and was able to pinpoint a general location where the necklace from the Widower was lost. We received the information a week ago and realized the location was just off our coast but knew it would have been discovered by now with the number of divers in the area over the last fifty years.

"However, we are now told that this storm today created more turnover in the submerged Mayan ruins and reef structure than ever witnessed before, and there is an increased likelihood that the necklace, if it is indeed in this area, could be found. It was thought to be enclosed in a chest at the time it was lost, perhaps gold-colored, so that is our target."

Chaz, Silva's captain, spoke up. "This sounds like a needle in a haystack to me, Iggy, but my crew will spend from daylight to dusk tomorrow and days after that if el Jefe wants us to."

"Is there a reason you will not be using night dives as well?" Iggy asked.

"Not at all. We will put plans in place to ensure we cover every square inch of the area and have boats and divers running 24/7. Consider it done."

"How many boats do we have available?" asked Bobby.

"About fifteen."

"We need more. Umair, I need you to contact all the dive outfits in the area and tell them to cancel all dives tomorrow. Gonzo will need their boats for the next few days. If they ask how long, tell them to ask Gonzo. That should shut 'em up. And tell them they will be compensated well for their trouble."

"Yes sir."

"That should give us about forty boats," continued Bobby. "Iggy, how many divers can you get ready?"

"You get me the total number of boats and I will get you six divers per boat. Two or three hundred divers will be ready."

"This game is driving me crazy," said Reagan. "I want to see Jaden do something."

"Me, too, honey, but there may be some scouts here. See those radar guns in the crowd? They may be scouting the pitcher Wilson to buy his rights, but if Jaden could just get on base and show his skills, they would be impressed. I've been watching his stats this year. Can you believe how many stolen bases he has? You would think that would get noticed." Shelly always sat straighter when discussing her talented son.

The announcer yelled, "Now batting, shortstop Donte Ramirez."

His walkup song was "Baby Shark." After three times of hearing it, the novelty had worn off. They ran through the motions. He struck out on three pitches.

"Now batting, second baseman, Buster Kadero!" He didn't fare much better, flying out to right on the second pitch.

"Now batting, Jaden Baxter!"

"OOH!" the fans cried in unison. He was hit on the first pitch in the rib cage and fell to the ground. The hushed crowd waited until Jaden got up and ran to first.

This was Wilson's first mistake of the game with no runs, seven strikeouts, and no walks. After eight consecutive throws to first, he went home, but it was a pitchout. Jaden wasn't going. Two more throws to first and then another pitchout. Jaden sat on first. Another pitchout and Jaden was off to second. A perfect throw to second caught him, but it was close. This was likely Jaden's last shot tonight before the All-Star break.

"Mom, I hate leaving Jaden, but since we can see him play three or four more games after the All-Star break, why don't we head home now? Jaden won't get to bat again unless it's extra innings, and we still need to go see the turtles. Jaden will take the bus back to Tulum, so we can catch up with him tomorrow."

Shelly was disappointed, but Reagan made sense. She nodded her approval grudgingly. Exiting the stadium, Reagan checked her cell phone for messages.

Hello, Ms. Prefontaine. We're so sorry, but we will need to cancel your dives tomorrow. We do not know when we will be open again for dives, and we regret to say that no other

dive shops will be available for dives until further notice. We
will notify you when we are once again available to serve
you. Good evening.

"This really sucks," Reagan said. She replayed the message
on speaker for her mom.

"All may not be lost," said Shelly. "We have tanks at the villa."

"But all our gear is at the shop."

"We have a car now, so all we need to do is go get the gear in
the morning. We don't have to tell them we're diving, just that
we need it to snorkel. Then we can do our own dive tomorrow."

"You are a genius, Mom! I knew there was a reason you
came along!"

Once home, they retrieved two long flashlights, with lenses
covered in red cellophane held on by rubber bands. They walked
cautiously down the road.

When they passed the last villa, they found a breach in the
landscaping and headed down a narrow pathway that led to the
beach. Reagan trained her light on a mound about forty feet
away and whispered, "There's one covering the holes with her
flippers."

"There's another one headed for the water," Shelly whispered
back. "Let's sit on that rock over there and watch for a while."

Enjoying the gentle breezes and incoming tide, they watched
six loggerheads take advantage of the circadian influences and
warm malleable sand, burying hundreds of eggs in holes they
had dug about five feet wide and a few feet deep. Even though
the eggs would hatch in a couple of months and the hatchlings
would head toward the ocean under cover of night, most would
not make it.

When they arrived back at the villa, they both found a text
from Jaden.

Thank you both for coming. The game went extra innings
and I scored the winning run! Afraid the scouts left after
they pulled Wilson in the 8th. Love, J

"Ouch," Reagan said. "My bad. Did you see Jaden's text?"
"Yes, just read it."
"I'll respond."

Congrats on winning! Wish we would have
stayed. What are your plans t'morrow?

Owner taking Chris and me to a tournament. New
sport that I might be good at. Called PokBall.

OK, Mom and I are diving on our own. Dive shops
all closed. Let us know how PokBall is. Never
heard of it.

Neither have I. Couldn't find it online. Presentation
I saw was impressive.

Do you know where it is?

Nope. On the team bus headed home. Just us
players and the driver. Chris doesn't know, either.

Keep in touch! Love you!

Mom and I love you, too!

CHAPTER 10

Eating some fruit and granola the next morning, Reagan and Shelly drove the short distance to AAK diving and retrieved their gear.

"With the storm moving things around and bringing colder waters in from the Atlantic, I'll be wearing a dive skin, Reagan. The visibility will be a problem, too, so we'll also need protection from fire coral," said Shelly.

They quickly slipped into their dive skins and loaded two of the four tanks on a tank sled. They put on their dive computers and BCDs, grabbed their regulators, masks, snorkels, and fins and walked to the edge of the water. It was a relatively calm morning on the water.

"What's going on over there?" An armada of dive boats about 300 yards dotted the coastline.

"Wow. Maybe it's a search-and-rescue effort? Could that be why they told us last night that all dives are cancelled?"

"There's nothing we can do now, but maybe we'll hear about it later. Dinner at the Blue Conch?"

"Yep. Thought about mahi-mahi this morning."

They continued to gear up during their conversation. When everything was in place, they did a quick buddy check, verifying each had over 3,000 psi, then did the stingray shuffle as they entered the water. Shelly had stepped on a ray in 2008 when she was kicking off in Bonaire, and she taught Reagan early on how to scare away any unsuspecting animals that could be buried, particularly at this time of day.

"Let's snorkel to the reef to conserve air," Shelly said. As they swam the 100 yards, the current carried them farther away from the glut of boats.

Submerging to the reef base, it was apparent the storm had unleashed a swath of devastation on the underwater environment. The familiar finger projections from one of the largest reef systems in the world that Shelly had explored for decades were torn to shreds, leaving broken coral, toppled outcroppings, and an underwater demolition that destroyed their vision of an underwater rainforest.

It was like a carefully crafted and assembled puzzle had been dismantled by an impetuous child bent on ruining everyone's day. They both stopped finning in stunned disbelief, taking in the defoliation. After a few minutes of reflection and anguish, they regrouped their senses and explored.

Caribbean octopuses scampered about, hoping to create some camouflage. Animals and fish were recessed into a new architecture of ruin. In this absence of life, something shimmered in the murky pea soup of the Caribbean. It wasn't a fish or the tank of another diver because it continued to shimmer like gold. Reagan edged closer, where the object punctured the white sand. Finning closer, she realized it was manmade.

It budged slightly when she attempted to dislodge it from the sand. She rubbernecked, hoping to see her mom but couldn't find her. She scooped sand away, scaring a gobi back into its hole. Goatfish showed mild curiosity as they scoured the surrounding sand. Rocking the object back and forth, she found a purchase point by grasping . . . a gold chest! She pulled it free and set it on the sand. Locked. She flipped it and inched closer to squint at the beautiful insignia. The chest did not have a handle, and it didn't fit inside her BCD.

Although she knew Shelly would be fine as an experienced diver, Reagan was still unsettled. Eyeing her compass, she navigated back to the spot where they had dropped down. Still no sign of her. Their family had established an agreement: If anyone got separated, they would return to the starting point of the dive, the only exception being drift dives, since no one ever got lost on a drift dive. She stayed in the spot, studying the chest. Worn, intricate patterns like palm tree leaves interspersed with newer, raised patterns. A sudden tap on her tank made Reagan jump.

Shelly waved at her, and Reagan held up the chest, then pointed to the surface. Shelly nodded and they began ascending. Reagan glanced at her computer and was relieved to see that she would not need a safety stop. They broke the water and lifted their masks. Reagan's first comments were not about the chest. "Where did you go?"

"I was wondering the same thing. I tried to find life—any life among the reef, and before I knew it, you were gone. I didn't want to waste the dive, so I explored for a while, but this storm scared everything back into hiding and scrambled the reef enough to cause some long-term damage. It's like an underwater nuclear wasteland. Mainly I spent time being sad. Is that chest heavy?"

"Not really. Feels like the chest itself is the weight. It might be empty, but the lock tells another story."

"Are you sure you want to tote that back to the beach?" She glanced over Reagan's shoulder. "That big group of boats is a lot closer. Have they not found a body yet?"

They flipped to their backs and finned toward shore. "I'm sure glad we didn't see a body down there, but for all we know, we could have gone right by it. It would've freaked me out." Reagan placed the chest on her stomach and the sun made it glow. "I'm also glad we came up when we did. Another fifteen minutes and the boats would have been on top of us."

After a few minutes, they felt the sand beneath their fins and stood up. Backing up toward the edge of the water, Shelly searched the horizon. "They have so many divers. Too bad the viz is so bad. I feel sorry for them."

CHAPTER 11

This is too weird, Chris thought. What can be so secretive that they wouldn't want us to know where it is? They had all been blindfolded before boarding the bus, with the explanation, "We have an obligation to keep the location of the stadium secret because the owners are in negotiation to sell it, and we have signed a nondisclosure that says we will not bring new suitors who could potentially outbid them."

The ride was without incident, and although blind, he felt the many turns and some uneven terrain. No other vehicle sounds could be heard, so Chris knew they were in a remote area.

After three consecutive sneezes, a voice from the front of the bus said, "Damn Mexican cedar!"

Chris had heard that voice before but couldn't place it.

Their blindfolds were removed as they arrived at the stadium and a representative led them away from the bus. "OK, I think everyone has checked in, so let's head down to the holding area where the lockers are." Bobby addressed the eight young, confused men who would be on Gonzo Silva's team.

"The location of the stadium is not to be revealed. It's on sacred ground and tourism will make a land grab if we're not careful."

This story shifted from the original, which concerned Chris, but he was getting paid well, so even if the story changed, he'd overlook it for now. Two other men approached but stood apart from the group, lagging behind as the group was led to the end of the stadium. Bobby walked down seven stone steps, where the ground gave way to concrete lateral walls. He removed a set of keys from his pocket and unlocked a metallic door, opening it to the inside.

"Let's go, guys!"

A long hall stretched before them to an area under the field. Scents of rust and motor oil filled the air. Jaden and Chris stayed close together. It was eerily quiet until the metal door closed behind them with a click and the sound of a turning key. Both men who had joined them held AK47s pointed at the group. The group became uneasy.

"Let me assure you," Bobby said, now wielding a Glock 19 semi-automatic pistol, his voice echoing off the solid walls, "you will not be harmed. We found it necessary to restrain you until the conclusion of the tournament, as anyone leaving would cause our team to forfeit the tournament."

Chris thought of engaging Jaden in a conversation to help ease the tension but didn't dare with guns trained on them.

Bobby continued, "If you are concerned about any essentials while you are here, you have no worries. You each have several changes of clothes in your locker and any toiletries you need. No one wants to smell your ass this week. You will find your name on your locker, by the way, and a number assigned to your name. You will be fed well, and you each have your own restroom. We also have a workout facility that you are free to use." He buried the gun into the back of his pants. "The walls are all concrete, and this means no cell signal. We apologize, but we found that when the team has fewer distractions, they stay more focused. The tournament starts tonight."

Montgomery, a player with a buzz cut and goatee, spoke up. "The video I saw showed it during the day. Is this different?"

"Good observation. Yes, the tournaments are played at night. The video we produced was a dramatization. It was shown during the day so you could easily see the action."

There were a few murmurings from the group.

"I know some of you are wondering, so I will answer the unspoken question. No, there is no way to escape. At game time, an electric fence is activated that surrounds the stadium. It has a radius of 125 meters and is unseen. Trust me. You do not want to venture outside the safe zone. But again, you will be free to go after the tournament. I want to emphasize that. Any questions?"

Tabani, a short, bronze-skinned man with glasses, asked, "A better unspoken question is when do we get paid the fifty thousand?"

"You will find your first payment in your lockers, gentlemen," Bobby replied. "I'm surprised that question took so long." This seemed to break some of the tension building to an uncomfortable level.

One of the players was at least six inches taller than the others and he asked, "Are we all playing tonight? The video showed it was one player going against another guy."

"No, not all will play tonight. The rules state that a random number will be called to play each round. Each night's activities are timed, so it starts at nine and ends at eleven, or until the last game started prior to eleven o'clock is over."

Now it was Chris's turn. "Will we be allowed to practice? I've never played this game."

"I'm afraid not. But keep in mind that your opponent has

the same disadvantage. We do have some of the balls down here so you can get a feel for the weight."

"I have a girlfriend who's expecting me to call," Montgomery complained. "If you knew her, you would know she is going to explode if I don't contact her."

"Give me her name and phone number, and we will let her know you're fine. We'll also invite her to the tournament so she can see you haven't abandoned her."

"OK, thanks." Pulling his cell out of his back pocket, he powered it on and clicked on her contact. "Here you go." Bobby took a photo of the screen with his own cell.

"Consider it done. Any more questions for now?"

Jaden didn't trust Bobby with any personal information so he didn't want Bobby to contact Shelly and Reagan, although he knew they would be worried.

"Lunch will be served at noon in the dining hall. Follow me and I'll finish the tour."

Chris glanced over his shoulder and saw the two men still held their rifles. The group followed Bobby down the hall to an opening on the right.

"This is where you will eat. Three squares a day. Don't miss the meals or you won't eat. Seven, twelve, and six. No snacks. Dining room is open for exactly thirty minutes." He continued down the hall and inserted a key into a hole on the wall to his right. A glass dome slowly descended to the hallway ground floor. "This is where each of you will come when your number is called." He opened a door outward. "You will walk into this dome, shut the door, and push this button just below the inside door handle." He pointed to a jungle-green circular compressible button. "It will deposit you onto the playing field where you will climb out and the game will begin."

The tall guy named Jaffer asked, "Will it begin immediately, or will we take positions and then be told to start?"

"Part of the challenge is knowing very little. Don't consider the dramatization video you watched as gospel. This is a contest of foresight, ingenuity, agility, and speed. That, along with the video you saw, is the only information at your disposal to explain what will occur once you enter the field of play. As you likely surmised, there is no internet coverage down here, either, and finding information on the game will be impossible."

"But we saw crowds in the video," said Tabani, a professional poker player from Malaysia who was in Tulum after winning a time share from another player in the back room of the famed Crockfords Hotel in Pahang.

"Again, that was a dramatization. Our crowds are closely scrutinized and extremely limited in numbers."

A cold chill crawled up Chris's spine. Like Jaden, he didn't trust Bobby. How could they all be paid so much money with so few fans?

"But my girlfriend will be here," said Montgomery. "Right?"

"Of course, Mr. Montgomery. Of course. However, I am not sure you will even play a game this evening, but I will be sure to let Bonnie know if you don't, so she won't be worried."

Bobby led them farther down the hall that took a ninety-degree right turn. He unlocked another metal door. Chris hesitated but followed along with everyone else. The room opened to a windowless, expansive area lined with bunk beds on each wall and an eight-foot wooden table in the middle of the room surrounded by eight chairs. An eighteen-inch-wide clear plexiglass tube extended from the thirty-foot ceiling, terminating at the hardwood floor. *Looks like a laundry chute,* thought Chris, *with no way to extract the clothes.*

"This is the underground bunker. We all call it the UB. You will have free reign of the premises up until game time, but you need to be back in the UB by nine where you will await your turn to play PokBall. The door will be locked at nine. Please do not be anywhere else but here by that time each night."

No one spoke. The entire group formulated their thoughts, none of which were inspirational, some of which were rational, and all of which were apprehensive.

CHAPTER 12

"There they are." Standing inside the living room of their villa, Reagan pointed through the glass sliding doors to the armada, the leading edge parallel to their villa. They jettisoned their diving gear on the patio to dry and put on their wraps to take some of the chill off from the central air. They decided not to take a postdive dip in the pool until the body-seekers were past their section of the beach. Reagan grabbed her phone and began searching.

Typing in "drowning Tulum" only produced a story from 2007 when a forty-one-year-old man's body was found floating in the sea at Tulum. Trying "body missing Tulum," she found a story of a family of four from Iowa last year, but their bodies were found. There was a missing Israeli from 2011 but nothing else. "I guess this is so new that the slow news in this area hasn't caught up."

"Maybe they're hunting for that chest you found," smirked Shelly.

"Oh, the chest! I forgot about it." She hurried over to the table where she had placed it. "Let's find something to open it with."

"I saw a letter opener behind the bar," said Shelly, "and there's the set of keys we use for the villa on the counter. Let's at least try them." The keys did not work, and the letter opener's tip broke off when they twisted it in the lock. "Crap. Maybe we need a locksmith."

"This is ridiculous," Reagan said, thrusting her hands skyward. "I am not wasting time or money finding someone who *might* be able to unlock this. I saw a hammer down by the bikes." She hurried out the door and returned with the hammer.

"You should see the boat parade passing near our beach. Divers were getting into some boats and falling backward off others. Workers on the decks changed out tanks, and one boat was packed with tanks but no divers. I wish we knew what they were searching for."

Shelly peeked out the window. "They've passed us now, so let's go outside. We can bang on the chest without worrying about breaking something in the house."

"Mom, stand back." Reagan placed the chest on the concrete rim of the jacuzzi, then lightly tapped the lock, using a downward strike. Increasing the force, she struck again. Nothing. Doubling the force again, the hammer head slipped off the edge and she banged her knuckles on the side of the jacuzzi. She tried not to cry out to avoid bringing attention to anyone lingering in the water. She then slammed the chest against the rock patio out of exasperation and the top of the chest popped open. They both laughed and Reagan temporarily forgot her throbbing knuckles.

The contents had partially spilled out of the top. At first, it appeared to be a black leather strap, but when Reagan picked it up, they realized it was a necklace. It had an unusually large pendant in the shape of a starfish. The pendant had an iridescent sapphire-green hue with yellow circles ringed in magenta evenly spaced down each arm.

"This is pretty, but hardly worth being locked in a gold chest. I guess it really was a child's chest. Must be why I was able to break into it. I'm going to see if it matches my cover-up." She placed the necklace over her head and the starfish rested gently against her chest.

"Where am I?"

"Stop being silly, Reagan."

"My name is Reagan? Who are you?"

"Quit playing around."

Reagan gave her mother a confused look, then took in her surroundings. "Where are we?"

"This is no longer funny, Reagan."

"If I'm Reagan, then who are you?"

"Reagan, take that necklace off!" Shelly jumped up, eyes wide as she tripped over the ottoman and sprawled headfirst onto the carpet.

Reagan stared at her mother. "Hey, I knew you were going to fall just now."

"Please take off that necklace."

Instinctively, Reagan removed the necklace. "Mom, why are you on the floor?"

Shelly got up and hugged Reagan tightly. "Oh, baby, I don't know what that necklace did, but don't put it on again."

"Why? All I did was put it on and take it off. You're not making any sense, and I don't understand how you tripped."

"I think I know why that necklace was locked up. When you put on the necklace, you didn't know who you were or who I was."

"How could a necklace have powers? I don't think you heard me right. Maybe we should test it again. I have an idea. It's crazy but it may help you feel better and prove you are wrong . . . or prove you right." She walked to the kitchen and rummaged through some drawers. "Bingo!" She walked back to the couch and placed a piece of paper on the coffee table. She spoke out loud as she wrote, "The necklace I have on makes me forget that the lady sitting next to me is my mother, Shelly. This is normal and all I have to do is remove it to remember her. My name is Reagan."

"This makes me nervous, Reagan."

"Mom, it's fine. Just don't fall on the floor again." As she placed the necklace over her head again, her confused eyes stared quizzically at the room.

"Look at the piece of paper in front of you," Shelly said, pointing.

Reagan read it, then removed the necklace. "See, nothing happened!"

"But I told you to read the paper. Do you remember that?"

"No, but I believe you. The best way is to have you wear it now so I can see what's going on. Write a message to yourself." She handed Shelly another piece of paper and the pen.

You are wearing a necklace that makes you forget who you are and who you are with. Take it off to bring you back to reality.

Shelly started to place it over her head, then hesitated. "What if something goes wrong? This necklace has powers that we should not be messing with."

"Just put it on. I'm right here."

Shelly placed the necklace over her head and the starfish rested awkwardly on her ample cleavage. "Well, I know you're Reagan. And I'm Shelly, and I'm not even looking at that paper I wrote."

"Well, well. Maybe it only works on smaller boobed women."

"That's not funny."

"OK, let me try it again, but let's spice it up. I'm gonna add to my message."

As a test, go to the refrigerator and get an apple. Bring it back and put it in your lap, then take off the necklace.

"OK, here goes nothing!" She placed the necklace on, bringing once again an unknowing stare.

"Read the paper in front of you," Shelly once again directed her.

As she read it, she shot a puzzled expression at Shelly, went to the refrigerator, opened the bottom drawer to get the apple, then returned to the couch, and removed the necklace.

"Oh my god. There's an apple in my lap and I don't remember getting it. This necklace . . . now it's scaring *me*."

"I watched you but didn't tell you where the apple was. It was on the top shelf, but last night, I straightened up and put it in the bottom drawer. You opened the bin immediately and didn't even look on the top shelf."

"You mean I can see through closed drawers?"

"Or something like that. Maybe you just *know* stuff when you have that on."

"Hmm . . . OK, next experiment." She went behind the bar and found a set of dice she had seen, then returned to the couch. She took a selfie and placed her cell phone face up, showing the photo.

Adding to the already lengthy note, she wrote,

My picture is on the phone by me, and it is a selfie. Take the two dice and roll them, but first tell the woman in the room what the roll will be. Do this five times, then remove the necklace.

Shelly returned to her seat but inched closer to Reagan so she could see the dice rolls.

Reagan placed the necklace around her neck, returned to the confused state, read the paper, and picked up the dice. I am about to roll a 4." She rolled the dice. Two twos. "I can see what I will be rolling. Is this a dream?"

"No, it isn't. Roll the dice again."

"Six this time." A five and a one.

"Eleven." A six and a five.

"Seven." A four and a three.

"Another seven." A six and a one.

Reagan removed the necklace.

"You were five for five, Reagan. You can see the future with that necklace on. Maybe there are more powers, but do you really want those powers?"

"An ethical paradox?" Reagan asked.

"More like dangerous consequences. Knowing things you would rather not know but forgetting your past to know the future?"

"That's not a paradox, actually, but it reminds me of the phenomenon of hormesis."

"Hormesis? What the hell is that?"

"It's something that's seen in toxicology usually. It involves a biphasic-dose response to an environmental agent of some kind."

"Speak English, please."

"For example, a medication at a low dose might have one effect on you, while at a higher dose, could have the opposite effect. That's hormesis."

"So, the necklace can do good things but with the memory loss, might create some problems. That's hormesis?"

"Just hang with me, Mom. I'm still not believing this is really happening, and I don't know why it doesn't work on you.

What if it has to do with the DNA change in me that Dr. Brancaccio discovered? He seemed to be really fascinated with that."

"Yes, I know he was intrigued. He hadn't ever seen it and spent years studying the science behind it. It's so sad that he died."

"Does this mean I'll be burned at the stake like the witch you told me about? We both have starfish birthmarks and now I have special powers?"

"Reagan! Stop that!"

"Just kidding, but I know of one more experiment I want to try," said Reagan. "We need to try the necklace on one more person to see if I am the special one or if you are for not being affected."

"Jaden?"

"Well, he's related. I don't want to add genetics to the equation, so I'd rather get someone else, but we could at least try him if he's available. I'll text him." She picked up her phone.

> Hey J! Join Mom and me 4 lunch? Is that PokBall
> game over?

"While we wait for him, let's—hey, the maid just pulled up. We have a victim."

In a few minutes, Marta walked through the door with her young helper, Tahira. "Buenos dias, Marta!"

"Buenos dias."

"Can you do a favor for me?"

"Of course!"

"May I see how this necklace looks on you?

"Yes, ma'am."

Reagan slid the necklace over her neck and said, "You look very pretty!"

Marta grinned. "Gracias, Señorita Reagan."

Reagan then removed the necklace carefully and rubbed her

own starfish mark. "Marta, we will be fine today. Please take the day off, and I will make sure you get paid." After the maids left, she walked back to the couch.

"I'm thinking it has to be the DNA, Mom. Last experiment of the night. I want to see how far out I can predict something." She grabbed the paper and added one final set of instructions.

This necklace also allows me to tell the future. Close my eyes and think hard. Try to see something happening in the future. When you see it, write it down below this paragraph.

She placed her phone again where she could see her selfie, then placed the necklace over her head. She was confused, until she read the note. She shut her eyes and explored her memory. She remembered nothing from the past, but events came into focus in the future. She wrote on the paper:

Halep upsets Williams 6–2 6–2 to be the first Romanian to win Wimbledon.

She removed the necklace and stared at the paper. She then checked her phone and searched for "Wimbledon." Williams and Halep were set to play in one hour.

"OK, why did I see this? Is it because it's happening so soon? Because it's on a national stage? Because I like tennis?"

"I don't know, honey, but this is upsetting. Who knows what kind of side effects the necklace will have on you?"

"Mom, if it's a connection with the starfish mark on my arm or altered DNA or both, I don't think it will create any more distress on my body than has already occurred."

"You're rationalizing."

"Let's just see what happens with Wimbledon. Then we can discuss this again. We need to eat but no text from Jaden. He must be busy."

CHAPTER 13

"Things are rounding out nicely," said Kara, sitting to Silva's right at the mahogany table in the library. "All eight players are tucked away in the underworld. Zoom invitations have been sent to the twelve apostles, and drone instructions have been couriered to the two Danes and the Saudi, since they are new."

The twelve apostles for this tournament included the Saudi and two Danes, a German, a Belarusian, an Austrian, a Sri Lankan, a Tunisian, a Japanese, an Israeli, an Egyptian, and a Czech.

"Did the damn Saudi sign the hundred-year nondisclosure agreement?"

"Yes."

"He didn't get the discount, did he?"

"No. He paid in full."

"He better not win this one. I'll shit a brick."

"Don't forget how much money he's paid us."

"I don't care about his goddamn money! You know what the Saudis did to me. One thing I don't do is forget a wrong. I'm going to see if Bobby can rig something for me to make sure he doesn't win."

"You know that would be in violation of the agreement you always make with the apostles, dear." She caressed his right leg.

"And you know that turns me on."

The eight players huddled around the table, playing Mexican Trains. They knew the room might be bugged, though some had to be told. The IQ level in this group failed to average eighty, so the discussion ranged from how hot their girlfriends were to who was going to the World Series this year. Chris begged off to take a nap, and Jaden said he was ready for a pregame shower. They both met by the shower, clothes on, shower steaming up the bathroom. "What do you think, Jaden?"

"I don't know, but this is all kinds of wrong. I know they've paid us, but I've never heard of this game. No one on our team has ever participated, so what's happened to the other teams? Do they all retire after a tournament?"

"I can only hope so," replied Chris. "Maybe we sign an NDA later. I'm worried about what Reagan and your mom are thinking. No one is counting on me, but they will be putting out an APB on you for sure. You're one of the reasons they flew here."

"I know. I'm worried about them but didn't want to give Bobby any way to contact them. Didn't seem smart. Maybe tomorrow if I feel better about this whole thing."

"I think I want my number called just to get this over with."

"I agree. I wish I had said 'no,' but something tells me it's too late for that."

"I'm sure you're right, Jaden." Chris looked toward the ceiling. "See that vent?"

"Ah, yes. Like your thinking. A bit small for us, though."

"I'm sure it opens up to larger ductwork and we have to

assume they wouldn't have cameras in here, but for the time being, let's be considering what steps would need to be taken to get up there, remove the vent cover, and expand the entry."

"The table in the room we're in could get us high enough . . . if we're including the others in the plan, but we'd have to be confident they wouldn't be watching. Maybe they don't watch 24/7."

"OK, we'd better get back before they get suspicious. I didn't see any cameras or audio equipment, but we have to assume we're being watched." They opened the bathroom door and heard muffled shouting from down the hall that morphed into an adrenaline-packed argument as they neared the bedroom door. Apparently, any fear they had of a bugged room was bested by the emotional need to be correct.

"You're a pussy for wanting to take this without a fight!" Montgomery engaged with Tabani.

"You really think those two guys with AK47s are all that stands between us and freedom?"

"How do we know if we don't try?"

"You're going to get us all killed, not just yourself!"

"I'm not willing to let some madmen orchestrate my—"

"Wow, big word, motherfucker."

Montgomery jumped over the table, sliding on domino trains, and lunged for Tabani when Jaffer and a beefy guy named Hornbeck grabbed and wrapped him up. J.C. Hornbeck ran a construction firm in Indiana and had seen his share of misplaced virility.

"That's enough!" Jaffer yelled through gritted teeth. "You guys are so paranoid. This is just a game, and you're getting paid well to play it, probably better than all of us make in a year, and we get to make it in a week." Montgomery calmed down slowly.

Chris and Jaden watched from the doorway with no intentions of engaging.

Shirt unbuttoned to reveal a tanned, expansive belly, Silva sat at a round marble table positioned under the awning of his greenhouse. His cell phone chirped. "Any news?"

"Not yet," Chaz said, speaking from his boat.

"Shit!"

"I know. Sorry, but the visibility's been a bitch and having so many divers in the water doesn't help, especially when we're turning over rocks and broken reef."

"What's your plan?"

"We did one pass-through of the radius Brancaccio had mapped out. We're about to head back through, but I'm considering expanding the radius so we can avoid the mess we've been kicking up. Brancaccio could have miscalculated—"

"I don't wanna hear that shit."

"But I'll also be getting the night crew to go back through what we just did. We're hoping the lanterns will help by bouncing light off anything metallic that we might have missed on the first go at it."

"I don't need to tell you that this needs to have the right conclusion."

"I am well aware, Jefe."

"I don't care if you have to tear up every goddamned reef or turtle nest in the Caribbean. Get that damned chest for me!" He reached over to smell the nearest cannabis plant. His plan this evening was to partake, chest or no chest.

Shelly read and napped in cycles in the lounge chair by the pool until Reagan interrupted. "Mom, I just checked Wimbledon. Serena is losing 6-2, 5-2. I guess I could really see the score with that necklace on. What could this mean?"

"It makes me nervous." Shelly put her book down.

"I've always asked Jaden when I have a life decision to make . . . after you, of course," she backpedaled, "but I've texted him a few times and my call went straight to voicemail. He probably forgot to charge his phone again."

"Why don't you put it in the safe for now while—"

"Already ahead of you. Put it there a few hours ago with the broken chest while you were eating your sandwich."

"Good. Your dad will be out of the mountains by tomorrow, and I'd love to get his perspective."

"Me, too," Reagan said. "He'll probably throw some statistics into the conversation, but he usually has a good head about ethics."

"He'll likely need to see proof for himself. You know the way he is, but at least he can be thinking about the possible consequences of knowing the future. I can hear him now. 'Forecasting is the art of saying what will happen, and then explaining why it didn't.'"

"That won't help me at all in making a decision, Mom. Oh dear. The final was 6-2, 6-2."

"We're fortunate that no one can hear this conversation, Reagan. It doesn't even sound believable to *me,* and I'm living it."

"I'm hungry," said Reagan. "Where are we going for dinner tonight?"

"Should you put on the necklace?"

"Very funny. We could always do the Blue Conch again. With my facial injury and your bruised shoulder, maybe the fewer new people we meet, the better."

"At least we know where it is, and we can drive our golf car there. Wait, let me call the dive shop real quick to see if they're open tomorrow." Shelly hit the number for AAK diving.

"AAK Dive Shop."

"Are you guys open tomorrow?"

"No, ma'am. We do not know when next we will open."

"Thank you." She ended the call. "Just what I figured. I wish someone would tell me what they're using all those boats for. Maybe we can ask at the Conch."

They arrived just as the sun decided to show off. It began sliding beneath the waterline in the distance, casting an amber glow destined to be the catalyst for a lover's kiss somewhere this evening. Shelly and Reagan asked to be at the same booth they had sat in on Thursday night.

The television above the bar showed highlights of the Williams-Halep match with a voice-over. "Simona Halep played a near-flawless fifty-six-minute final on Saturday, winning six-two, six-two against the game's best player. She becomes the first Romanian woman to conquer Wimbledon."

Unfolding the menus, they made their choices. They were enjoying their meal of mahi-mahi with a mai-tai for Reagan and sea bass with a house chardonnay for Shelly when they saw Blessy.

"Welcome back! The weather's a tad better today. Did you get some diving in?" asked Blessy.

"Well, yes, but speaking of diving, do you know what all the boats and divers were doing today? It appeared as if they were on a treasure hunt."

"You aren't the first ones to ask. We saw them float by us as well." A younger woman with unkempt brown hair stood next to Blessy. "They started incredibly early this morning, and someone just told me they saw them headed out again just a few minutes ago. By the way, how did you dive with all the boats in use?"

Shelly had a mouthful of sea bass, so Reagan responded. "We kicked off from our place, but the visibility was terrible. You don't have any idea what they're doing or what they're searching for? We assumed they were scouring the ocean floor for a body."

"That's what we all thought as well. I may have to get another tattoo from Alpheus to get the scoop. This is my sister, Rose. Say hello to our new friends, Rose."

"Hello." Rose's smile showed more teeth than the keys on a piano, but it was the tattooist who piqued Reagan's curiosity. "How would Alpheus have that information?"

"It's his special technique for painless tattooing. He knocks twenty-five percent off if you allow him to use nitrous oxide. You know, the laughing gas dentists use?"

"Yeah, I don't like it because I like to be in control, but Mom here insists on it every time she goes."

"Yes," Shelly offered. "I can see how that would help with the pain of a tattoo . . . or at least you wouldn't care if it hurts."

"Alpheus is at least eighty. He can also get you some opioids if you really wanna get loopy, and that's on top of the tequila he hands you when you enter his establishment."

"They don't let tattoo artists use anything like that in the states. They're regulated and could lose their license."

"How do you know that, Reagan? Did you get a tattoo and not tell me?"

"Mom, you have seen almost every inch of me on this trip. Have you seen one?"

"Well, I haven't seen every inch."

Changing the subject, Reagan asked, "Where is this Alpheus character?"

"Next to Banca Gonzo. Can't miss it."

They watched a sea of lights on the water. Hundreds of divers' lanterns gave the landscape a surreal effect perfect for a memorable photo op for a Nat Geo photographer. Reagan went outside to get her own photo. Other inhabitants of shops and villas along the seaside took their own photos, entranced by the procession.

Shelly followed Reagan outside. "It's beautiful. Reminds me of the fireflies you chased when you were young. If this could be fireflies and nothing sinister, I'd sleep better tonight."

"Yes, it's beautiful, but I have something to tell you that I probably shouldn't. I knew Blessy's sister's name before she introduced us."

Shelly brought her eyebrows a little closer together. "The necklace?"

"I think so. There must be some residual effect from wearing it, but I've been trying to see if I sense anything else before it happens. Nothing so far."

"Please keep telling me if this continues. I can't help but worry about what this has done to you."

"I really think it's the mark. I choose to believe it's a good thing. Let's call it a fringe benefit for me having to deal with this for the last sixteen years."

"Let's hope it's a benefit and not a curse."

CHAPTER 14

The players were all in the bunker room ten minutes before nine. No one wanted to get Bobby upset. It was eerily quiet for the next few minutes, but tension eventually created some nervous chatter. Jaffer spoke up first. "Are you guys gonna use your legs or try the bat first?"

A short Hispanic youth of about eighteen years named Sonmez spoke up. "Soccer is my game. Just like in the video, I plan on kicking the ball up the wall." He had traveled from Puerto Rico this week with some friends to try out for Cancun F.C., the local football team. Bobby spotted him and had no trouble recruiting Sonmez, using the pitch for a financial reward that he could not turn down.

"The video I watched showed the guy using the bat winning easily, so I plan on using it," said Montgomery.

"We obviously saw different videos," Chris remarked. "It's part of the game they're playing with our heads."

"I don't like this shit they——"

"It's PokBall Tournament time!" A jovial voice rang out from the speaker system overhead. "*Ivamos a* PokBall!" Conversation stopped as the voice spoke. Chris did not recognize the voice.

"Please have a seat at the table where you have been playing

Mexican Trains." Knowing they had been watched, they uneasily made their way to the chairs.

"Thank you, gentlemen," the voice continued as soon as the last player sat. "I need each of you to look under your seat. If you have the #1 taped to the bottom, you are our first player."

"I've got number one," Jaffer said shakily.

"Mr. Jaffer, please proceed to the field elevator."

"Wish me luck, guys!" He walked through the door and down the hall, but as soon as he was free of the door, it closed and locked.

Montgomery glanced up at the ceiling, not knowing where the voice came from. "Isn't there a closed-circuit TV or something we could watch to see how our team is doing?"

"No," the mysterious voice responded. "The element of surprise should be afforded every player. You will appreciate the element of suspense if you do not have prior knowledge of the activities above."

"Here come the first players," Kara purred in his ear. "I love to see the excitement in your eyes." Silva ignored her, more intent on making sure the twelve apostles had a good view and were ready for the winner . . . except for the Saudi. He considered turning off his feed. An 87.6-inch OLED smart monitor attached to the opposite wall broadcasted the action. A bank of twelve monitors decorated the left wall in this "situation room," allowing Silva to observe each of the apostles in their environment as they watched their feed on high-resolution CCTV monitors with zooming capabilities. Silva supplied these as part of the package.

Jaffer had just walked onto the field, unsure of his next move. Bright, forty-foot LED lights stood on robust stanchions and cast sufficient light to illuminate the field and sloping concrete walls. The two target loops on each stone wall glowed. No birds sung. No grasshoppers chirped. No girlfriends cried out their lovers' names. No fans in the stadium. Only pronounced silence. Another player, a shoeless middle-aged man appeared at the opposite end of the stadium. Scoreboards rose above the two ends of the field.

Hunahpú 0   Ixbalanqué 0

There were two rubber balls, the size of soccer balls, one at each end of the field resting on a line. A bat with flat sides lay beside each ball. Jaffer did his best to conceal his fear, then walked toward the ball on his end. When he made his first move, the other player sprinted toward his own ball. Jaffer picked up his pace and they reached their targets at the same time. The opponent showed soccer skills, punching the ball down the field. Jaffer did likewise, although not with such grace, holding his bat with both hands for balance.

As Jaffer neared midfield close to the wall on his right, his opponent maneuvered his ball onto the sloped wall on the opposite side of the field and headed for the glowing loop. Jaffer saw he was in trouble, so he picked up the ball, tossed it in the air, and swung the bat. The ball bounced once below the loop, but without enough velocity, bounded back down the slope. His opponent did not notice this. He was on the other side of the field, focusing on his own ball. However, when he got close, the ball got away from him and retreated down the wall. It picked up speed, bounced high, then lurched toward the other side of the field.

Jaffer saw this and knew he had a chance, already having retrieved his. He was able to kick it up onto the sloped wall and quickly met it to stop its gravitational pull. He worked slowly, knowing he had some time. Approaching the ring, he held the ball with his left foot and peered across the stadium. His opponent now moved toward his loop. Jaffer returned his attention to his own loop, steadied the ball with his left foot, and kicked it through.

As he raised his hands in celebration, he heard a scream from across the field. Lowering his hands, he jerked his head toward the source.

CHAPTER 15

"Jaden is really irritating me, Reagan," Shelly said after seeing no message from him on her phone. "He gave me his address when he was in the hospital, so maybe we should—"

"You're not planning on just showing up there, are you?"

"Maybe he just has a friend over." Shelly worried the gold bangles on her wrist.

"Knowing we're in town to see him? I doubt it. I'm pretty sure he would've left these two weeks open. But then, why hasn't he responded? I sure hope he's OK."

They rose, waved goodbye to Blessy behind the bar, and left. Michelle stood guard in the road. "She appears grumpier today," said Reagan.

"Jaden's car isn't here. Maybe you need to put that necklace on," said Shelly.

"Yes, I have been trying to see things in the future and from my limited experience, it seems like the residual effect of the necklace is only a few hours at best. I also noticed that I could see either events that occur very close to me . . . like when I could tell you which cards you were going to turn over, or big events that were on a national stage like Wimbledon. I was curious about the MTV awards. I could see Ariana Grande winning artist of the year next month, but when I tried seeing who I would marry—"

"You didn't!"

"No worries, Mom. I couldn't see anything."

When they unlocked the gate and entered through the front door, something felt wrong to Reagan, but she did not want to alarm Shelly. While Shelly headed up to her room to change into her pajamas, Reagan walked slowly through the kitchen and out onto the patio. The only item out of place were the divers' lamps and boats on the water. She headed back in and sat on the couch, hands fisted and perched under her chin. Was it a smell? She breathed in, paying attention to her senses, but nothing alarmed her.

She decided to get the necklace, so she could find Jaden, but as she reached the top of the stairs, she suddenly knew what she would find. The safe was open, and the necklace was gone.

Jaffer threw up his dinner on the sloped rock wall. The upper sheaves of a crane were positioned, out of the light from the end zone stanchions, and the upper sheave rotated over, dropped a loop around his opponent's neck and yanked him off the concrete wall. He was suspended in air, grasping at the loop in a futile effort to loosen the tension, shaking his legs in desperation, but as the sheave continued rotating over the field, a hole opened in the middle, the noose tightened further, severed the head, and dropped the body through the hole in the field. His head grotesquely sat inside the noose, resembling a bubble awaiting a burst of air to release it from a bubble wand. The crane carried the head twenty yards down the field where another hole opened and deposited the bloody mass into it like a hole in one on a par three.

In the UB, as the players sat around the table, discussing politics, religion, and sex in an effort to stay sane, they heard a thud. A few saw movement within the plexiglass tube. Vertical blood streaks appeared along the plexiglass and at the bottom rested a head. No one moved at first, but after a few seconds, Chris got up. "It's not Jaffer," he said, relieved. "He must have won."

Above the UB, Jaffer's legs wobbled. His paralyzed mind told him the same fate was in store for him. A booming voice came over the loudspeaker system from the corners of the field.

"Mr. Jaffer, your victory has earned you a gentleman's chance. Congratulations."

Jaffer froze.

"No one in this arena will harm you. The invisible electric fence that Mr. Hybal mentioned?"

Jaffer made no effort to acknowledge the question, either from fear or tactic, as the thundering voice continued.

"That fence is not always armed. To give you that sporting chance, there are five-second gaps in electricity, then fifty-five seconds when you do not want to cross. If you get across safely, you are free to go home."

Back in the situation room, Silva grinned. "Gentlemen, on your marks!" He scanned the bank of monitors, watching the apostles' excitement bleed from the screens.

"You're going down, Herr Gremling!" the Swede boasted. Gremling had won the last two tournaments, and the other apostles were out to get him.

"Get set!" The apostles leaned forward in anticipation.

"Lift off!"

They used their controllers to navigate each of their drones away from Silva's helipad a little over a mile away.

Silva had decided years ago to resurrect the Mayan legend of Pok-A-Tok and the book of *Popol Vuh*, one of the antiquities he collected.

The sacred book of the Maya related the story of the brothers Hun-Hunahpú and Vucub Hunahpú, who enjoyed playing Pok-A-Tok. One day, they played on the way to Xilbalbá, the underground world, or hell, but this annoyed the men of Xibalbá as they overheard the brothers playing with the ball.

It is unclear why this activity riled the men of the underworld, but they met as a council to decide how to punish the brothers. Their illogical decision was to kill the two brothers, cutting off the head of Hun-Hunahpú and hanging it in a jacara tree.

Silva's reenactment had taken some liberties with the story, but the theme remained. One player would lose his head and the other would die, but he decided he could make more money if he made a sport out of both watching the beheading and in killing the second player. With the drones approaching the field, the announcer once again came alive.

"Mr. Jaffer, we may have been remiss in telling you that twelve drones are on their way. Each one has a poison dart, but only one. You can escape these and run through the forested area at the ends of the field and to the electric fence to safety, but we do suggest starting your escape quickly, because the owner of each drone is very motivated to be the one to kill you." The announcer did not provide details, but Silva's prize was a doubled return of their million U.S. dollars.

Jaffer heard the buzz of the drones and saw their light beams probing the ground beneath. He sprinted as fast as he could away from the open field, finding a bushy Mexican sycamore for shelter, thinking the darts could not reach him there. He heard one come close and instinctively swung around to the other side of the trunk, not realizing he was not completely hidden.

The Japanese drone found a target in his upper right shoulder. Nausea hit him immediately and he dry-heaved. The poison seized his airway and clenched his throat. He stumbled, lost consciousness, and fell on his face, white foam oozing from his mouth.

"One point for Mr. Azuma. Congratulations! Round two begins in twenty minutes. We will see you then."

Winston entered the situation room. "Jefe, there is someone to see you."

"Dammit, can't you see we're in the middle of a tournament?"

"I think you will want to meet this person."

"I can assure you that no one can be as important as this contest."

"Even if this someone has found the necklace you seek?"

Silva swiveled around. "So Chaz was successful?"

"Not exactly."

"Then who is this messenger and how do we know this is the necklace?"

"One of the workers on one of the dive boats saw some divers ahead of the group this afternoon. One diver was holding a chest as they headed in from the dive. This worker's name is Nariz, and his cousin is the maid for the Villa Sueno del Mar. Nariz saw the divers enter this villa, so he pretended to be nauseous on the boat, and they let him go home. He then called his cousin to see if she could find the chest in the villa after the divers went to dinner, and she found it in the safe. Should I let Nariz in?"

"Please do. I would like to thank this man and reward him. We have about fifteen minutes until round two, so we need to make this quick."

Winston spoke to an unseen messenger through the doorway. "You can send in Nariz." A thirty-five-year-old Middle Eastern man entered hesitantly, head bowed at a forty-five-degree angle. He held a small burlap sack securely, both arms wrapped around it.

"Is there a necklace in that sack, son?" Silva arranged some players on a board game, speaking to Nariz as if he was an afterthought.

"Si, Señor Silva."

"What is on the necklace?" Silva pulled the head off one of the players.

"A starfish, Señor Silva." The man sweated through his pale white tunic.

"Have you tried this necklace on?" Silva finally acknowledged the visitor.

"No, no! I would never do this." He was now shaking enough for sweat droplets to loosen and fall to the floor.

"This is good," Silva said calmly. "Please do not worry. You have done the right thing." Nariz nodded a few times, more sweat catapulting onto the floor.

"Who knows that you have come to see me?"

"No one, Señor Silva."

"What about your cousin, the maid?"

"No. She only knows I have it. I paid her five hundred pesos to keep that quiet. She's a good person. She will tell no one."

"Thank you for your honesty. OK, I only have a few more minutes here. Please remove the necklace from the bag and place it around your neck. I know this sounds unusual, but I have my reasons." Silva's reasons were no different than his insistence on his personal chef tasting the food before he ate each meal. Nariz stood still for a few seconds, then nervously reached into the bag and pulled out the necklace.

Silva's eyes widened. "Those colors are amazing. Let's see how it looks on you." Nariz slowly placed the necklace, slammed his eyes shut, and waited for it to explode in his face. As the starfish rested on his chest, he slowly opened his eyes and began breathing again.

"We have a contest going right now. Who will win?"

"I do not know, Señor Silva."

"Will Clauvino da Silva successfully escape from his jail in Rio de Janeiro?"

"I do not know, Señor Silva."

"Who will win the Academy Award for best actor next month?"

"I do not know, Señor Silva."

Silva pulled a Glock out from under the table and shot Nariz just above the eyes, blood splaying behind him onto a photo of a recumbent nude before he dropped. "Get him outta here and take care of his cousin."

Winston grabbed the feet of the dead man and dragged him out of the situation room but not before Silva ripped the necklace off his neck and threw it into the fireplace. He returned his attention to the monitor showing the PokBall tournament, seething inside. He would deal with the necklace later.

"Round two begins, gentlemen. In the closet where you found your board game, there are a set of dice. Mr. Prefontaine, please retrieve these and I need everyone to roll. Low roll is our next contestant."

Finally, Andade, a pediatrician from Columbia, rolled a nine. The doctor was in Cancun to see his horse, She's My Kid, race at the Hipodromo de ls Americas in Mexico City. Bobby had struck up a conversation with him the week before while they watched the races. He was waffling on whether to return to Columbia or spend some time in Mexico. One hundred thousand dollars was a strong persuader, particularly when your horse loses and breaks her leg in the back stretch.

Jaden rolled a seven on the mahogany table. Chris rolled a nine. Montgomery rolled a three. "Shit!" Tabani rolled a twelve, sneaking a smug glance toward Montgomery. Sonmez, a soccer player for Querétero, rolled a seven. The 260-pound Hornbeck rolled a six.

Montgomery winced. "I have a plan. I'll whisper it to Hornbeck, and if my head doesn't roll down that tube, you'll know it worked." He leaned over to the large man and whispered his plan.

Hornbeck nodded. "Sounds like it could work."

Montgomery headed toward the door. "I hope my girl doesn't have to see me headless." The door locked behind him. He entered the elevator and pushed the button. He was lifted to field level. Seeing his opponent at the other end, he had a good feeling about his plan. His opponent was lanky and nervous, although at 130 yards away, he struggled to even see the guy.

They both ran toward the ball and bat, and upon reaching them, kicked their ball toward their right and down the field, bat in hand. As his opponent was halfway to his target, he dropped the bat to help his speed. Montgomery had been watching him out of his periphery and when he saw the discarded bat, he left his ball and ran toward the bat-less opponent. Unaware of the new direction Montgomery took, he began kicking his ball up the smooth rock slope toward the ring.

When Montgomery was within ten feet of him, he sensed his approach and whirled around, but not in time to avoid a bat slamming against the side of his head, knocking him unconscious. He tumbled down the concrete slope onto the grass field below. Montgomery raced to his ball and carefully nudged it up the slope on his side of the field. He paused to see if the guy had moved, but he was still out. He booted the ball closer, then sidekicked it through the loop.

CHAPTER 16

"I can't believe someone stole it. How did they even know it was here?" asked Reagan.

"The safe doesn't appear to be broken into, so someone had to know how to figure out the combination we programmed in. You locked it, right?" asked Shelly.

"Of course."

"What combination did you choose?"

"Jaden's birthday."

"I don't know how anyone would know to try that. Maybe someone knows how to circumvent these types of safes. Maybe Sabbi?"

"She's in Boston with her wife."

"Would the maids know how?"

"I don't see why, unless Sabbi tells them a trick in case a tenant like us forgets the combination. She said we could reach her on her cell."

"I hate to bother her, but don't you think we should tell her the safe was broken into?"

Reagan hunted for Sabbi's number on her phone. "Wait, I read about a guy named Jeff Sitar who could open any safe in about five minutes. He was a world champion, but there must be a bunch of safecrackers out there if they have contests to determine who is a world champion. I bet the criminal world has recruited the best, and if someone knows the value of a necklace like this one, they will do all they can to find one of those guys. Mom, check your drawers and let's see if anything else is missing."

They opened closets, doors, and cabinets. All the scuba gear was accounted for on the back patio, too.

"Jaden always knows what to do during uneasy times." Reagan glanced at her phone. "Still no response."

J! We need you! If you get this, please call!

"Montgomery didn't play the game like it was meant to be played." Silva had the attention of all twelve apostles. He was seething, trying to keep calm, but the veins on the side of his neck resembled a road map of downtown Portland. "We need to send a message, but first, we need to end this quickly. Lift off!"

The drones were on their way. Since Montgomery had an advanced showing of what would happen to the loser, he held it together well during the beheading but now considered his own escape should plans for his future not include living. He spanned the grounds when the unseen voice began, explaining the electric fence and the five-second gaps to freedom.

He took off as fast as he could run through the forest at the edge of the playing field and toward the perimeter, gauging where it would be. Nearing what he felt would be the edge of the safe zone, he hurled a stick as far as he could, but there was no hint of an invisible electric fence. The voice picked up again, explaining the drones and poisonous darts.

He soon heard the buzzing sounds of the approaching drones. He took ten more steps toward the perimeter, picked up a stick, and threw it, getting the same result. He decided not to take a chance on the poison darts and made the fatal decision to run for it. Three strides into his exit, he hit the electric wall and five amps coursed through his body, stopping his heart immediately.

"That bastard can't do anything right, but at least we can send *that* message. Sorry, apostles. That would be a draw in round two. Take your drones back to the base." He pushed a button next to a microphone and spoke into it. "Do not, and I repeat, do not take Mr. Montgomery's body to the furnace. I want his body dismembered and dropped, limb by limb, organ by organ into the tube."

"As you wish, Jefe."

"Montgomery's trick must have worked," Hornbeck said after they saw the second head slide down the tube. He then went to each player and whispered the technique Montgomery had told him he would be using.

After everyone had been told, Sonmez yelled "This is nuts! I can't do this! There has to be a way out!"

No one replied, fearing comments like that would invite retribution. "I wonder how many more rounds there will be tonight," Tabani said. "It's supposed to be a week-long tournament, if that's what you call this. We might not have any more tonight. It's almost eleven. Didn't they say it's over at eleven?"

Chris replied, "Yes, they said no new rounds would start after eleven, but that's ten minutes from now."

They heard some rumbles coming from the direction of the tube. A leg came shooting down, foot first, then an arm, followed by the entrails, after which it was too difficult to see what came down the tube, until Montgomery's head came last. His eyes were open and bulging, his mouth held permanently into a grimace.

"Shit!" Sonmez yelled. Chris was stoic. Andade wept. Jaden buried his head in his hands. Tabani paced. Hornbeck pounded the table three times with such force that it cracked the mahogany.

"Let's call it a night, gentlemen. It's almost eleven and I know at least Maximilian needs his beauty sleep."

"It's six o'clock in the morning here, Señor Silva," said the Austrian. "Sounds like *you're* the one who needs sleep."

"Fucking time zones. They always confuse me." Silva wanted to think about the necklace, not the tournament. "See you in twenty-two hours, gentlemen!" He flipped a switch that blacked out the twelve monitors.

He stared into the fireplace, empty save for a hurtled necklace buried in ashes, and contemplated his next move while considering his first and only son. Javier had eschewed the Mafia lifestyle at the early age of sixteen and joined a monastery, eventually becoming a Benedictine monk at the Monastery of Santa María y Todos los Santos in Zipolite. He harbored mixed emotions over his son's decision, at one moment being proud, then sorrowful, then angry. But the most lasting and powerful emotion was anxiety. He wanted what was best for his son but also wanted him to carry on the Silva legacy.

Javier would be the sixth and perhaps last of the line if he never married and had a son. A mountain-climbing accident when Silva was thirty-eight crushed his pelvis, severing the pudendal nerve, which made him impotent. This gnawed at Silva like a midnight ulcer after a dinner of spicy chilate de pollo. He ached to know if his son would bring an heir, and the necklace was to bring closure to his burden. He wondered if this had been the right necklace worn by the wrong person. Perhaps it was the wrong necklace. Was this legend simply fantasy?

He removed the necklace from the fireplace ashes and shook off the debris. He again admired the beauty and was convinced it was the one Brancaccio described a few short weeks ago. He placed the necklace with the broken strap on the mantel and decided to get some sleep, knowing it would be a night of restlessness and suffering. He hoped Kara could help him to forget, at least for a moment.

He awoke the next morning at 4:00 a.m. as he had done since early adulthood. Leaving Kara asleep, he contacted Chaz and told him to call off the search. He remotely tested the drones, making sure they were charged for the second night of the tournament, and checked in with Steffen, who was in Stockholm checking on a vase Silva coveted. Studying the necklace, Silva decided he would text Alpheus to see if he could help him. It was after 7:00 a.m. now, and he knew the tattooist was seeing clients.

"Jefe, how may I be of service?"

"I need to know anything you know about a necklace with special powers."

"That's easy, but you don't need me for that. There's a lady named Gerene Stephens. Goes by GiGi. She's been telling a story of a necklace that can help tell the future for many years. It was first owned by a girl named Omelia back in the eighteenth century, I believe. Most think GiGi is just old and nuts and full of stories that have been . . . well, shall we say, edited . . . for as long as they can remember, but the one about the necklace never changes. That necklace got Omelia in trouble, too. She was burned at the stake for being a witch."

"That's helpful, Alpheus. I'll go see this GiGi."

"Better do it soon. I hear she's at death's doorstep."

CHAPTER 17

Reagan climbed out of bed and checked her phone. Still nothing from Jaden, but AAK had texted her.

Ocean open again. Come C us 4 a dive.

She smelled bacon wafting from below, so she hustled down the stairs. "Mom, we can dive today. I guess the boats are back." She raced through the back door to see if the armada was in sight. Seeing only a few boats, she said, "Yep, let me call and see if they still have a spot for two."

AAK said they had room for both on the 8:30 a.m. boat.

"We need to leave in about fifteen minutes," Reagan warned. "I'll get our gear ready." She gathered everything they needed from the patio and loaded their mesh bags, then stuffed them into the back of the golf car. "Hey, Michelle! Who's your friend?" The iguana had brought a companion who eyed Michelle with suspicion or post-copulatory guarding after a sexual encounter.

Silva found Kara in the living room. "Mi amor, would you locate a Ms. Gerene Stephens for me, better known as GiGi?"

"I'm on it, darling. What would you like me to do if I find her?"

"See if we can drop by and visit. She's in Tepich. Sounds like she might know something about the necklace. I feel like I don't have all the information I need. She is not well, so I would not expect her to come here."

Kara nodded and sat down at a laptop in the library. In a few seconds, she said, "Found her in Tepich on Calle Sac-Be." She keyed in the phone number she had found online.

"Stephens's residence," a sultry voice answered.

"This is Kara with Mayan Holdings. May I speak with Ms. Stephens?"

"The last Stephens passed away yesterday. You're too late."

"I'm so sorry. With whom do I have the pleasure of speaking?"

"This is Barbra. I'm her great-niece. Can I leave her a message?"

Ignoring the smart-ass remark, she asked, "What do you know about a necklace with special powers?"

"That crazy bitch was always talkin' some old wives' tale about a necklace, but she was full of shit. Her mind was sicker than an Ebola monkey with diarrhea."

"That was rather graphic," replied Kara. "Can you tell me the story she told about the necklace?"

"That will cost you, Miss Mayan Holdings. How much is it worth to you?"

"I'll tell you what. I feel quite sure that you are not the only one Ms. Stephens related this tale to, so you can either give me the details and let us decide the worth or I will find someone else to help me."

Barbra didn't immediately respond. "All right, all right. The details are easy to remember because it was her favorite story.

There was a girl named Omelia back in the 1700s who lived with her daddy in Fajardo, Puerto Rico by the water." She recounted every detail Gigi had told with each recounting.

"Anything else?" Kara asked.

"Like I said, she told the story hundreds of times, so there are no more details, or I would have told you. When do I find out how much this was worth to you?"

"I will be in touch."

"You better be. I know people, Ms. Mayan Holdings."

"My name is Kara, and I will get back to you soon."

She ended the call and found Silva. "Ms. Stephens passed away yesterday, but I spoke to her niece who had heard GiGi's story many times. I think-"

"Did you take care of the niece?" he asked, without looking up.

"Of course. I made the call, and I must say . . . it was a pleasure. Anyway, there are six keys to the story that could help us. First, this girl who could tell the future was named Omelia. One foot had webbing, I suppose like a duck, and another had six toes. Finally, she was stung by a Man-O-War, and it left a mark on her wrist that looked like a starfish. The other differences between Nariz and Omelia are their ages and sex. You could let me try the necklace and we can rule out the sex part, leaving us with five differences."

"Good work, Kara." He went to the situation room and grabbed the necklace off the mantel. He quickly tied the ends together with a fisherman's knot and placed it around Kara's neck. "Will we make love tonight?"

"I don't need a necklace to know that."

"OK, can you see anything else in the future?"

She closed her eyes and concentrated. After some effort at

blocking out the present, nothing came. "I guess it's not a female thing." She removed it carefully.

Silva thought for a moment. "Do we know if Omelia had any children? Maybe it was passed down."

"I don't know. The niece did mention Omelia had met an untimely end, but I don't know if she had any children."

"Send an APB to our community. I need them all to be on the lookout for anyone who has webbed feet, six toes, or a mark on them resembling a starfish."

"I will get that sent right now, cariño." She strode to the computer again, this time swaying her hips for Silva.

Three couples joined Reagan and Shelly on the boat while they pulled on their dive skins. Carlos came on board.

"Hola, everyone! The visibility is still not very good in most places since the storm, but we have a site that is perfect . . . well, as perfect as it can be under these conditions. It's called SeaDrop. It's the only site worth going to, so this will be the only dive we do today."

He introduced everyone to the boat and then did his dive briefing, including safety features, buddy rules, computer details, and rules for the dive ahead.

One couple was a man and his teenage daughter, appearing very comfortable together. There were two older women—sisters—who took turns correcting each other. The last couple were young newlyweds.

"Are you guys here on vacation?" asked Reagan.

"Sort of," offered the girl. "I work for the Travel Channel

and my boyfriend, Aaron, is a NatGeo photographer."

"That's interesting! Are you doing a story on the diving in Tulum?"

"I was going to, until the storm happened, and now my story will be about the way a storm can devastate the reef system when it's not in season. I'm Robyn, by the way.

"Nice to meet you, Robyn. This is my mom, Shelly." They all shook hands as Aaron worked with his camera gear.

"Yeah, we were diving yesterday and it's awful," Shelly said.

"You dove yesterday? We couldn't find any boats."

"We had some tanks at our villa, so we just kicked off from shore."

"I don't think your boyfriend will get any good photos." They continued to ready themselves, and Aaron put his camera gear in the camera well.

The dive, after reaching the drop, was stunning. Four big tuna hung above them, suspended and awaiting lunch. Large schools of snapper, almaco jacks, and amberjacks also hung out, waiting on a plankton meal. This was why Reagan liked divemasters. They always knew where to find the hidden treasures of the sea.

When they were back on the boat and headed in, Reagan asked Felipe, "Did you get some good shots?"

"We'll see. That was beautiful."

Reagan and Shelly removed their gear, skins included, and stuffed it in their mesh bags for the freshwater cleaning. They took fifteen-second showers, then wrapped their towels around their waists. Nearing the dock, no one noticed Carlos taking a photo of Reagan's wrist with his cell phone.

CHAPTER 18

The group spent most of the day anywhere but the UB. The site of the human remains in the tube made them queasy, and no one wanted to be reminded of the horror. They ate meals in the dining area and engaged in talk about anything besides their current grim circumstances. Chris and Jaden met again in the bathroom with the shower running.

Chris started, "Some of the guys are talking about rushing the guards by the doors. They're saying they have a better chance that way than in the game they know nothing about, especially after they saw the winner and loser killed."

"I can't argue that perspective convincingly," said Jaden. "I'm just hoping there's a third option, but from what everyone's been saying, there's not another exit besides the one we came in that's guarded by a gun. If you want to consider that it's a better way to die, then maybe, but we also know if we play the game the way they told us to, we might have a chance."

"I wish we knew what happened to Jaffer."

"Me, too, but we don't, and I doubt we ever will."

"Maybe," said Chris, "we could all rush the guards with the table in front of us. Problem, though. They would see that coming from the end of the hall and would have the table shot up by the time we got halfway."

"Keep thinking, Chris. There must be a way. One thing I've been wondering, seeing this from a 40,000-foot view, other than seeing two people try to win a game and then seeing them get killed or killing them yourself, what is their motivation for doing this? I can't see there being a stadium full of people with the loser getting killed. That would never work, even in Mexico where they kill bulls. Doesn't it look like an elaborate undertaking for the perverted pleasure of just one person?"

"Depends on the level of perversion or the wealth of the twisted, warped monster."

"I see this as a bigger play. I know Gonzo, and there is no doubt he is the puppetmaster. We're the puppets, but who is the audience for his play?"

Chris considered this. "You think he's selling seats to this tournament of death?"

"Yes, I do, and I doubt the seats are cheap. The last thing he wants is to see the game not played well. That's why he dismembered Montgomery. It was a message."

"OK, Jaden, so do you have a plan?"

"Not yet but think about it. Would he want the guards to kill us all? What kind of tournament would he have if all the players were dead? So, what instructions do you think he would give the guards?"

"Maybe they're not deadly bullets. Is that what you're getting at?"

"Exactly," Jaden whispered. "But do we feel good enough about that theory to rush the guards?"

"Like a game of chicken?"

"More like Russian Roulette." He flipped off the shower.

When they got back to the dock, Carlos asked, "Will you be diving with us tomorrow?"

Shelly replied, "We aren't sure, but we'll leave our gear here. Even if we don't, we'll probably come back when my husband gets here on Tuesday."

"Great! I will enjoy meeting Mr. Prefontaine."

Walking to their golf car, Reagan said, "Mom, I don't think they'll let him fly out with the alert level so high."

"I know, but it makes me feel safer to think he's coming, and I like people to think he is."

"Makes sense. Mom, don't make fun of me for reversing course, and I admit you were right to suggest it, but can we drive to Jaden's place to see if he's home?"

"Of course, I was about to suggest that myself. I've got his address. I think it's about a mile or so from here." She punched in his address to her phone's GPS system as Reagan headed out. They arrived in ten minutes and knocked on his second story apartment door. After receiving no response, Reagan tried the door to find it locked, then looked through a slit in the drawn curtains inside a window and detected no movement.

"I don't think he's here, Mom. Nothing looks unusual and with the door being locked, I don't see any signs of forced entry. Why is he doing this to us?"

"I don't know, sweetie, but let's get home." When they arrived, the maids were still working.

"Buenos dias, Marta," said Shelly. "Where is Tahira?"

"She not show up dis morning, señorita."

"Is that unusual?"

"She not miss a day whole year. I go by apartamento and knock on door, but she no answer."

"*Lo siento,* Marta. Please don't worry if you can't get it all done.

We will be fine."

Reagan yelled from the back door, "Mom, I'm going to the hammocks to read . . . or maybe sleep. I checked and Jaden still hasn't responded. Think we should file a missing person's report?"

"Read my mind, Reagan." She found the phone directory and called the number listed for *La Policia*. When she was handed off to an English-speaking woman with a Scandinavian accent, she supplied her with the details and the last time they had heard from Jaden. The policia agreed to post a missing persons' report, but Shelly could tell this would not go to the top of their priority list.

"Please let us know when you hear from your son so we can remove him from our list, Ms. Prefontaine."

"Of course." Shelly ended the call and considered what their next move would be.

CHAPTER 19

It was getting close to nine o'clock, and although the players had stayed away from the bunkroom for most of the day, they knew it was time to return. They filtered in slowly, orienting their backs toward the ghoulish tube. Some sat on their bunks, some at the table. No words were spoken. At nine, the voice no one wanted to hear came alive.

"Good evening, gentlemen. I hope you have enjoyed your day in our facility. You have been model citizens. Now for the next round. I need you all to place your right hand on the tube." No one moved.

"I'm waiting."

One by one, they walked over and placed their right hands on the tube, looking away or down as they did. Jaden and Chris were last, but they got up from their bunk and walked over. Jaden placed his right hand and the voice returned.

"Mr. Tucker, you were the last one to follow orders. This makes you our next contestant."

He remained stoic. Jaden looked toward him, saying "I'm sorry" with his eyes.

Everyone watched Chris walk through the door and down the hall. He saw the elevator in the distance and shivered. At six-four and 230 pounds of muscle, he was built to compete, but what would this game be like? He decided he would use the bat, knowing he could hit better than whoever they put out there. He could probably get at least two shots at it before the guy could kick it up to the loop. He pressed the green button and was lifted to field level where he walked out, taking in the surroundings.

He saw his opponent at the other end of the field but couldn't make out much about his physique, even with the bright LED lights illuminating the field of play. It mattered little to Chris. He had a plan. He ran toward the bat and ball on his side and kicked the ball down the field. He glanced at his opponent, who made a bowling ball look trim. Rather than kicking the ball as the rules stated, he picked it up and lumbered up the concrete-sloped wall toward the loop. A crane swung over the top of the wall and a noose slipped around the rotund player's neck, lifting him thirty feet in the air. His legs were kicking, and Chris instinctively knew what was about to happen, so he took off with his bat and headed toward the forest on the outskirts of the stadium.

After running what felt like 200 yards and out of the light from the stadium, he saw some wildlife, and he knew he was in his element. He had been running so hard that he missed most of the message from the stadium announcer but did hear something about "drones with darts for killing" and "five-second gaps in electricity." That was enough. He knew they would not want him getting out alive. In his last few strides before slowing down, he stepped on a startled rabbit and broke one of its back legs. Chris stopped and picked it up. "You might have saved my life, little guy," Chris whispered.

He found an opening in the trees large enough to see the bright field. He knew how far the center field fence was at Estadio de Beisbol Beto Avila, so he converted the number to meters and estimated the distance to the fence. He wasn't quite there. He backpedaled and kept an eye on the field as the drones appeared over the forest at the far end of the field. He was getting close to what he felt like would be the edge of the safe zone. He reentered the thick of the woods and crouched down. The drones were at the middle of the field and closing. He felt good about his hastily made decision to wear a drab forest green shirt and coffee brown slacks this morning.

Finding a long stick to pair with his bat and holding one in each hand, he let the rabbit go, directionally herding it toward danger. The drones crossed the field and were now in the timber, but his forest-colored clothing prevented them from zeroing in, especially in the dark. He heard them but could not see as one flew directly over him and beyond what he knew to be past the perimeter. He continued to guide the hare until a harrowing crackle accompanied by sparks lit the night sky and suspended the electrified bunny in the air. The light show had temporarily blinded Chris as night orbited to day. The frying of the rabbit continued for another twenty seconds, then abruptly stopped, dropping the animal onto the forest floor, leaving a smoking, sacrificial pile. *Five seconds!* He jumped to his feet and propelled himself forward into a somersault that carried him past the now invisible fence into safety, just as the voltage began its second course on the sacrificed rabbit.

Silva grabbed the attention of the twelve. "Gentlemen, we have another runner who made another bad decision. Return your drones to base and prepare for round four. The extraction committee will retrieve the remains of Mr. Tucker and transport him to the oven. Good luck in the next round!"

Chris didn't know what the drones would do, so he hunkered down under a Montezuma cypress and buried himself in a bed of tall grass. When he heard the buzz of the drones fading into the distance, he had two distinct concerns: *They won't find my body, so they will come after me*, and *I don't know where the fuck I am.*

Realizing he might have little time, he rose and ran through the forest, using the small amount of light from a three-quarter moon to avoid fronting a tree trunk head on. He heard a noise and stopped to listen.

Shit! It's a drone!

He found a downed alligator juniper and crouched between some of the larger, upturned roots, then tried to remain motionless while his heaving chest objected. One lone drone drifted back and forth. It may have realized the rabbit had been electrocuted, but if Jaden had been right, this guy wouldn't want to tell the other competitors – he would want to claim victory.

His breathing slowed and he craned to hear the position of his would-be assassin. Holding his bat in a readied position, he waited, knowing that if he could destroy this drone, the owner would be so humiliated that he would tell anything but the truth.

The drone continued its reconnaissance, buzz volume ebbing and flowing. On another pass by his root fortress, it hung in suspension for a few seconds, hovering within three feet of his face. Knowing a dart could come quickly and using the instincts of a baseball player with a ninety-eight-mph fastball bearing down on his head, he lowered his bat in defense and felt the impact of the dart thud into the opposite side. He sprang from his support and swung like he was trying to drive a slider into the left field alley, connecting solidly with the drone, shattering it into several pieces. Taking no chances, he located the main body in the darkness and drove it into the forest bed with his foot, delivering maximum damage.

That son of a bitch'll never fly again.

Dropping his bat, he continued his escape. The wind picked up and cooled the sweat drops that had released into his cotton shirt. The dark forest was his ally . . . his terrain. Beginning to see less forest density after an hour, he hoped civilization would welcome him soon. Running . . . walking . . . running . . . walking . . . his energy waned. Fatigued muscles begged him to give them respite. Now past midnight, he would have to make a decision in the next few hours if he didn't find friendly help. He knew they would send dogs as soon as they realized the rabbit body wasn't Chris Tucker. They would get some of his clothes in the UB and instruct the dogs to track the scent. *That's what I would do.*

After another hour, he realized he wouldn't make it somewhere safe tonight. He removed his pants and shirt and threw them into the upper limbs of a ceiba tree, hoping the scent trail the dogs chased would end here. He sprinted in his boxer shorts for another mile. He used the moon as a nightlight and allowed the moss-covered tree trunks to guide him north. He hoped the forest would soon transition into civilization.

The night became cool, so he jogged to keep his body temperature at a manageable level. Finally, the fatigue overcame him. He crawled inside the root system of another alligator juniper to shield him from the wind and other elements, closing himself in with some greenery and branches. Sleep overtook him quickly as the cooing of the Inca doves sang him a lullaby.

"Apostles, we've had a hard time so far, but it is my pledge to bring you more excitement. Watching heads roll is one thing, but I know you get your real kicks with the drone competition. I'm thinking of turning off the electric fence in the next round so you can have more fun. What say ye?"

Of the twelve voting lights, eleven shone green and one red. "Heir Gremling, I am surprised. Our reigning champion would prefer seeing our runner fried than to hunt him down?" He was on his monitor, nodding, but said nothing.

"Majority rules," Silva continued. "No fence for the next round. We will decide after that if we like the new format."

He awoke with a start to the distant barks of an unknown number of dogs. He slipped out of his makeshift bed, muscles and joints objecting, and slowly walked away from the far-flung howls. As his joints became oiled by synovial fluid, he picked up the pace, realizing boxers were not meant for the running male species. His multiple scrapes, scratches, and cuts from his romp through the dark appeared in the early morning sun. Adrenalin kept him from feeling them at first but seeing them made them sting. He knew he could make better time in the light, but still didn't know where he was going.

After a ten-minute fast jog, he came to a stream flowing north, away from his pursuers. It was only six inches deep, so he walked carefully down the uneven creek bed for a mile before he came to a bridge with trails leading both ways. He took the left trail and came upon a trailer park. He thought it was Monday and considered the occupants would be at school or work. He found a Schwinn leaning up against the peeling skirting of an RV and found it unlocked. He felt sorry for the kid who lent this to him, but it didn't prevent him from straddling the bike that was a decade and a half too small and headed down the road. His short journey drew some curious eyes from mobile home windows, and he soon came to a Pemex masquerading as a convenience store on his left. Drawing more stares, he went inside and walked to the counter.

"Do you speak English?"

"Si, señor."

"May I use your phone?"

"Customers not use."

"What if I give you my bike?"

"Ugly bike."

A guttural voice came from a few aisles over. "Hey, you can use my phone, you big glass-a-water, but what'dya do with yo pants?" A middle-aged woman wearing overalls approached Chris with a cigarette dangling from the chapped right corner of her lips. She had a six-year-old boy on a leash.

"It's a long story."

"Sounds excitin' to me!" she said, eyebrows lifted, accentuating the years of earned forehead wrinkles. Her eyes traveled up and down Chris' body like a butcher sizing up a hanging piece of meat.

"I appreciate you letting me use your phone. By the way, where are we?"

She winked at the uncooperative Mexican at the counter. "OK, now I *knows* it's excitin'!"

"Trust me . . . you don't want to know anything else."

"How'd ya get all beat up?"

"He's bleedin', Grandma!" said the boy at the end of the leash.

"Now be nice, Peter." She handed her phone to Chris. "We're in Tepich, by the way."

"I need to look up a number. Is that OK?" Chris was not sure when her benevolence—or perhaps curiosity—would end.

"You come by here every day, stripped down to your boxers, and I'll give you *my* phone number, sweetie."

Ignoring her, he searched for Villa Sueno del Sol, found a number, and punched it. After a few rings, "Villa Sueno, this is Sabbi."

"Hello! I'm trying to reach the villa. I have some friends there."

"Oh, I see. The number inside the villa is unlisted. Who are you?"

"Just a friend of Reagan's."

"Oh, she's a sweet girl, but I must protect my tenants. Tell you what. Give me your name and the number where she can reach you and I will call her right now to see if she's in the villa, but she might not be there."

"Do you have the number I'm calling from?" He put the phone on speaker.

"Is it 832-487-6439?" The woman nodded.

"Yes, it is. My name is Chris Tucker. Please try your best to reach her."

"OK, Chris. I'll call right back if they don't answer."

As he waited, he wondered what he would do if they weren't at the villa. "Thank you so much for letting me use your phone." In what felt like an eternity for a baseball player in his underwear inside a Mexican convenience store with a grandma ogling his muscles, the phone mercifully rang.

"Hello?"

"I'm sorry, Chris, but they didn't answer."

His hopes shrinking, he said, "Thanks for making the effort. Will you keep trying?"

"Of course."

Holding his hand over the phone mic and turning to the unhappy man behind the counter, Chris asked "What is the exact address of this establishment?"

Crossing his arms, he said "Calle X-Lapak and Calle San Jose."

"Thank you." Uncovering the mic, he said "Hello, Sabbi?"

"Yes?"

"If you reach her, can you ask if someone can come get me at the Pemex on the corner of Calle X-Lapak and Calle San Jose in Tepich?"

"I know that store, so yes, I can do that."

"I don't guess you're in the area, Sabbi?"

"No, I'm in Boston. Sorry."

"Thank you so much." He terminated the call.

"Hey, Boxers!" the woman said. "I need my phone back."

Chris replied as he returned the phone, "If you take me to the villa, I'll give Peter here my bike." He grinned at the boy.

"That's Denzel's bike, Grammy!"

"Well, now it's yours. Let's go, Boxers!"

CHAPTER 20

"Still no trace of him, Jefe," Winston announced. Winston's nickname was Black Bluto, a nod to his size and bulk.

"He got rid of his clothes. With any luck, he got deliveranced by one of those fuckin' backwoods boys, but we have to find him, dead or alive. Can't afford for him to tear apart our operation. Fourteen years. Fourteen years! No one has ever escaped! How the fuck did this happen?" Silva fumed. His scar glistened when his blood pressure rose, and it was climbing steadily.

"Don't worry, Jefe. We'll find him."

"Kara . . . feedback from the apostles?"

She grimaced. "As you expected, they were livid. Several mentioned that you should have had better security to keep anyone from escaping. Most are very concerned about their anonymity, and all want their money back."

"Goddamn Saudi incited them." He threw his fedora against *The Flower Carrier*, a painting by Diego Rivera, and a purple piece of the flowers floated to the floor. "They know there is no way to trace their involvement. The drones are coded and can't be linked to them, and the links to the video were erased. Their funds were deposited in a Cayman account and they can be returned from that same account. They need to calm the fuck down. Were any of them willing to keep the money on hold for the next tournament?"

"I did offer that," Kara said, "and although a few originally said it would be fine, others think the run is over and that there will be no future tournaments."

"We're in damage control, and if we can find Tucker before he fucks up our operation, the collateral contamination will be limited. Winston, what do you have in place?"

Winston Magee had graduated from the school of Jamaica knocks at an early age. He towered over his friends and outwitted them on the streets. His parents wanted him to stay and work on their small sugar cane field, but he knew the world was bigger than Maroon Town, Jamaica. When he turned fifteen, he travelled to Montego Bay and wrangled a job as a guard at a resort by passing himself off as an eighteen-year-old high school graduate. He waited for his opportunity, which came nine months later, when he was asked to stand guard for a VIP in one of the butlered villa suites. When he bit the head off a Jamaican yellow boa as it slithered toward their suite, Gonzo Silva had him on his payroll the next day.

"We still have the dogs out. We're going door to door to ask if anyone saw a man with no clothes, and I'm sending a few men to the villa where one of his friends is staying. Our police friends have also stepped up their patrolling in the area."

"That's not enough. I need the helicopter using our infrared scanners to cover the area southeast of the stadium to start."

"I will take care of that immediately," said Winston.

"You should have thought of that before I had to tell you. What did Hiro find on Tucker's phone?"

"Not much to help us. He wasn't in communication with anyone here except Jaden and Cunningham. No family here that we could find. There were some older texts with a few girls, but those leads got us nowhere. Hiro is still investigating, though. He may find something we can use."

"Were you able to clean the UB?"

"All clean."

Reagan awoke to another cloudless day, checked her phone, and decided to contact Raul. She removed the card he had left from the drawer by her bed and punched in his number.

"Detective Isuega."

"Detective, this is Reagan over at the Villa Sueno."

"Hello, Ms. Prefontaine. To what do I owe the pleasure of your call this fine morning?"

Impressed that he remembered her last name, she continued. "We're very worried about Jaden, my brother. He hasn't contacted us, and we haven't been able to contact him since his baseball game Friday night. We're only here for two weeks, and it isn't like him to go this long without being in touch. We held off for a while, but I can't ignore this any longer."

"Are you sure he didn't go anywhere for the weekend?" he countered.

"Even if he did, he would still contact us, but all he said was that the owner was taking him and Chris to some kind of tournament."

"You mean the owner of the Tigres? Gonzalo Silva?"

"I'm pretty sure that's who he meant."

Raul hesitated, then asked, "What else did he say?"

"He said it was a tournament for a sport called PokBall, but he didn't know anything about it and couldn't find anything about it online. I searched myself and all I could find was a sport called PokeBall named after PokeMon." Reagan heard him taking notes on the other end.

"Ms. Prefontaine, this may sound like an odd question from a detective, but due to your amazing recall and attention to details in your surroundings, I'm wondering if you can draw any connection between the bombing at the SOC and your brother's disappearance?"

Reagan considered his question. "I haven't tried to make a connection, but thinking back, maybe this Gonzalo guy also owns the bar? But why would he want to blow it up, except to deflect suspicion away from himself?"

"Interesting perspective," replied Raul. "And by the way, we've got a few leads on the SOC bombing. Forensics has uncovered a few things."

Reagan asked, "Have anything to do with the jukebox?"

"Impressive, but I can't say anything more about it. I'm sure you understand."

"All I care about right now is my brother, and if he said the owner was taking him to a tournament somewhere, I know where I would start my search."

"You don't know Gonzalo Silva - deeply involved in many illegal activities, locally and in other countries, but he's insulated himself with more layers than my Italian grandmother's seven-layered lasagna, may she rest in peace." Raul made the sign of the cross.

Raising her voice a few notches, Reagan asked, "So you can't talk to him?"

"Oh, I can talk to him, and I plan on it, but chances are that the conversation won't bring much fruit."

"Please try, detective."

"It will be my pleasure. I always enjoy having a reason to visit his villa. Anything else related to the bombing that could help?"

Reagan stopped listening and hung up when Chris walked through the door. Fear gripped her as she saw his physical condition and she didn't see Jaden. "Chris! Where's Jaden?"

"We need to get out of here first. Fill you in on the way."

"The way to where and why is there a rush to leave?" Reagan was unable to piece together anything now that made sense, and it was obvious to her the effects of the necklace had worn off.

"Anywhere but here," he said. "Don't have much time. Please find your mom and get everything you need for a few days and be back down in five minutes."

Reagan pleaded. "Not that I don't trust you, Chris, but why are we in danger here?"

Chris remained calm. "Have you guys left this villa today?"

"No, why?" Reagan said.

"I talked to the owner, Sabbi, and she told me she would call the villa to see if she could reach you. She called me back and said you weren't here. I had a strange feeling she wasn't telling me the truth."

"I can see why you don't trust her," Reagan said. "One thing you don't know is that someone broke into our villa and stole a necklace out of the safe the other day."

"More proof that this is not a safe place. Now please get ready!"

Shelly and Reagan hurried up the stairs to pack while Chris grabbed some water, a package of bagels, and a bag of flaming Cheetos he found in the kitchen.

In a few minutes, they rushed down the stairs with their suitcases and a robe for Chris.

"We have nothing here that will fit you, so this will have to do," Shelly said.

They almost ran over Michelle as they sped away.

"Have you decided where we're going?" Even in a tense moment, Reagan giggled at the man in a bathrobe driving the getaway car.

"I have a friend in Cancun we can stay with for a few days."

"Please tell us where Jaden is and what the hell is going on!" Reagan demanded just before Shelly did the same. Chris spent the next twenty minutes as they drove the 307 toward Cancun detailing their last forty-eight hours, being respectfully delicate when discussing the grisly murders.

Reagan struggled to hold back tears while Shelly wept in the back seat. "What about Jaden?"

"I don't know if Gonzo would keep the tournament going, once he found out I escaped or if he would take off and try to separate himself from the ungodly game he must have invented. I've thought about this a lot over the last day and still don't know what he would do. For all I know, the rest of the guys may still be down in the UB."

"We can't take any chances on that," Shelly said through sobs. "Why aren't we calling the police?"

"It doesn't take long living here to realize that Gonzo owns the police. We go to them and they call Gonzo. Then Gonzo finds us. We could try to find the stadium where we were, but they blindfolded us on the way, and all I know is that it's about three miles from a Pemex in Tepich. The problem there is that they know I know you guys and that you will probably convince me to go back and try to rescue Jaden. They could be laying a trap."

"But you're just guessing," Reagan said through clenched teeth. "Do we just let him die in that damned prison?" She trembled. "The police might be crooked, but I trust Raul. I have his number in my phone now, so I'm calling him to get some advice."

Chris quickly glanced at Reagan. "Who is Raul?"

"He's the detective in charge of investigating it. We told him about you, but maybe you were in that awful prison when he tried to contact—wait, he's calling me now."

"Detective Isuega, I'm so glad you called."

"I'm here at your villa. Where did you guys go?"

"Chris Tucker is with us. Silva has been playing evil games and killing men for entertainment. Other than Silva, we don't know who else is involved. And no, we have no proof right now, before you ask."

"That is typical. As I said, he's insulated himself very well."

"We don't trust the owner of the villa we were in, which is why we're headed —"

"Reagan, don't tell me where you're going right now. I'm not sure how secure . . . wait a minute. There's someone in the villa right now."

"Is it the maid?" Reagan asked.

"No, I've been at the front gate since I called. I see two men in there and they must have come from the sea side of the villa. I'm going around back."

Instead of walking by the side of the Sueno, Raul hustled down to the next villa and negotiated some uneven terrain and thick black mangroves to reach the beach side. A couple walked along the water's edge toward him, and a young girl rowed in a kayak about twenty meters out. He kept his gun pocketed. No one appeared to be home in the villa next door, so he found a good vantage point on a couch under a pagoda and watched the sliding glass door, waiting for any activity. None occurred. He watched several other walkers and a boy hunting for shells, but after thirty minutes of surveillance, he decided there were only two possibilities. Either they had exited out the front or they were hiding in wait for the Prefontaines to return. He called Reagan.

"They never came out the back of the villa, so it's possible they're in there waiting for you to return. It's also possible they were sent by the owner to get some repairs done, so I don't have probable cause to enter the villa. How long will you be gone?"

"We may never return to that villa. I have to find out about Jaden first. When are you going to arrest Silva?"

"Let me talk to Chris," Raul said.

Chris got on the phone.

"Chris, this is Detective Isuega. I am with the Policía Federal Ministerial, not the local police, and I am not on Gonzalo Silva's payroll. Is that clear and may I proceed?"

"Do I have any choice?"

"You do not have to believe me, but it is true. What can you tell me about the events that occurred after the baseball game on Friday night?"

Chris related to Raul what had happened, as Reagan and Shelly listened quietly, gently crying. He named the six others besides himself and Jaden.

"Thank you for being so helpful, Mr. Tucker. Please tell Reagan we will do all we can to find Jaden alive and healthy."

They pulled up to a small green house with a brown '95 Ford pickup parked in the front yard. Chris had known Rocky

Lancaster since his early years in elementary school. He was their next-door neighbor in Beaumont, Nebraska. Chris's family owned a cattle ranch, and Chris' dad always used a bale spear to move hay from the field to the barn. The hydraulics malfunctioned one day, and it dumped a silage-wrapped group of thirty-two bales on top of the tractor he operated, breaking his neck and turning a virile and proud man into a depressed quadriplegic. He slowly spiraled into an angry alcoholic, eventually committing suicide by grabbing a knife between his teeth and slitting his paralyzed left wrist.

Chris was four at the time and Rocky became his surrogate father. He went to every game Chris played, encouraging him when he needed it and disciplining him when he earned it. He also taught him to hunt, and Chris became an accomplished marksman after hours at the gun range during off seasons.

Rocky would save baseballs that had lost their usefulness and use an electric pitching machine he built to launch them. He claimed he gave the idea for the machine to Paul Giovagnoli who got credit for it but says Giovagnoli screwed up by not creating different launch patterns that would also work for outfielders catching flies. Rocky played minor league ball in his day, and he was the driving force for Chris to become a third baseman.

Rocky moved to the Caribbean when Chris caught on with the Tigres. His early career found him doing rescue diving with the navy, so he also planned on resurrecting his diving, although he would do little rescuing at his advanced age. He was pushing eighty-five now and the filters had taken a hiatus, if not a permanent vacation.

"Well, who are these fine-lookin' bitches you brought, C-Dog?"

"Rocky, you have to use what manners you have left around these ladies. They don't know you yet."

Rocky was a country boy at heart, and his well-worn blue jeans were held up with a cowboy belt fastened with a bronzed representation of a bucking bronco. His long-sleeved gray chamois pearl snap shirt was tucked in neatly to reveal a flat stomach, and a Tigres baseball cap was pulled down to his bushy eyebrows. Years of ranching had leathered his face, but his cobalt eyes drew attention away from the abused skin.

"Sorry, ladies. You'll have to pardon an old man's deviation from propriety. I assure you that it was meant as a compliment. But Chris!" he said with a raised voice, turning to find him leafing through a photo album. "What the fuck are you doing in a bathrobe? I could speculate right now with some tawdry guesses, but I'll stand down and await a believable response."

Chris closed the album. "It's a long story. Do you have anything I can wear?"

"Come right this way. Let's see if I have anything that'll fit that frame." He found a pair of gray sweatpants that ended mid-ankle and a white wife beater.

"Do they have a Walmart here, Rocky?" asked Shelly.

"Does a whore have tits? Oh, sorry again. Yes, that's where I do my shopping. By the way, C-Dog, why didn't you warn me you guys were coming?"

"Because you still don't believe in phones, and I still haven't learned Morse code."

"Oh yeah. That makes sense."

"Can I get you to put us up for a few days until things blow over?"

"I have a feeling you're about to tell me a story, C-Dog."

CHAPTER 21

A clean-shaven, neatly coiffed man of thirty-five years, wearing a Givenchy suit and zebra boots rang the bell on the counter at 10:15 p.m. Alpheus emerged from around the corner. "You must be Mr. Wilson."

"That's right." His lips didn't move.

"Have a seat. What are you offering for this specific tattoo?"

"Five hundred thousand pesos."

"Very well. Here is the account number," Alpheus said as he handed him an index card. "When I see the deposit, the tattoo will be delivered." Mr. Wilson punched in some numbers on his cell, hesitated a few seconds, then nodded to the tattooist.

Alpheus opened his laptop, found what he had hoped, then closed it. "You can find the starfish tattoo at 4315 La Cepra, Cancun."

Mr. Wilson stood. "If we do not find it there, we will be back." Then he was gone.

"That's unbelievable," Rocky said, head shaking to accentuate his incredulity. "I've never trusted Silva, but I never thought he would take my mistrust to this extreme. I know the Hetacalín is known for their willingness to kill anyone who gets in their way, but these are innocents. You're a wanted man now, C-Dog, but hopefully you're safe here and I got a spare bedroom for the women. You get the couch."

"Thanks, Rocky. We owe you big."

"We're all in danger," Shelly said, "so let's get our priorities straight for now. No one knows we're in Cancun, so let's stock up on some food before any news spreads."

Rocky said, "Why are you ladies in trouble? Just because of your association with this guy?"

"We have our own worries, Mr. Lancaster," said Reagan. "Someone tried to run over us, then someone broke into our villa and stole something out of our safe, and right before we drove here, there were two strange men inside our villa. We're not sure why someone or someones are after us, but we're paranoid."

"If I knew any sombitches were in my residence, I'd go in shootin'," declared Rocky matter-of-factly. "Any chance anyone followed you over here?"

"We weren't really paying attention, but don't you think they would have broken in by now if they were after any of us?"

"Not sure you aren't rationalizin'. He reached under a cushion on his couch and retrieved a Glock and handed it to Chris. "The safety's on, but it's loaded. You remember shootin' this one back home?"

"Sure do. Shot many a rabbit with this."

"Take it," Rocky said. "After hearing your story, you need it more than I do. Besides, I have my Browning semi-automatic in my bedroom, so I'm well-armed."

"I appreciate it, Rocky. Just hope I never need it. Do they require a license to carry here?"

"I made sure to get one that's approved to use for self-defense here. You don't need no license to carry. 'Course, whose gonna make the decision on who was defending and who was offending in this country? I just feel better if you have that on ya."

Their suitcases had not been unloaded, but they decided to leave them in the trunk until they returned. "OK, Rocky, we'll be back in a few hours. We haven't eaten, so we'll probably get something to eat while we're out. Do you want us to bring you anything?"

"Nah. I'm good. Had me a ham sandwich before y'all got here."

"Anything we can get you at Walmart?"

"Bring me the new edition of *Playboy*," he grinned. "Hey C-Dog. By the way, you had a great game the other night. That off-balance throw to nip Hernandez was big-league talent and that opposite-field screamer over first showed me you were takin' what they gave ya. If those scouts didn't take notice, they wouldn't take notice of . . . aw, never mind. Forgot we had ladies present."

Reagan wanted to get Chris some clothes to wear so she put the Walmart into her GPS and began giving Chris directions. "Mom, you think we can find out about Dad flying out tomorrow? I'm using my phone for directions, so can you find the travel restrictions for government employees? Might be best to search under the Department of Defense that Dad falls under."

"Give me a minute to get on the Google."

"Mom, it's . . . never mind."

"OK, I found something. It says, 'All DOD civilians and their family members will stop all official travel, such as permanent change of station or temporary duty, through July 31, 2019. This is an amendment and extension of existing restrictions put in place on July 10, 2019.'"

"I bet he can get an exception, since he has a missing son. Surely that would draw some sympathy. Turn right at the next light, Chris. What time does he get within cell range, or do you know?"

"I know he's back in town by tonight, but he didn't tell me when he would be back to civilization where he would have access to a cell tower. I've been texting him every hour today just to make sure he contacts us before his DC people."

They spent half an hour getting enough food and drinks for three days, some toiletries and medicine for Chris's cuts, and some shorts, sneakers, and shirts to switch out for Rocky's wardrobe. They spent the next hour in a Carl's Jr., letting Chris regain some calories. Three large hamburgers did the trick. Reagan plugged in Rocky's address, and they took about twenty minutes to get back to La Cepra.

As they approached Rocky's home, Chris slowed down and said, "Something isn't right."

"What do you mean?" Reagan asked.

"He *never* leaves his door open. It's wide open and not moving. Drives him crazy to waste the AC. I've learned that lesson."

"Maybe he carried something in and hasn't had a chance to close it yet," Shelly said.

Chris put the car in reverse and backed it up a few houses down the block. "Stay here," he ordered Reagan and Shelly. He placed the Glock into the pocket of his sweats and eased out of the car, leaving the door open. He walked quietly to an area between two houses, then walked sideways along the fronts of two more houses, hoping no one came out and made a scene. When he reached the edge of Rocky's house, he crouched down and edged toward a window, straining to see through the frosted barrier Rocky had installed. The door remained ajar. He stood near a sprinkler assembly, so he picked it up and tossed it onto the front porch, creating a loud clanging noise. No activity. *Dammit Rocky, why can't you get a phone?*

With his gun aimed at the front door, Chris inched his way to the porch, then enough to see inside. The smell of pizza drew his attention to the left, and he saw a box on top of the kitchen table, lid closed. Walking through the door and into the bedroom, he noticed some water trickling underneath the bathroom door. "Rocky!" he yelled as he yanked the door open, fearing the worse.

Rocky popped his head out of the bathtub water. "What the fuck, C-Dog?"

"Hey old man. You had me worried. Why didn't you answer me?"

"Still got a touch a' that narcolepsy. I doze off sometimes and when I'm in the tub, it happens more often, you know, the warm water."

"But your front door was wide open!"

"That ass-lickin' pizza boy musta left it open. I knew I shouldn't tip him."

"You said you weren't hungry."

"That was two hours ago."

"Just don't scare me like that again. I thought someone had come in here and killed you." Chris' heart rate slowly descended. "I better go tell the girls."

He walked out and gave them the A-OK sign, then pulled the car into Rocky's driveway. They unloaded the suitcases and the sacks of clothes and other items they had bought. Chris quickly got a shower and changed into some khaki shorts and a blue polo. "I feel like a man again."

"Let's get those injuries taken care of," said Reagan. She made sure they were free of debris, adding some antibiotic ointment and some gauze bandages over the worst ones. "I know you resemble a Tetris game midstream, but they'll heal faster this way. You should've seen my cheek four days ago. You'll heal faster in this salty environment."

"Thanks, Reagan."

Shelly got a text from Carlisle. "He's back!" she exclaimed with little effort at restraint. She read the text to Reagan.

> Back to civilization. Just got through all your texts. Still no word from Jaden?

Shelly said, "What should I tell your father, Reagan?"

"How about the truth? He deserves to know. You may not think he can do anything about it, so why upset him, but maybe he has some pull in Washington, even if he might not be able to get here."

"We should really just talk, then."

> Can I call you, honey?

> Yes, please.

She took the phone into the bathroom and closed the door.

CHAPTER 22

"How many have you located so far, Kara?"

"We have six in the cellar, cariño. Two with webbed feet, three with six toes on one foot, and one with a birthmark that resembles a skinned chicken instead of a starfish, but she's the closest we've found. We've had reports of a girl with a much better mark, but we haven't located her yet. One of the six-toed visitors is a young boy, by the way."

Silva was reviewing tape of the POK escape. "And have the visitors been tested?"

"Not yet," Kara replied, apprehensively. "I wanted to talk out the method we'll use to see if anyone has powers when wearing the necklace. We need a test we can trust that they can't fake. They were all told they would be paid handsomely for helping us with an experiment, but there could be one special visitor who would find a pot of gold."

Still somewhat distracted, he said, "The Yankees and Red Sox are playing tonight. Ask them the final score and the total attendance numbers announced at the end of the game."

"And if anyone gets it right?" She took notes.

Silva grinned. "They get treated like a queen. They don't need to be told it would be like the queen held in her castle.

The collectors ensured that their captors were taken without witnesses, yes?"

"This is what I was told, cariño. And what is to become of those who prove not to be accurate prognosticators?"

"Winston has plans for them."

"Ooh . . . can I watch?"

Sabbi's beachfront home in Tulum was majestic. Surrounded by coconut palms, it had a penthouse decorated with unique and expensive pieces of art. She walked out onto the balcony that had a view of a crimson-tinged Caribbean as the sun set behind her. Mario was let in by the butler and joined her at the rail. "Was the intel good, Mario?"

"Not sure yet," he stated reluctantly. "The first pass was negative, but there was some old coot taking a bath. I walked in on him, but he was asleep, so I let him be. I found no sign of her, so she might not have shown up yet. He also had a pizza delivered. I'm sure it was just for him."

"Now how would you know that?" She cut her eyes toward him, questioning his premise.

Smugly, Mario said "Because I order pizza from the same place—The Italian Paraíso—and they always ask how many the order is for. They place a separate container of parmesan cheese in the inserts for each person, and there was only one container in his box."

"And the reason you didn't interrogate the old guy in the tub?"

"Didn't want to alert him. He could send the girl away if he knew I was coming for her. I figured we had time."

She glared at Mario. "Did you take care of the tattooist?"

"Not yet. Have to make sure the intel he gave me is accurate. We may need to bleed more information out of him if we don't find the girl there but don't worry, he won't be feeding anyone else the intel on her whereabouts."

Sabbi's mood deteriorated quickly. "Did you leave someone at the old man's house to watch for the girl showing up?"

"Didn't have anyone to spare. The Durago brothers are looking into the Tepich report. I've got Murphy at the Villa Sueno. That leaves me, and I needed to report to you."

"You could have done that with a phone call," she said disapprovingly.

"I might as well call Silva directly and tell him what we're doing."

"Point taken. Just get back out there and find the girl and get some more help if you're stretched that much."

Shelly returned from a fifteen-minute debriefing with Carlisle. "Dad wants to come, even though the DOD won't allow it, but he also said the cartel has tentacles within the transportation sector and has no doubts they will know his time of arrival. He said he would likely never make it to see us, and DC has no intentions of facilitating his safe arrival or transport."

"So, he's not gonna try to come at all?" Reagan's disappointment was transparent.

"He's not giving up. Said he would see about speaking to the embassy here regarding who they trust in Quintana Roo. I promise he's not giving up. Not with Jaden missing. He has to make the best decision, and we all know that about your dad, right?"

"Of course. This does give me some motivation to do something ourselves, though." Walking toward Chris, she asked "Do you think you could lead us back to the killing field?"

"I can't know until I try. It was dark when I made most of my getaway."

Reagan glanced out the window on the west side. "It's about to be dark soon, so the look and feel should be familiar to you. We can drive to where you came out of the woods and listen for the dogs to see if they're still searching for you. If dogs are out, we return to the car. Deal?"

"That sounds acceptable. You patched me up rather well, I must say."

"I'm going with you," Shelly said emphatically. "That's my son out there, and I need to be part of the solution for bringing him home."

"Then I'm going too!" Rocky blurted enthusiastically.

"No, you're not," Chris said. "I've been in that forest with its uneven terrain and invisible trees when the moonlight betrays you. I don't want to lose you in the forest or leave you behind after we get there."

"Oh, all right, but let me get some guns for the ladies."

Reagan placed her hand on the bony shoulder of Rocky. "Do you have any archery supplies? Compound bow with some arrows?"

Rocky smiled. "Can you really shoot?"

"She's been shooting since she was five," Shelly said. "She can probably shoot better with a bow than most can shoot with a rifle."

Rocky sized up Reagan. "You may be in luck. I've got a Bear compound that I bought for my granddaughter this year. Looks like you would have the same draw length."

"Why doesn't your granddaughter have it?" asked Reagan.

"I didn't want to mail it to her because I wanted to show her how to use it. Well, really, I just wanted to see her. It's been over a year."

"I'll bring it back safely, Rocky. You'll still get the chance to shoot with her. What's her name?"

"Anabelle."

"I'll be proud to use Anabelle's bow."

Rocky smiled and retreated to his bedroom to get the bow and a gun for Shelly. Raindrops gently pattered on the window as a breeze diverted them northward. Reagan walked outside to see very few and no menacing clouds in the dusky sky.

Just a little dusting to cool things down for our trek, she thought.

Rocky soon emerged with the Bear for Reagan and a Walther P22 for Shelly. "Chosen especially for you, my dear."
Shelly leaned over and gave him a kiss on the cheek. "We'll take good care of these, Rocky, but we're praying they won't be used. If we're not back by the time you wake up in the morning, here's Carlisle's number." She hurriedly wrote the number on the pizza box lid. "Can you contact him and let him know exactly what our plans were and that we haven't returned when we were expected?"

"Sure will, honey. I'll say three Hail Marys myself."

CHAPTER 23

Chris drove south on the 180 toward Tepich with intermittent rain coming from a friendly but darkening sky. "The Pemex is on the corner of Calle X-Lapak and Calle San Jose. We should see it on the left in a few minutes." Chris hoped his sense of direction would serve him well once they were on foot.

Reagan's cell buzzed. "Inspector Isuega! Do you have anything for us?"

"I wish I had better information, but for now, all I can tell you is that I contacted the owner of your villa."

"Sabbi?"

"Yes. She had some repair people in the house this morning working on a plumbing issue."

"We had no plumbing issue that I was aware of. I don't trust her. What do you know about her?"

"Not much, but as far as I know, she's got a clean slate. Also, Silva has suddenly gone dark. I know it's their all-star week and there aren't any games locally, so he might have left the country, but no one has been able to reach him. Our drones show his helicopter is still on the pad, but he has many other ways to leave. We won't give up."

"Thank you." She argued with herself, wondering if she should have told him what they were doing, but the other self won the argument. He would find out soon enough.

They pulled into the Pemex and parked like they had every intention of making a quick getaway after a snatch-and-run. Chris hoped to speak with the uncooperative Hispanic behind the counter but found a portly, middle-aged woman of fifty-five years loading cigarette packs into shelf recesses that reminded Chris of a queen bee laying eggs in a honeycomb. "When will the Mexican man with the goatee be back?"

She responded without turning her head. "He won't be back." She tucked a pack of Winstons into a dusty slot.

"Why not?"

She pivoted to face him, stone-faced. "Someone killed him this morning."

An electrical current ran through Chris. The chilling effect choked off any words he attempted to speak.

"Did the police investigate?" Shelly asked.

"Hell, no. There was a note nailed to his temple that read, 'Skyrockets in flight, afternoon delight.'"

Chris and Reagan eyed each other. "What does that mean?" asked Chris.

"You must not be from around here. It's the Hetacalín cartel's hit squad's signature . . . kind of a code they like to use. They always leave a nail in the temple with the SIFAD signature. I can't remember what it stands for. Something like, *'Secreto Intelligentsia Favor Asesina Dildo'* or something. What I *can* tell you is if they left the message in English, it was meant for someone who speaks English, so I won't be working here after today myself. Soon as I get my hours in, my ass is gone!"

Chris peered over the counter onto the floor and saw the signs of wiped-up blood. The cigarette loader wiped her hands on her Pemex apron and gave him an unapproving glance.

"Do you know why they killed him?" Shelly asked.

"They had pulled out all of his fingernails before killing him. At least that's what the owner told me after he had the family come get him."

"You think they were trying to get some information from him?" Chris asked.

"Hell if I know. It's the cartel. They gotta have a reason? Nothing surprises me about what they do around here, but if they were trying to get information, I knew that prick pretty well and if he knew something, he'd have squealed like a pig gettin' fucked by a rhino."

Chris's knees were weak, but he did his best to act calm. They bought some water bottles, put them in their packs, and walked back to the getaway car, glancing up at the dusky, damp sky. "The Mexican behind the counter didn't know where the lady and her kid were taking me, and he didn't speak English very well, so I doubt he was much help for the guys that did this." They drove to the trailer park where Chris had borrowed the bike. They found the bike again but leaning against a different trailer house. "I know who's in there," said Chris. "Let's move on."

They entered the edge of the forest, then stopped and listened. There were no sounds other than a few nightingales and the trees shedding leftover rain from their leaves. It was more difficult to see with tree shadows accentuating the waning minutes of remaining daylight. Their light beams found a moist but navigable forest floor. "Wish I had thought to leave some type of trail. I'm fairly sure I came out at this angle." He pointed at a thirty-degree angle to the forest edge.

He led Reagan and Shelly, who had their lights aimed at their feet to illuminate any sudden change in the anatomy of the ground. All three were in good enough shape to walk the three miles, provided Chris's bearings were reasonably intact.

"This is an easier walk when you don't have to depend on moonlight," Chris said. "We should make better time than I did."

Reagan's bow and quiver were slung over her shoulders, and she held them close to prevent snagging on the branches straining under the weight of the recent downpour. Chris found the alligator juniper he had slept in. "We're on the right track. We need to cut off here and take a different path than I took coming out. It'll be a much straighter shot."

After another mile, Shelly suggested they rest for a few minutes. They each found a tree stump and sat, taking a swig of water from their bottles.

"Chris, have you thought about what we'll do if Silva has an army there waiting for you to rescue your friend? "asked Reagan.

"Since they know I've escaped, they don't know who I might have told, so my guess is they've disappeared."

Shelly wiped her eyes.

"It's OK, Mom. I know what you're thinking, but Jaden could still be in that horrible bunker, so we have to stay strong."

"I know, honey. I'm just scared."

Chris said, "We should have about one more mile."

They continued to follow him, lights down or held against their bodies to prevent any unnecessary beams beetling into the dark night. After thirty minutes of decelerated walking, Chris motioned for them to get down. He saw the still-illuminated field through a break in the forest. "Turn off your flashlights," he whispered. "We'll just use the light of the moon and the LED lights on the field to help us from here on."

They moved closer with as much stealth as they could, Chris motioning them toward the entrance Bobby had led them to on the first night. They were on hands and knees now, but both Chris and Shelly made sure they could get to their guns quickly, if necessary. They saw no movement. It was as void of life as an airport lobby during a pandemic lockdown. Chris surveyed the horizon for the cranes but saw no sign of them. They stayed in the shadows until they were thirty feet from the stone steps.

At the edge of the shadows, Chris whispered even more softly, "Stay here. I'm gonna see if the door's unlocked." He walked toward the steps, ready to flinch at any unexpected sound. He quickly descended the stone steps and tried the door. Locked. It was too thick to break through, and they would need much more force and firepower than they had.

He returned to the shadows. "OK, plan B. There's an elevator that goes down to the bunker. I think it's up." He pointed to a clear cylinder on the other side of the field. "No shadows to hide in on the way over there. Stay here until I wave you over."

"That's not going to happen," whispered Reagan. "We're going with you."

"Why not let me go first and—" but the girls were already marching toward the elevator.

Shit.

When they reached the cylinder, Chris said "Only one of us will fit at a time, and don't fight me on this because I know the geography down there."

"You're leaving us up here to get strafed by machine gunfire while you're safe down below?" Shelly was doing her best to help the strained mood.

"I'll send it back up after I'm down. In the meantime, get under that rock ledge until it comes back up." The sloped walls used for the POK contest had a rock ledge that extended out, forming a short and narrow roof. They slid under it as Chris closed the door on the elevator and descended.

Five minutes passed.

"I don't like this," whispered Reagan to Shelly.

"I don't either. Nothing we can do right now but pray."

Five more minutes passed. "We have to do something," Shelly said with a panicked voice. "I'm really afraid something bad has happened." The ground finally moved, and the elevator rose.

The door opened and Chris said, "It's empty. No sign of anyone. Remember the death tube I told you about?" They both nodded hesitantly. "It's gone. No sign of blood or death. If I had to guess, I'd say we could walk this field and not see any sign of the murders."

They walked to the center of the field. "This is about where they dropped the heads and bodies. No sign at all. . . as if nothing sinister ever happened here."

"No sign of Jaden at all down there?" Reagan asked.

"None."

Shelly sobbed uncontrollably while Reagan held her tightly. It was just after midnight.

"Let's go home, Chris," said Reagan. "I don't want to worry Dad." Just before Reagan entered the trees, she wheeled, pulled an arrow from her quiver, drew the string back and unleashed a projectile of hate, shattering the sixty-foot-high LED enclosure and blacking out the elevator side of the field.

Someone's going to pay for this.

CHAPTER 24

Kara's bronzed body contrasted with her yellow bikini as she reclined in a lounge chair on the deck of Silva's yacht, the *Cauliflower*. He bought it in 2016 from a Russian billionaire who had bought it from a sheikh in the United Arab Emirates. The name would be cruelly ironic to others with a deformed ear like Silva's, but he never got around to changing the name.

Silva was bringing her a martini . . . her third. The lights from the *Cauliflower* made Vegas at 2:00 a.m. look like it was shut down. Kara peered up from her iPad. "Thanks, my cariño. Interesting day, eh?"

"Indeed. We may stay out here a few days until things cool off. Been in contact with Winston?"

"Yes. The interviewees have been taken care of. No one guessed the correct score. But there's some good news. Our people in Mexico City tell us there are reports of a young lady in the area with a tattoo that—"

"Tattoo?" he asked. "Something our Alpheus could create?"

"I should have said birthmark. They said it's a birthmark, not a tattoo. Sorry. Anyway, the *birthmark*," she said with emphasis, "is almost identical to the one Omelia had . . . much better than the one on our earlier potential. We will find her quickly."

"Love your confidence," he said, as he cupped her left breast and kissed her on the cheek. "It's two a.m. You coming to bed?"

"I have more work to do. I'll be in soon."

The car clock read three-thirty when they pulled up to Rocky's house, the silence of the night and inadequate light from a broken streetlamp casting an eerie presence. Chris interrupted the mood. "You guys go in and let Rocky know we're here and safe. I'll get the backpacks and Rocky's bow."

"Thanks, Chris," a sleepy Shelly replied. They entered the house using a key Rocky had told them about on the transom above the door, easing into the dark front room. "What's that smell?"

"It's your friend." A man approached them from Rocky's bedroom, but it was too dark to make out anything other than the racking slide of a revolver. They didn't move until a light was switched on, revealing a well-built Hispanic wearing a black suit and an unbuttoned white shirt smattered with crimson.

"Where's Rocky?" Shelly demanded.

"He's taking a nap," the gravelly voice said. Beads of sweat appeared on his forehead. "I need both of you to roll up your sleeves."

They each wore dark, long-sleeved cotton shirts. Shelly shook but managed to roll up her right sleeve. Reagan followed, and when he was satisfied with what he saw, he raised the gun to Shelly's forehead. The sound and blood spray caused Reagan's heart to cavitate, seizing her in a suspended position that felt like minutes. The man's head exploded, sending pieces of hair, skin, and skull in a splayed pattern on the wall. Blood splattered across Shelly's face as she collapsed to the floor.

Chris ran over and hugged Reagan, then reached to lift Shelly off the floor. "Are you OK?" he asked, shaken. Shelly slowly nodded. The dead man lay at Reagan's feet, blood drenching the beige shag carpet. "Where's Rocky?"

Chris rushed into Rocky's bedroom, still holding his gun, to find Rocky lying naked on the bed, hands and feet tied to bed posts and duct tape over his mouth. He had seven vertical incisions stretching from nipple to groin like the race lanes in a swimming pool. But he was alive. Chris first removed the duct tape.

"That son-of-a-bitch better be dead. You get him, C-Dog?"

"He won't cut you anymore, Rocky. You're going to make it." He untied his hands and feet.

"Bastard gave me a slice for every hour you didn't come home. At least it kept me awake." Once he was loose, he gingerly put on some pants and went to the bathroom to survey the damage.

When Shelly and Reagan had recovered enough to enter the bedroom, Shelly stared, fury building. "Rocky, do you have any of the gauze left that we used to fix up Chris?" He rifled through a drawer and pulled out a package. Shelly cleaned the wounds, provided some antibiotic ointment, and bandaged them as well as she could with the materials she had. "You'll need stitches and ideally soon. For now, just be careful. The medical tape will have to do." She wrapped his torso with the roll of gauze and hoped it would hold for a while.

When he managed to get a shirt on, Rocky asked, "Anyone know what the fucker wanted?"

Reagan walked over to him. "I think this is all about the starfish on my arm." She pulled up her sleeve.

"What the hell?"

"We're also confused," said Reagan. "People have been staring at this since we landed a week ago. It's from a Man-O-War sting when I was young. Some think this gives me some special powers, but then why would some people out there try to harm or exploit me? The dead guy in the other room was going to kill Mom once he saw I had the mark, then probably kill you and take me somewhere. We all have Chris to thank for saving our lives."

Chris asked, "Hey, Rocky. You think there's a chance the neighbors heard the gunshot and got curious?"

"Nope. If it did wake them up from a drunken stupor, they'll just think it was a caddy backfirin', but even if they did think it was a gun shot, they don't want to get involved. Those pricks would just roll over and go back to sleep."

Reagan said, "Think you can sift through the dead guys pockets and see if we can learn anything?"

"I've never killed a man," Chris whispered.

"I don't think any of us have," said Shelly.

"Not so quick," Rocky chimed in. "Diggin' around in the bastard's pockets won't bother me in the least." He gingerly walked over to the contorted man, straightened him out, then rummaged through his pockets, locating some cash, a billfold, and a cell phone. He pocketed the cash. "To pay my medical bills and for pain and anguish." He handed the billfold and phone to Reagan. "I don't even know how to turn the damn thing on."

Reagan looked through the billfold quickly, finding nothing of interest except his name, Mario Narvaez. She used the dead man's thumb to log on to the phone. She attempted to remove the thumbprint logon but needed the phone code to do so. Using information from his wallet, she tried every code she could think of but had no success. She went to Rocky's kitchen, and finding a butcher knife and baggie, returned, extended the man's arm and with a chopping motion, brought the butcher knife down, separating the thumb from the hand. She placed it in a ziploc baggie.

Chris and Shelly watched wide-eyed, but Rocky rooted her on. She opened his text messages and found a long thread between the dead man and a Sabrina Chavez-Escano. She realized Sabrina must be Sabbi. Reading through these removed any doubt of her complicity.

Sabbi and a guy named Ephraim were angling to use Reagan in the financial industry through a company called Berringer Investments, but they were trying to find her before the cartel did. The Hetacalín cartel wanted to use her talents for their interests, too. She added some contacts from his phone to hers, then opened his calendar. He had a meeting with someone named Alpheus today at two-thirty. Alpheus must be the tattooist, so she rolled back both sleeves to inspect but found no visible tattoos.

Chris asked, "Can you explain what you just did?"

"I didn't want to take the phone because they may use tracking software to find it, and I don't want to be in possession of it when they do."

"But you cut off his thumb."

"Yes, and I will put the phone in the microwave I saw in Rocky's kitchen. Do you think there's a chance this house gets burned down or blown up?"

"That wouldn't surprise me," Chris replied.

"If it does, the phone shouldn't be destroyed. We can get back in and get the phone. They wouldn't try to track it after an explosion. They'll assume it was destroyed, and the police wouldn't know to miss it."

"Remind me to never play you in a game of chess."

Ignoring the comment, she said to Rocky, "We have a dilemma. Someone may show up in the morning when Mr. Mario here doesn't respond to Sabbi. I considered texting her from his phone, but we may not be here when she responds, and I don't want to take the chance of alerting her too soon. I suggest we find a no-tell motel and get some sleep. Do you have anyone in town you trust?"

He downed two ibuprofens. "I was already thinking about that. I met an old guy at a bar a few weeks ago and we were talking about the war. Not sure where he lives, but—"

"Wait! I saw a home boarded up two houses down. If we stay there, we can keep an eye on this one and see who comes to visit."

Rocky replied, "I think they just boarded it up a few days ago. Old lady lived there. She was pushing a hundred, and I say lived because they wheeled her out with a white cloth over her face last week. No living kin and didn't leave a will. Probably going to probate court to see if they can find some long-lost relative. Likely to be boarded up for some time."

"Perfect," Shelly said. "Let's go there instead of the hotel. Chris, can you park the car around the corner? I saw a church parking lot I'm sure you could leave it in. Rocky, let's take all the medicine and gauze you have left, plus any food and water for a few days."

"We should have plenty. Hey, mind if I set a little trap for our new friends who might show up?"

"That depends, Rocky. What do you have in mind?"

"Great. Don't ask too many questions, but I've got an incendiary that explodes with friction. I can set it so when the door opens, the room and the bastard that opens the door are sent straight to hell."

"This is your house, Rocky!" said Shelly.

"Not exactly. I lease this dump. If it blows, no skin off my back." He held his bandaged torso as he laughed at the irony.

"OK," Chris said. "It's all yours!"

"I like your style," said Reagan. "I'll go to the other house now to see if I can find a way in." She grabbed a flashlight and ran to the boarded-up house, finding a gate open to the backyard. There was no sign of a dog, but a few chickens rebelled at the invasion. She opened a window that groaned under the effort and slithered through it onto the kitchen counter. She unlocked the back door, then found two bedrooms with both beds made up. She found a thin vertical space between two of the boards that covered the windows and thought that would be a perfect view of the street.

After returning to Rocky's house, she asked, "Everyone ready? Rocky, if you have extra sheets or blankets, can you bring them for Chris? He gets the couch. Make sure everything that's supposed to be gone is gone. We have to make sure it appears as if we've left the area completely."

CHAPTER 25

"Stayed here all night?" Silva found her in the same chair on the deck, iPad lying beside her, wearing the same yellow bikini.

"Yes. I've taken about thirty naps, so not sure how much sleep I got, but we've been trying to find this girl all night and she's vanished into thin air."

"Unacceptable." He wore plaid shorts with a blue T-shirt sporting a sexy caricature of Kara.

"I know, but we will not stop. We have many boots on the ground. I also heard from Bobby. He went by the stadium this morning and found one of the stadium light casings shattered. He's thinking maybe a hawk flew into it, but he didn't see any blood or a dead bird, so he's not sure. He asked what you wanted to do with it."

"May not use the stadium for a while. Any luck finding Tucker?"

"Last known location was a Pemex on the corner of Calle X-Lapak and Calle San Jose in Tepich. That was yesterday evening. He's picked up two women, but we know nothing about them. We thought Tucker might have been trying to retrace his route back to the stadium, but we found no signs that he did."

Agitated, Silva said, "When we get POK cranked back up, we need to implant trackers in the contestants. We can't afford to let this happen again."

"Why not stop the five-second pauses in the current from the electric fence? They'd never escape."

"But then the players would know there is no hope of escape. Part of the excitement is seeing in their eyes that they think they have a chance out."

Kara grinned. "Well, they wouldn't have to know there was no chance."

Silva considered this. "That's what I like about you, Kara. OK, it's settled. No pauses . . . and no escapes."

Sabbi was up with the sun, but the sun was not her alarm. Her sleep was fitful and racked with disoriented dreams. She called Mario. "Goddamn it, Mario! Pick up!" Sabbi paced, biting her lip and cursing simultaneously. She ended the call and connected with one of the Durago brothers.

"Victor, I need you to check out 4315 La Cepra in Cancun. Mario isn't answering and I need to know if he found our target there."

"OK, I'll get Javier and head over now."

"Listen, you damn fool. I said you, not you and Javier. I need him to stay at the villa because she may show up there. Is that understood?"

"Yes, ma'am. I'll be there in about forty minutes."

"Make that thirty. Call me when you get there."

They awoke to an explosion. Rocky held his torso and scratched his balls through droopy white underwear. "Let's go see the damage!"

"Not so quick. This might draw a crowd, and when the police get there, they'll be very confused by a separated thumb . . . if the eviscerated head doesn't alarm them. On the other hand," Reagan was thinking out loud, "I can act like a concerned citizen. I can grab the phone when I get inside."

Reagan dressed in a tank top and boxers, then ran down to the smoking house to survey the damage. The front door wasn't there, so entry was easy. She noticed some interested onlookers standing in their lawns, but no one left their safe place. Reagan found very little remaining of the unfortunate visitor, but she only cared about extracting the phone from the microwave. She walked casually to the door to see if any police were in view. Seeing none, she held the phone to her ear, feigning a call to the police as she walked toward the boarded house. Knowing there would be eyes following her, she walked two houses past the boarded one, then through a gate to an alley that would lead her back to the group.

"The guy who set off the bomb have anything left to bury?" Rocky asked.

"It'll take a while to find the pieces," Reagan replied. "Your work was very effective, but they'll now redouble their efforts to find me. We can't stay here long, so one by one, we need to head to the car. Go by the alley in back."

His partner Garvey called. "We found him."

"Silva?" Raul was hopeful.

"Yes. His goon tried to shoot down our drone as we got close, but we know it was his yacht."

"We need to get the navy involved now. Can't wait for him to return to his villa, and I don't see that he has any plans to help us."

"On it, boss."

"No, I'll contact them. The admiral and I go way back, but I also have some additional information I need to pass on. I'll fill you in later. Text me the coordinates the drone registered. How many minutes ago did the drone see him?"

"Six to seven at the most."

Isuega began some mental exercises as he punched the number for the navy. *They should get there within five minutes of me calling, so twelve minutes at five knots only puts them at maybe four hundred yards . . . shouldn't be difficult to find . . .*

"Armade de México."

"May I speak with Admiral Espinosa? This is detective Isuega with the Policía Federal Ministerial."

"Just a moment," said the soothing voice on the other end.

"Raul! How's the family?"

"They're fine, Admiral, but I don't have time for pleasantries. Is this line secure?"

"This is 2019, Raul. Nothing is secure, but this line is as close as we can get."

"Thanks. We have a missing person . . . I should say persons, but one is the son of a U.S. DIA officer at the Pentagon and this could turn sour fast. He reports only to the director. He's their key statistician. He knows about his son, Jaden, who is missing, and our fear is that he will board a plane and be here soon, even with the threat level. We don't know what intel the Hetacalín cartel has on the travel itineraries of government officials, but we must assume the worst."

"Go on," Espinosa said.

"We have new information that the Hetacalín, specifically Silva, has lured the son into an activity that has likely led to his death."

"Why are you contacting me about this?"

"Silva has been spotted at 19.97 by -86.26 as of . . ." glancing at his watch, "eight minutes ago on his yacht. I make his top speed at five knots, putting him maybe a quarter of a mile from those coordinates if he began moving immediately. Can you send a vessel to intercept him and bring him in for questioning?"

There was an awkward silence between them. "Now Raul, I'm not trying to subtract us from this maneuver, but what intel do you have on Silva that would warrant what would essentially be an arrest?"

"It's solid, Admiral. We have a baseball player who was also lured into this game of—"

"You're taking the word of a baseball player?"

"No!" Raul said emphatically. "I assure you this is legitimate and we're wasting time. I don't want that yacht to disappear."

"Don't worry about that, my friend. With those coordinates and with our birds, we can easily find him, even if it's an hour later. I just need some reassurances that this is going to stand up. The cartel has powerful lawyers, disreputable as they may be."

"OK, I'll get through this quickly." He related the series of events, starting with the video the players were shown, ending with Chris's escape.

When he finished, Espinosa said, "That sounds barbaric and frankly difficult to believe, but since you have a witness willing to discuss the case, I have a reason to detain. I will alert the capitán closest to these coordinates and get this started."

"I appreciate it, Admiral."

After the call, Espinosa punched a number on his cell.

"Hello, Admiral. What can I do for you?"

"Consider this a favor, Gonzo. Head south for the next few hours."

"Is this about the drone?"

A dial tone responded.

CHAPTER 26

The *Cauliflower* anchored near the beach at Zipolite. Silva said, "You guys stay here. Going to visit my son."

"I'm going, too," Kara said, "but I'll stay on the beach while you go to the monastery. They have a nude beach here."

"As you wish, *mi amor*. Winston, make sure the others stay on the boat, and I'd better not catch any of you looking toward that beach." Winston nodded, though reluctantly.

They deboarded into a small motorboat that had been lowered onto the water, fifty yards from shore. Kara descended the ladder first, waterproof lime-green bag slung over her shoulder. "Oh, Winny! I forgot my tanning lotion! Be a dear and toss it to me?"

As Silva climbed down the ladder, he saw Kara come close to falling in as she reached for the tossed tube. He drove the boat to the shore and stopped the motor, pocketing the key. Two teenaged boys watched their arrival. Silva pointed to the yacht and said, "See that big man standing there?"

They nodded in unison.

"He has a gun, and this is his boat. Would you like one hundred pesos to guard it?" They nodded vigorously.

"Doscientos pesos," the shorter boy said as he slowly backpedaled.

Silva handed the smaller boy the hundred-peso note and said, "You're the businessman here. You get to decide if he gets any. And remember, my friend has a gun, and he's a good shot." He walked away as the smaller boy smiled smugly at his friend and Kara parked herself under an umbrella, sans bikini.

It had been three long years since he last visited his son. Anxiety slowly robbed his serenity like a thief meticulously withdrawing valuables as he neared the monastery to which Javier had escaped seven years ago. Silva saw his son's sojourn to the monastery as an escape, as did many who knew their relationship, but friends of Javier knew he was on a journey to find himself—to wrestle the demons that chased him from his envelope of awareness.

Walking up the graveled path, Silva hesitated, then used the knocker on the baroque, ten-foot oak doors. In a moment, the door opened to reveal a bespectacled, white-headed robed man who, seeing that this was not a man seeking solace among the brothers, said, "Are you here to see someone?"

Silva bowed faintly, then replied, "I am here to see my son, Javier Silva."

"Just a moment," the monk replied, closing the door. It was a few moments before the door reopened. The same man stood there. "Your son is in prayer right now. If you did not know, he is in temporary profession."

"Of course, I knew that" Silva replied unconvincingly. "Do you know when he will be . . . out of prayer?"

"That is not for me to say," the white-headed man said calmly.

Silva thought for a moment in protracted silence. "What if I made a sizable donation to your monastery?"

The man's matter-of-fact expression morphed into one of disdain. "Sir, Epictus said that wealth consists not in having great possessions but in having few wants. Your son's affections are not for sale here." The door closed on a distraught and confused Silva. He stood there, feet planted. He finally walked back toward the beach. He was not accustomed to not getting his way, but his son vexed him. He pledged not to give up and to visit the monastery once a year until his son would see him.

The two teenage boys sat on a log and stared in Kara's direction. They nervously stood as he approached, noticeably sweating. The shorter businessman offered, "Your boat is safe, señor."

"You're lucky my man didn't shoot you. OK, my boat hasn't disappeared, so here's the next hundred," he said, pulling the bill from his pocket. "Now go buy you a whore and stop jerking off." They took the money and sprinted out of sight. He walked toward Kara, who was now on one elbow, exposing her breasts to the boys as they made haste. "Kara, get dressed. The peep show is over, and we need to get moving. We have another few hours to go."

As she slipped on the bikini bottom and fastened the top, she said, "Did you get to see Javier?"

"That son-of-a-bitch didn't want to see me."

"I'm sure that's not true," she said, trying to reassure him.

"This discussion is over."

Sabbi's phone chirped. "Well?" she barked.

"This ain't smellin' good, boss," Victor Durago said. "The door's blowed off and half the house is burnt down."

"Get your ass in there and find out what happened, you damn idiot!"

She heard some shuffling and scraping noises, then a gasp.

"Uh, boss, Mario's pretty dead. He's got a big hole in his head."

"Anyone else around?"

Victor did a cursory inspection, not wanting to discover anything unsavory and reported back. "Not a soul. I've searched the whole house and they ain't no trace o' life."

"OK, get out of there. I don't need the police seeing you there."

"I don't think we need to stay in this car," Reagan said. "Mom, you do remember who got this for us, right?"

"Oh my god. You're right. She knows what kind of car we have, and she could have even put a tracker in it."

"Exactly," Reagan replied. "Any ideas, Rocky?"

Chris answered for him. "No need to ask Rocky. I can't pass on all the secrets he taught me, but any car we find, he can have us behind the wheel inside of sixty seconds. It would take me sixty minutes."

Rocky grinned. "Well, with this new artwork on my chest, it might take me ninety seconds. Let's find a shopping center before we head out of Cancun. I think there's one in a few blocks on the right." They pulled into the parking lot and he pointed to a white Tzuro sedan. "Let's take that one. White is the most common and that model is used by taxis. We can blend in easier with that."

They pulled into a slot three cars down and Rocky went to work, leaving the others to watch. He removed a small bag from his larger bag in the trunk and found a hammer, wrench, and screwdriver, then removed the license plate of a Volvo and switched it with the plate on the Tzuro. As he prepared to break into the driver's door, he found it unlocked. He inserted the screwdriver into the keyhole slot and hit it with the hammer to dislodge the key cover. He inserted the screwdriver and turned the ignition switch, bringing the sedan to life.

"Only forty-seven seconds!" said Chris, as they transferred bags to the sedan.

"An unlocked car saves me time," Rocky replied.

Chris pulled away nonchalantly. "Where to now?" he asked no one in particular.

"We can't get too far away," Reagan offered, "Dad might fly in and we need to be diligent in finding Jaden. I have an idea." She took Mario's baggied thumb out of her backpack and used it to activate his phone, then found Sabbi's cell number. "Rocky, I need you to help us again."

"Whatever you need, my lady."

"OK, we need Sabbi to implicate herself. I want you to call her and say you're the one who took care of Mario and the messenger she sent as well. Then tell her you have me and are willing to turn me over to her for fifty thousand pesos. I'll have Inspector Isuega on the phone. It's a three-way call, by the way. Just trust me, and we'll see what she says."

"You'll have to dial the number for me."

"No problem. Do you understand?"

"Got it."

She called Raul and said, "Rocky is going to call Sabbi and offer to bring me to her for fifty thousand pesos while you listen in."

"OK, this wouldn't hold up in court, but it'll at least confirm what we suspect, and I can bring her in on charges of conspiracy to murder and a few others. We can't keep her long with a good lawyer, but let's see what she says."

Reagan looked at Rocky. "You ready?"

"Let's nail this bitch." She added Sabbi's number to the call and handed it to Rocky.

After one ring, she answered. "Mario?"

"Nope, he's a bit incapacitated right now and the guy you sent ain't lookin' too good, neither."

"Who is this?" she demanded.

"That's not important, but what *is* important is that I have who Mario was hunting for, and I can get her to you for a finder's fee of fifty thousand pesos."

There was a momentary pause, then Sabbi responded, "Where are you?"

"Again, not important. I don't have all day, so let me know if we have a deal."

Sabbi replied, "You must be crazy. I don't know what you're talking about." She ended the call and Rocky handed the phone to Reagan.

Raul said, "Well, good try, guys."

"What did she say?" Reagan asked.

"She said nothing. I can't bring her in on this. Oh, Reagan, we found some photos on one of the teen's phones who was killed in the explosion that might give us a better lead."

"I'm listening," Reagan said in anticipation.

"This girl caught a tall, olive-skinned, teenage boy in the background putting a coin in the jukebox, just like you said, but she took several, and it's not clear, but his hand is pulling away from the spittoon in one of the photos, so he could have also dropped something in it. We did find evidence of a very sophisticated device in the aftermath, but we had doubts, as this would have taken some advanced planning and the technology is in its infancy. We now think that the word 'wicked' in the song is what set off the bomb. From what we have been able to gather through our research, it would have only been triggered by the word when sung. The inventor didn't want someone to accidentally set a bomb off if the word was spoken."

"Thanks for trusting me with that information, Inspector," Reagan said. "Would ten minutes be enough lead time to set it up? That's about how long it took me to get there from the villa."

"Did they know you were coming?"

"I called them to make sure they were open, and they asked my name, so yeah, I guess so."

"But the group of teenagers was there when you got there."

"That's right."

"Our interviews with other survivors place them there for at least thirty minutes before your arrival."

"You don't know how good that makes me feel. I'm now hoping that all of the close calls were just bad luck."

"We've also found out that one of the teens killed was the daughter of a clothing manufacturer in the U.S. that had recently signaled they would be bidding on a contract for school uniforms in Mexico. These have always been supplied by Oaxaca Clothing here, and we're thinking the killing was a message."

"That's horrible," she replied, subconsciously fingering her scarred cheek.

"It's reality here, unfortunately, but at least it indicates you may not have been the target of the explosion. The next—"

"Hey, Sabbi's calling back! Let me add her to this call." She selected Add Caller and handed it to Rocky.

"You rethink your position?" Rocky asked when he connected.

"I have someone who is interested in your property," Sabbi responded.

"Great. I'll call you back in ten." He disconnected Sabbi's line. "So, what's the plan now?" He handed the phone to Reagan.

"Inspector, what would you suggest?"

"Call her back and mention the fifty thousand pesos again. We need her to commit to the amount and that it's for the girl. That's all I need. Just say you'll meet her at the villa at . . . three o'clock. No need for any of you to be there. Then I'll let you all know once I have her in custody."

"Copy that," Reagan said. "Hang on." She added her number to the call and handed it to Rocky.

"This is Mario's friend. Do you agree to the fifty thousand pesos to bring the girl to you?"

"If it's Reagan you are referring to, yes."

"We will be at the villa at three o'clock." He ended the call. "She took the bait."

"Nice work, Rocky," Reagan said. "Let's head to Alpheus Blizzard's place, Chris. Mario's appointment was at 2:30, so we should just make it in time."

"What's this about?" asked Chris.

"When I saw he had an appointment with Alpheus, I knew it had to be the tattooist, but he had no visible tattoos and didn't fit the type, so I knew he must be seeing Alpheus for information. However, he already knew where we were, so I'm thinking he was going to close the loop by killing our tattooist."

"Hmm . . . you might be right," said Rocky. "Most people know he owns many secrets, but that they can be bought. What you don't know is that I've been stashing money for a rainy day, and it's raining . . . and he don't take credit cards."

Reagan considered the offer. "We'll pay you back, Rocky. We could use some information ourselves."

"What will you want to ask him?"

"A bunch of things," Reagan replied. "What does he know about Gonzo's game? What about Sabbi? What has he heard about the SOC explosion? Who were the teenage kids, especially the tall one who played the jukebox?"

Chris cut in. "What does he charge for this information? If it's a sliding scale, I bet the charge for information about Gonzo's game is priceless."

Shelly asked, "Know where the Banca Gonzo is?"

"Yes, I remember." He made an immediate right, tires screeching. In twenty minutes, they pulled up to the tattooist's place of business.

It was just as Reagan had pictured it in her mind, nestled between the Banca Gonzo and the Farmacia Escaño, a nondescript wooden facade with a door that blended well enough to confuse the uninitiated. Other than some painted seahorses that appeared to be an afterthought, no art graced the shop front. A sign to the left of the windowless door read, By Appointment Only.

"We're right on time," Shelly said. "But something tells me he won't buy that we're Mario."

A brooding, heavily tattooed young woman adjusted a multicolored yarmulke on her ink-black hair. "We only see people by appointment," she muttered through a piece of metal protruding from her lower lip as she continued to bother with her phone.

Chris spoke up. "We're aware of the policy. Our name is Mario. It's a nom de plume for our group."

"A nom de what?" She raised her thinned eyebrows.

"Just tell Mr. Blizzard that Mario's here. He'll understand."

Alpheus walked through the door and stopped. "Where's Mario?"

"We aren't Mario, but we're here to save your life. May we come back and share some information with you? I think it's in your best interest."

Alpheus sized up the group, then motioned them back.

"Jasmine, hold all calls."

The room they entered was an interesting blend of tattoo parlor and dental office. A patient dental chair sat in the center of the room, nitrous oxide hose and mask draped over the headrest. There were seven beanbag chairs in various shades of orange and green scattered along the walls and two loveseats filled in the gaps. In one corner was a desk with a lacquered chair and a laptop in screensaver mode.

"Have a seat anywhere," Alpheus said, waving his hand over the room like a circus ringmaster introducing his animals. "Let's see what this is all about. I must admit to being disturbed at seeing Mario's name on the schedule this morning. That's why I have this gun." He reached around the back of the laptop to retrieve a sawed-off shotgun. "I assume you're here in his place because you have rearranged his schedule?"

Reagan scanned the room and replied from one of the loveseats. "Yes, we believe he was coming here to kill you. We don't think you're safe here, even with Mr. Mario's rearranged schedule, and we're willing to take you out of harm's way until it's safe to return."

Alpheus said, "You seem like a very bright young lady, Miss—"

"Reagan. Call me Reagan."

"Miss Reagan, but I am over eighty now and I've lived a good life . . . an extremely comfortable life, free from running scared. I have a wonderful business and have no desire to run and hide."

"That's all fine and good, Mr. Blizzard, but we can't afford for you to be tortured into telling Silva's men that we've been to see you. Now gather what you need for the next few days and we're going to get you to safety. Send Miss Jasmine home . . . better yet to a friend's house. We don't have room for her in the sedan."

Knowing he had little choice, he agreed to go with them, "as long as I can take my binoculars." They loaded a few of his belongings into the trunk, shotgun included, and began the thirty-minute ride to Villa Sueño del Mar. They had barely left the tattooist's shop when Reagan's phone began playing "Poker Face." She had set this song to play when the number calling wasn't in her phone.

"Hello?"

"Is this Reagan?" a male voice asked.

"Who's this?"

"This is C-Ham, one of Jaden and Chris's friends on the baseball team. They haven't been answering their phones and Chris gave me your phone number, so I thought I'd try you. Have you seen them?"

She quickly put her hand over the receiver and whispered to Chris, "Is C-Ham a friend?"

"Yes, let me talk to him." She handed him the phone.

"Hey, man. What's going on?"

"Not much, dude. Been visiting my girlfriend in Miami since Saturday. Just checking in."

"Glad you're getting some R&R," Chris said. "I'll be glad when this break is over. I'm ready to play ball again."

"I hear ya," C-Ham responded. "Where are you guys spending your week off?"

Chris glanced at Reagan, shaking his head, wondering why C-Ham hadn't asked where his phone was. "We've been at the beach. Did some diving, partied, you know, just taking it easy."

"You seen Jaden?"

Chris stiffened but stayed calm. "Nope. Last I knew, he was going to see his mom."

After an uncomfortable pause from the other end, C-Ham said, "I'll try to give him a call again, but—Achoo! Achoo! Damn Mexican cedar! Anyway, he hasn't been answering. Let me know when you can meet for drinks. I'm flying back in tonight!"

Chris did his best to conceal his sense of betrayal by a friend. "Tell ya what. We're about one hundred miles from Cancun. We've had a road trip and are headed to Cozumel for some diving. I'll just catch up with you after the All-Star break."

"Can I reach you on Reagan's phone?" C-Ham asked.

"Probably not. We're trying to spend some time together." He glanced sideways at Reagan. "So, we don't want to be bothered." He ended the call.

"Son of a bitch," Chris said as he handed the phone back to Reagan. "That asshole was on the bus with us when we were blindfolded, but he wasn't one of the players. He must be working for Silva."

"What do you want to do?" asked Reagan.

Shelly said, "I say we get to the villa but let's call Raul first to make sure it's clear. He hasn't told us he got Sabbi yet."

Reagan called the inspector. "Sorry I didn't report back after arresting Ms. Chavez-Escano aka Sabbi. We arrested her as she was pulling up to her villa."

"Was there anyone else there?" asked Reagan.

"Yes, there was a guy there, evidently guarding the property or maybe searching for you, but we flushed him out."

Reagan replied, "Do you think it's safe to stay there? We need to be in the area, and I have a plan."

"Yes, because I did leave two men there, but don't worry. You won't even know they're around."

"OK, we should be there by about six-thirty. We have a friend you might like to interview, by the way." She ended the call, then got Alpheus's attention in the back seat. "We need you to cooperate. Do we have a deal?"

He pursed his lips and replied, "Do I have a choice?"

CHAPTER 27

Although Silva didn't want to be on the lam, his yacht was the envy of the Caribbean and afforded him every luxury he could want. It was over 120 meters in length, powered by 19,200 horsepower that pulled 8 diesel engines. It had been built in Germany in the Lurssen shipyard and had decks laid with teakwood and zero speed stabilizers that allowed him to comfortably, although not without generating damage, navigate narrow Caribbean waters. There was a gambling pit for his horse-racing bets, a recording studio, a cabin for his in-house doctor, a helipad with a Bell 505 bird for transporting him to his villa, a submarine for clandestine meetings on Caribbean islands, a pool with retractable roof that Kara always left retracted, a cinema, jet skis, a massage room, and a gym.

Even though it was admired by many, the naturalists and diving community decried its use locally, as it displaced so much water that reefs were destroyed in its wake. A reporter for the *Riviera Maya Times* who launched a campaign to have the *Cauliflower* banned from the Caribbean was found beheaded in her front yard. No one had spoken out against it in the last eighteen months.

"Where do I tell the captain to head now, boss?" A shirtless Winston, having landed on the helipad a few minutes before, addressed Silva.

"Let's head toward Belize for now, but I need an update on Mr. Tucker and the girl with the birthmark."

"Let me direct the captain, and I'll be back to give you some new information."

Silva asked Kara, who sat in her chair, "Anything from your sources yet?"

"Yes, but first, you need to know that there are several apostles who want a refund on the last tournament that wasn't completed."

"Bunch of fucking idiots. They couldn't kill the guy with their drones, and they blame it on me?"

"They're blaming the hole in the perimeter and your inability to capture him after he escaped. They say the tournament could have continued if you had caught him."

"OK, tell them they'll get a discount on the next tournament."

"Already ahead of you, but they said they don't believe there will be another one with the breach."

Silva picked up a lounge chair and hurled it into the ocean. "Tell them they can all go to hell."

"That might not go over well, but if that's the message, I'm on it."

"Do I look worried? Send the fucking message!"

"Yes, my cariño." After seeing something on her laptop, she said, "You want more good news?"

He tried to find a deckhand to shove into the sea, but finding none, he tossed another chair.

"Your sister was arrested."

"That might not be so bad. Do we know if she went rogue?"

"Not yet. She wasn't sharing her information with us, but I don't know what her plans were if she got the girl first."

"She had her right there in her villa and never knew it. That's fucking unbelievable. That wife of hers must have really screwed with her brain."

Kara ignored the comment and searched for more news from her sources. "The dive shops are all back in business. There was some unrest, but it's calm now. We've gotten some more images of the girl's birthmark. I don't think there's any doubt she's the one. The forensic examiners at our lab compared the best photo of Omelia's mark. It's just a depiction and not an actual photo, of course. They compared it to hers and they say there is virtually no difference between them, especially to the naked eye. I believe she was destined to find the necklace."

"Where are we concentrating our search right now? Do we know if she's left Quintana Roo?"

"We don't think so, but only because she still doesn't know her brother's fate." She looked up at Silva to get his reaction.

"What do you know about Silva's PokBall game at the secret stadium?" Reagan was determined to get as much information out of Alpheus as she could.

"Not much. He was always tight-lipped about that, although I do know he kept the location secret." Their Tzuro sedan's back seat width wasn't meant for long rides with three passengers, and the business end of Rocky's gun created a firm dent in Alpheus's right hip.

"Alpheus, I told you we needed your cooperation, and I'm not feeling it. No one knows you're with us, and we'll take you wherever you want to go after we get the information we need, but if you do not cooperate, Silva will hear that you cooperated fully. Is that clear enough?"

He hung his head but didn't have to think about this long. "Very clear."

"Let me ask this again," she continued. "What do you know about his secret game?"

Alpheus resituated himself between Shelly and Rocky, cleared a scratchy throat, and prepared to betray a confidence, but he knew it was not the betrayal that caused his unrest. It was the repercussions. He had seen what the man could do to someone who simply spilled his coffee, and he did not want to consider what he would do if he found out he cooperated with someone with a goal of uncovering his pleasures. "OK, it will mean my death sentence, but at least I'll have a clear conscience. Everything he does is for money . . . or for his son, who is a monk in a monastery somewhere in Mexico.

"He's secretive about the location, for obvious reasons, but he's impotent now due to an accident and his son is his only heir. It's tearing him up, not knowing if his legacy, if you want to call it that, will live on without his son having a son himself." Alpheus stopped talking, hoping to stop the interrogation.

"And the killing field?"

Without enthusiasm, he continued. "He brings players from all over Mexico under the guise of playing in an unusual game, but for a large payday, and it's too tempting for almost anyone to turn down. It's a secret location that I have never seen or been given directions to, so don't bother asking me where it is."

"We already know the location," Chris stated with disgust as his foot became heavier on the gas. "Tell us something we don't know."

Alpheus bristled. "Did you also know that benefactors from around the world pay millions just to watch through closed-circuit television? He has a group of very wealthy foreigners. I have no idea who they are, but I've heard Silva reference his apostles because he limits the audience to twelve."

"That's sick," Shelly said. "Do they come to the contest or do they view remotely?"

"Oh, I'm sure they aren't there in person. These are some big players in the industrial world. They may all be in the drug business, but again, I don't know who they are. I just know he charges the apostles more money than any of us will make in a lifetime just to watch one tournament."

"Suspected that when I saw there were no fans in the stadium. They must have been the ones controlling the drones," said Chris. "There were about that many chasing me during my escape. I managed to disable one of them but didn't have time to collect the evidence."

"You played the game?" Alpheus' bushy gray eyebrows became animated. "I've never known someone to survive it."

Shelly quietly wept.

Chris immediately regretted telling him, not knowing what they would do with Alpheus after they finished their interrogation. "Yes, but that's not important. What is important is what he would have done with the players if the game was stopped. Where would they be?"

"Oh, I'm afraid I can't help you there—"

"Then what good are you!" screamed Shelly, shocking the other four into a short moment of silence.

That's the mom I've been missing, thought Reagan.

"What else can you tell us about his operation?" Reagan asked.

"I know he has a girlfriend. Her name's Kara Wilder. She helps him run the operation. Winston is his bodyguard. He loves gambling on horse racing . . . even owns a few thoroughbreds but also loves to collect art. He must like Posada more than the other artists because I was asked to tattoo a likeness of *La Calavera Catrina* on his back a few years ago."

"Or maybe because *The Elegant Skull* is now part of the Day of the Dead holiday," Reagan said.

"He also has one of the most expensive yachts in the world . . . the *Cauliflower*. I've never been on it, but it's his baby. No one messes with his *Cauliflower* because if they did—"

Reagan's phone came to life. "Inspector Isuega, what do you have for me?"

"She made bail."

"How did she get out so quickly? You couldn't have held her at least for the night?" The others in the car didn't have to ask who "she" was.

"She had her attorney at the station before we even got there. She made no calls from the car, so I have no idea how she communicated with him. I had too little to hold her, especially with her high-priced attorney knowing which buttons to push."

"Well, that puts a wrench in our plans," Reagan said. "Any idea where she went?"

"We have a tail on her, and she went south, away from the villa you guys might be going to."

She considered that for a second. "Will you be tracking her until you know for sure?"

"Of course. We plan on keeping an eye on her twenty-four-seven for the next few days."

"Today's been a bitch, but you can make it better. Did you send him?" Sabbi was in a better mood now but anxious to get business taken care of.

"He should be there sometime today."

"Good. He has the villa address?"

"Yes."

She ended the call, showered, wrapped a blue-flowered robe around her torso, cinching it closed with a white strap. She sat on her porch with a gin and tonic, watching the end of the Caribbean waters change from cerulean to amber to crimson to sangria and finally to indigo. Maybe it was the gin talking. She took another sip of her drink and lit up a blue dream, thinking about her brother's reaction if he knew she was smoking legal weed. She chuckled to herself.

CHAPTER 28

The blond, heavily bearded man of European descent carried a khaki backpack with a passport for Boris Johnson. He weaved his way through customs with little trouble and hailed a cab. Throwing his backpack into the back seat, he said, "*Sólo toma el 307 hasta que te diga que detenga.*" He dropped five hundred pesos onto the front seat beside the driver.

"Si, señor."

After the driver had navigated his way out of the airport and onto 307, he texted.

Villa in under an hour.

The reply came immediately.

Splendid.

He placed his hand on the shoulder of the driver and said, "Do you know how many frogs it takes to change a light bulb?"

The driver spoke into the rearview mirror. "No hablo inglés."

He nodded, then tapped a number on his phone. "This is Blue Pigeon. May I speak to 302?"

"Just a moment, Mr. Pigeon," a soporific voice replied on the other end. The on-hold music was a French opera. Then another voice with a British accent said, "Blue pigeon, what's your favorite red?"

"I favor the 1979 malbec."

"Good year. Listening to Neil Sedaka here."

"I'll be purchasing a sewing machine . . . a yellow one."

"London bridge is falling down."

"Sad to hear. Get some rest." The call ended.

He kept to himself for the next forty-five minutes, and as they crossed Figuero Street, he told the driver, "*Détente aquí.*"

The driver glided to a stop. He stepped out onto an uneven patch of dirt, rocks, and a hint of grass and texted.

> Walking from the highway.

Motion detector lights came on as he passed by villas. Dogs barked from a yard across the street. Approaching the target, he slipped through the unlocked gate.

Shelly ran out the front door and grabbed him by the neck, crying tears she had been saving. "I'm so glad you're here."

"Where's Reagan?" He set his bag down and walked toward the living room.

"We just got here and she's upstairs. I'm sure she'll be down soon but let me introduce you. This is Chris, one of Jaden's friends on the baseball team."

Chris stood and shook Carlisle's hand. "Nice to meet you, sir. I've heard so much about you."

"Yes, I'm afraid my family hasn't quite discovered the value of secrets." His smile was strained.

"And this is Rocky, who's one of Chris's old friends but now he's one of our new friends. Saved our life."

They shook hands and Carlisle said, "I'm not sure what happened, but I certainly appreciate whatever you did."

"And this is Alpheus. He knows where the Tulum skeletons are buried, and he's been giving us a map. We know much more about Silva's organization now than we did a few hours ago."

"Nice to meet you, Mr. Alpheus. Thank you for helping us out."

"By the way, I'm the old one," he said.

"Daddy!" Reagan raced down the stairs and jumped into his arms.

He held her until Reagan had time to wipe away some tears. "We still don't know anything about Jaden. If anyone would know, we were hoping it would be Alpheus here, but he couldn't help, either."

"OK, I've had considerable time to think about this on the way over. I contacted the embassy here."

"Oh no, Dad. I'm not sure that was the right thing to do."

"I know what you're thinking, Reagan. You're afraid the cartel will react to our involvement and if Jaden's still alive, he would be in more danger."

Rocky said, "The cartel here has long tentacles and most of the police force is part of the tornado Reagan speaks of."

"I realize we're undermanned here, but I've just gotten permission to use satellite imaging to locate Silva and also use infrared technology to see into the stone bunker you told me about."

They gathered on the couches and told Carlisle all that had happened and all they knew.

"I picked the wrong two weeks to clear my head," Carlisle said.

"Hey guys," Reagan said tensely, but with an audible whisper. "I heard something on the roof. Sounded like footsteps. Everyone get their weapons and get in a place we can defend ourselves." She cut the lights.

Rocky took his gun out of his bag, gave another to Carlisle, and hid behind the refrigerator in the kitchen. Chris slid behind the bar with his. Alpheus got his shotgun and crouched behind the couch. Reagan ran up the stairs with her bow and Shelly took her gun and followed Reagan. Carlisle took Rocky's gun and went out the front door to get a view of anyone coming from the road. As he headed toward the gate in the new glow of the moon, he heard a loud thud on the grass to his right. A man in a uniform lay motionless, his left leg bent behind him. The badge that tore loose from his fall read Hector Rosales. Blood pooled around his head. Carlisle laid down and crawled back to the front door. He listened but only heard the crickets and frogs exerting their behavioral overtures. He slowly opened the front door and wriggled in, allowing it to softly close. The moon over the ocean allowed him to see a shadow moving along the back patio. He was sure the others could see it as well.

A loud blast from behind the couch exploded the sliding glass doors, sending both shotgun pellets and glass shards in many directions. When the cacophony abated, he saw the outline of a man, sitting with shoulders slumped, in obvious pain. Alpheus and Rocky walked toward the man, guns raised. A shot rang out from the right of the pool, and the squatting man lurched, then grabbed his right arm. A uniformed man appeared from behind the pool and shouted, "I'm Officer Rosales with the Policía Federal Ministerial. We were placed here by Inspector Isuega to protect you."

Chris held his gun on the man. The injured man's torso had several shotgun pellets in it, and four shards of glass protruded from his shoulder, side, leg, and neck. His right arm had been shattered by the bullet of the officer.

"He killed the other officer out front," said Carlisle.

Officer Rosales raised his gun toward the bleeding man,

gritting his teeth, but then lowered it. "I don't want him dying yet. He needs to suffer." Rosales removed his badge and dropped it on the wounded man's lap. "Bad news for you, asshole. I'm off duty now."

"We need to get information out of him first," said Rocky.

Carlisle replied, "Who sent you?" He didn't answer, so he reached inside the wounded man's jacket and removed an airline ticket stub for Caesar Avila. "We don't know if that's your real name, but it doesn't really matter. For now, we'll call you Caesar."

Carlisle twisted the glass in his shoulder. Caesar winced and moaned.

Carlisle whispered loud enough for all to hear. "You're not mortally wounded, by the way. The glass in your neck missed the artery and neither pellet got a lung. It's really your choice if you live or die tonight, and we can make it miserable for you to live. Will you cooperate and just go to prison or would you like to die here tonight after some painful lessons?"

Alpheus then walked over with his sawed-off shotgun and pointed the barrel toward Caesar's groin. This appeared to be an effective stimulus.

"Sabbi sent me."

"OK, we're getting somewhere now," said Carlisle. "Keep cooperating and you get to keep the family jewels. Tell us what you know about Silva, or Gonzo as you may know him."

"Sabbi's brother."

This brought a moment of shocked silence. Carlisle said, "That shouldn't surprise me, but that means you know more about Gonzo."

"Can you take me to the hospital?"

"In due time," Carlisle said, "as long as you give us the information we need. You're losing blood, so I figure you have four or five hours, anyway. The sooner you cooperate, the sooner we can save your lousy butt."

Still sitting, he managed a sigh. Speaking slowly, he said "He . . . wants . . . the girl."

"We know that," Alpheus said behind his shotgun. He looked at Reagan. "He has the necklace and knows you're the only one who can use its powers."

"Can you corroborate that?" Reagan asked the bleeding confessor.

He nodded. Speaking appeared to be a struggle with the glass lodged in his neck.

"OK, now we need to know about his pet game of death at the stadium. Tell us everything you know about it."

He closed his eyes and said, "I will tell you everything if you take this piece out of my neck and bandage it."

"Today's your lucky day, Caesar." Shelly used some bandages from their Walmart run and used her experience as an emergency room nurse to remove the glass shard and apply a butterfly bandage. "What happens to the players in Gonzo's draconian game?"

"First, you must know I have nothing to do with his operation."

"Keep talking. We'll decide your involvement," Carlisle said.

Caesar said, "He never allows a player to leave."

"What does that mean?" Carlisle pressed.

"He has a crematorium that he uses on all players to ensure no one finds the evidence."

Carlisle quickly went to Shelly before she collapsed. No one spoke for several minutes, not knowing what to say, as Shelly sobbed uncontrollably into Carlisle's chest. Reagan had feared the worst and was closer to believing it now. She had to be strong for her parents and find a way to avenge his death. She would risk her life in this pursuit, and although her parents would likely object, she knew what she needed to do.

Suddenly, Rosales fired three successive shots into Caesar's chest, who lurched, then collapsed against the pavement. "The man this bastard killed tonight . . . was my brother." He picked up his badge and slipped it into his pocket, then headed back through the villa to the front door. His brother awaited him on the other side, a victim of the cartel like Jaden.

A light shone through the dead man's jacket. She pulled the cell phone from the pocket, finding a text from Sabrina.

Did you get the girl?

She used his thumb to turn it on. She replied with a quote from *Rubicon*, adding a little flair.

The die is cast. Et tu, Sabbi?

Who is this?

The girl you sent him for.

Reagan, I meant you no harm. I was trying to keep my brother from using you for his own gain.

Explain.

Gonzo wants you to help him see the future of his only son. It aches him to think he may not have an heir to carry on the family name.

Did he steal my necklace?

Yes, and he had Tahira, the maid, killed. She was very special to me. I think we can help each other. Remember when I said I might call in a favor when I cleaned up the mess behind your villa?

Yes, but sending someone with a gun voided that debt. He killed an officer here.

> I am so sorry. That was not supposed to happen.

Why should I help you?

> Because it would help you. We both have
> the same goal. Gonzo must pay. I know what
> happened to your brother, and I want to help you
> in whatever way I can.

How can you help me?

> I know his motives and I can predict his moves.

I'll be in touch. Can your cleaners get rid of
Caesar here?

> We'll take care of that tonight.

She hesitated, then typed.

What happened to my brother?

Sabbi waited for an interminable minute before sending her reply.

> I have nothing to do with my brother's actions, but I am
> sure you will never see your brother again. I am so sorry.

Reagan stood with the phone and hurled it over the sandy beach into the incoming waves. The silence that followed was palpable. No one had to ask, but Reagan said it anyway. "Jaden's never coming back." She knew the effect this would have on her parents but hoped this would break the counterfeit hope they clung to and start the grieving phase. They hugged each other tightly, Carlisle remaining stoic while his wife wept into his chest.

"Mom and Dad, I need to speak with Chris for a while. Caesar here is to be left where he is. He won't be here in the morning. I'll be down soon."

She said to Chris, "Can we go upstairs?"

Alpheus had been sitting on a lounge chair by the pool, taking in the ebb and flow of the incoming tide. He stood and asked Rocky in a hushed tone, "What next, Lancaster?"

"Three bedrooms upstairs . . . we get the couches tonight. After our day, these couches and the rhythm of the waves will feel like heaven."

Carlisle put his arm around Shelly, and they headed upstairs. Once in bed, they held each other, Shelly crying softly into his shoulder. "Shelly, we still don't know if Jaden is . . ."

"Just say it," she said through sobs.

He grabbed his phone and punched a number.

"Federal Bureau of Investigations. How may I direct your call?"

"750992, please."

"Bible here."

"Hey, James. It's Carlisle. I knew you'd be up there late. I need a favor. You know why I'm here, and I have confirmation that Jaden has been killed. We know it's the work of Silva. His precious yacht has a heat signature that would be easy to find."

"How do you know that?"

"I did some digging around. I would like nothing more than if an MGM-140 ATACMS found its way to the belly of that boat."

"Consider it done, buddy. For Jaden."

The next morning, Reagan woke up to pounding on her bedroom door.

"Reagan! You up?" Chris asked.

She jolted to a sitting position. "Yes, what's going on?"

"You've got to come downstairs. You won't believe it."

She threw on some shorts and a T-shirt and headed down. The back of the villa was intact. The sliding glass doors were back, and it appeared as if nothing had happened. The body, blood, glass shards, and bullet casings were gone.

This is unreal, she thought.

"Unbelievable, huh?" Rocky observed from the couch. Shelly was making breakfast and Alpheus was out by the pool. "He got up before the sun did and didn't see a hint of whoever did this."

Carlisle came round the corner. "Reagan, let's talk for a few minutes."

They walked outside and around the pool toward the hammocks away from Alpheus. "I thought you should know. I was able to convince our guys to order a strike on Silva's yacht."

"That's too good for him, Dad."

"I know, but the strike already occurred. The *Cauliflower* is now a future reef."

"Do you know if he was on it?"

"My sources tell me they don't think so. The helicopter was gone, and they intercepted a call from him to someone in Greece about thirty minutes after the strike, but at least he's out about eight hundred million with that loss."

"Are they still trying to locate him?"

"Of course, but I'm told they've had no luck." Carlisle chose to wait on any news of the reconnaissance mission before he told her about the efforts being deployed.

"Wish there was something I could do."

"I understand, but this isn't your field, sweetie. Remember your history degree? Leave the military maneuvers to the military."

"OK, but I don't have to like it. Can you take Mom, Rocky, and Alpheus to Sabbi's villa?"

"What makes you so sure you can trust her now? She sent men to kidnap you and one of them killed a policeman."

"I understand your hesitance, but no one knows her brother's operations like she does, and it's obvious to me that she wants Silva to pay, just like us. As far as I'm concerned, we're on the same team now."

"Where are you and Chris going?"

"We'll follow in a few days. Have to pick up a friend of his at the airport. His brother played with Jaden and is also missing. We need to spend some time with him and fill him in. As soon as we get him settled in here, we'll head to Sabbi's. We'll keep in touch, but you have to tell me anything your guys find out. Deal?"

"I don't feel good about you staying—"

"Dad. We handled it when you weren't here. What's a few more days? Besides, maybe Chris's friend has some information that could help us."

After they were picked up by Sabbi's driver, Reagan told Chris of her father's news regarding the bombing of the *Cauliflower*. "Does this change your plan, Reagan?"

"It doesn't look like he's dead yet, so no."

"And you really trust Sabbi?"

"No, but she has information we need, and we have a common enemy. I do believe she hates her brother. Let's just say I'm using her."

"But getting kidnapped from your hammock is crazy risky."

"I've thought this out, Chris. Like I said, once I prove that the necklace will only work on me, I'm completely safe."

"OK, assuming you really go through with this, you know I'll do my part."

"I'm counting on it, Chris. Did the hypnosis seem to work?"

"Oh yes. You were quite susceptible."

CHAPTER 29

Silva threw two lamps through windows and kicked a priceless vase into the fireplace. He wondered if an apostle would dare do this. He had plenty of enemies, but the only ones who could pull off the bombing of his *Cauliflower* were the billionaires or a few nations he managed to upset over the years. He didn't expect anyone to claim responsibility, and none did. Towergate had refused to insure it after learning of Silva's refusal to remove it from the shallower Caribbean reefs, fearing reprisal from environmentalists. Efforts to get Lloyds of London to insure also failed, so this was a total loss for Silva.

Kara's phone vibrated. "Sabbi, you're calling at a bad time. Did Tabani get you released?"

"Yes, I would like to thank my brother for that, but I also have some good news for him."

"He could use that right now. I've been afraid to talk to him since the incident this morning."

"Yes, I heard about that on the radio. He wasn't answering his phone, which is why I called you."

"OK, let me get him." She walked hesitantly into the den where Silva had his head in his palms, sitting in his favorite chair. "It's your sister. She says she has good news for you." She extended the phone to him.

"Sabbi, this better be about the girl."

"How did you know?"

"Because that's the only news that could make me forget about that damned boat for a few minutes."

"I have her at the Villa Sueno del Mar."

"You're not playing games with me are you, because if you are—"

"No, I'm not. I'm not there, but I have a spotter and have been told she's in the hammock on the beach right now."

Silva put his hand over the phone and said to Kara, "Get Winston and his team to go to the Villa Sueno del Mar. Go along the water from the south and have them grab Ms. Prefontaine and bring her here but don't hurt her. Is that clear?"

"Of course. This could be a very good day, my cariño. No more worries about the *Cauliflower*." She sprinted through the doorway to find Winston.

Bible called Carlisle with an update. "We found the crematorium and enough teeth to extract DNA and make positive identifications. We should know something in a few days."

Carlisle bit his lower lip. "I know in my heart that Jaden is gone . . . Can you save some ashes for us?"

"Of course, Carlisle. Of course."

The nightmares returned, not allowing her a deep sleep, but instead a tortured form of stage two, somewhere between alpha and theta waves. She's trapped under a table . . . people shout and cry . . . someone grabs her necklace and pulls her out . . . standing in the water now, unable to move . . . water getting deeper around her . . . still can't move . . . water rising to her chin . . . jellyfish stinging her neck, and she's floating now, but the night sky is above her . . . then . . .

Two men wrapped Reagan up in her hammock, the larger one throwing her over his right shoulder. "What if she wakes up?"

"She'll be out for a few hours. That injection is powerful. Stop worrying." They trudged through the sand, then between two villas and back to the Ford SUV they had parked on Sunset. Carefully laying Reagan down in the back seat, they drove south.

When they arrived at Silva's villa, they took her inside and laid her on the couch in the den. When she awoke, it was dark. She reflexively rubbed her eyes and the back of her neck, then managed to slowly move some words through her thick, dry lips. "Must be this headache that woke me up." She began to raise herself into a sitting position to clear her head when Silva appeared and stood over her.

"I want you to know . . . no, I *need* you to know, that you are a guest in my house, and no one will be allowed to hurt you. I pledge this to you."

Reagan applied direct pressure to a few tender spots on the back of her head. "Feels like someone isn't aligned with your mission statement."

"Sorry about that, Ms. Prefontaine. The rohypnol you were given can leave one with the nastiest of headaches." Silva relaxed into an easy chair by the fireplace.

"Why am I here?" she asked as she laid her head on the

armrest to apply more direct pressure to the pounding behind her left ear and to stave off her wooziness.

"As I said," Silva deferred, hands folded into his lap, "you are my guest."

"Where am I?"

"Why, you're in my home." Silva grinned broadly. "I am Gonzalo Silva, and back to your first question. I have a proposition for you."

"I'd rather have some ibuprofen." She was having a difficult time concentrating.

"Of course." He pushed an intercom button on the wall to his left and yelled, "Maria!"

"Si, señor."

"*Tráele a la Sra. Prefontaine dos Motrin.*"

"Si, señor."

Maria brought her two white pills with a glass of water. "How do I know these are ibuprofen?"

"I have my reasons for wanting you alive and healthy. If I wanted you dead, you wouldn't be sitting here. I know you have little reason to trust someone who has spirited you away from a morning nap on the beach, but you will soon know my reason."

She swallowed both pills with a drink of water, exposing the starfish on her wrist as she did so. "I'm quite impressed with the marvelous mark on your wrist."

"Most people think it's a tattoo, but it's certainly received a lot of attention since we arrived a few days ago." A bronzed girl in a pink sundress entered.

"Hello, I'm Kara." Kara kissed Silva on the cheek. "Would you like something to drink? Mr. Silva is such a boorish host."

"No, this water will do, although I'd love some more. My mouth is so dry."

"Ms. Prefontaine," Silva started. "We would like to know about a special necklace."

"You have my necklace?" Reagan asked, looking from Silva to Kara and back.

Kara responded, "Did you lose a necklace?"

"Yes, it was stolen from the safe in my villa."

"Was it *your* necklace?" Silva asked, "or did you find it in our ocean?"

"What do you want?" Reagan's dizziness was now gone.

Kara asked, "Did you ever put the necklace on?"

"Yes, I did."

"And?"

"I was able to see the future."

Silva and Kara eyed each other with faint smiles.

"May we try it out right here?" Kara asked.

"One problem. When I put the necklace on, my past is erased from my memory. I won't know who either of you are or why I am here."

"That could be a good thing," Silva said in jest. Kara shook her head.

"It can be confusing, so we need some visual clues to make sure I cooperate."

Silva stood and slid the necklace off the fireplace mantel, starfish dangling free. "I'm sure it will work out."

His duplicitous grin would have made her uncomfortable except she knew he needed her. *Should I bargain with him? Tell him I'll help him if he tells me what happened to Jaden? No, that wasn't in the plan and that could make matters worse. I'll find out soon enough.*

He handed the necklace to Reagan and she made a quick inspection, noting the repaired leather strap and a nicked arm of the starfish. She slipped it over her head and erased everything she had learned in her twenty-one years. She looked at Silva and Kara, confused.

"Your name is Reagan, and I am Mr. Silva. This is Kara." He then pulled a gun from his waist. "I'll explain later, but I'm hoping this persuades you to cooperate. Is that clear?"

Reagan slowly nodded.

"OK, I want you to close your eyes and tell me if you see any events that happen in the future."

Reagan trembled but closed her eyes to concentrate. *What will he do if I can't come up with something?* She buried this thought and peered through closed eyelids into the future, then opened them. "Very soon, some guy named Epstein will die in jail. Is this significant?"

"That doesn't sound important to us. You must try again. Concentrate on this house. Something that has not yet happened."

She closed her eyes again and pictured the parts of the house she had seen. Without opening her eyes, she said, "I see you playing cards."

Silva pulled a deck of cards from his pocket. He had anticipated using them for a test. "Well, you got that one right. Now let's see what you've really got. I'm going to lay a card down on the table. These have been thoroughly shuffled. What will it be?"

She closed her eyes. "Three of diamonds." He turned the card over, and Kara clapped. "And the next four," she continued, "are the four of spades, the jack of clubs, the queen of hearts, and the seven of hearts." He flipped over the next four cards, largely grinning at Kara with each card laid.

"You have a gift," Silva said, laying his gun on the coffee table and grabbing her by both arms. "We will do great things." He removed the necklace from her neck.

"How did I do? And why was the gun necessary?"

"It wasn't necessary," Silva replied. "You did very well. Please put the necklace back on. I have a question about my son."

She did as he said. He went through the introductions and explanations again. "My son is a Benedictine monk at the Monastery of Santa María y Todos los Santos in Zipolite. I need to know if he will ever marry and have a son. Close your eyes and do your best to see Javier."

She saw the monastery, then a picture. Not live people, but a picture showing a man with a wife and three children. "I see your son with a wife and three children. Two boys and one girl. They're happy."

Silva's eyes welled up as he struggled to conceal tears of joy. He couldn't allow this emotion to show. He rushed to Reagan, removed the necklace then grabbed her in a bear hug and lifted her off the ground. "You just gave me the best news of my life." He released her, then left the room.

"You made him very happy," Kara said.

"I'm glad to hear that. May I go home now? My family will be concerned."

"Not yet. You're a bit like a unicorn, but we'll treat you like a queen. You have nothing to worry about."

"What if I go home now, then come back tomorrow? I can see it's dark outside." Reagan made these requests, knowing they would not be granted but needed to preserve her authenticity.

"Sorry, you can't leave just yet. Winston!" she yelled down the hall. In a moment, he lumbered into the den. "Winston, please show Ms. Prefontaine to her room."

"Yes, Miss Kara."

Reagan followed Winston out the door. "Am I a prisoner?" she asked Kara over her shoulder.

"Only if you want to be. It's your call."

Her room was understandably impressive. With the ostentatiousness and eccentricity of the residence, nothing should have surprised her, but the stuffed javelina standing guard and staring at her from a bay window was unexpected. A poster bed with drawn canopy protruded from the north wall. She poured herself a vodka tonic as a reward from the wet bar. The first sip reminded her she hadn't eaten all day. As if they read her mind, a knock at the door made her jump, sloshing some of the drink onto the hardwood floor. "Come in!"

A uniformed man appeared, pushing a food cart. "Your dinner, ma'am."

"I would tip you, but I kinda left my place in a hurry this morning and didn't get a chance to pack any money."

"I would not have accepted it, Ms. Prefontaine, but thank you for the thought." He bowed and left, closing the door.

After she had gorged herself, she found a card propped against a cotton-filled jar in the bathroom that read:

If you have difficulty sleeping, one or two of these should help.

In a shot glass at the base of the card were two white pills.

What have I gotten myself into? She climbed into the bed. *What did they ask me today? Did they ask about Javier? That must have been what made that SOB hug me. I'll never get to sleep now.*

She climbed out of bed, retrieved the two white pills from the shot glass, and downed both with a glass of water, praying they weren't roofies.

When she awoke the next morning, there was no pounding headache and no wooziness. A handwritten note, face side up on the floor, greeted her by the door. A cell phone acted as a paper-weight.

Someone must have opened her locked door during the night. She shivered, then picked it up.

Breakfast is at 9. Use this cell phone to text "Ready" to 46732 when you would like to join us. Kara

She dressed in white shorts and a blue polo with a large "S printed on the left breast and then texted.

Ready.

While she waited by the door for it to be unlocked, she heard a muffled discussion. She held her ear to the door.

"Sabbi . . . eleven o'clock . . . road . . . ambush . . . report." Shouts from the kitchen and landscapers outside her window prevented her from hearing more. She jumped at the knock on the door.

"It's Kara. May I come in?"

Reagan opened the door and Kara walked to the bathroom and turned the faucet on.

"What's this about?" asked Reagan.

"I'm with the CIA. I've been undercover for the last two years. I get a sense you have something planned, and I can't allow it to upset the operation."

Reagan avoided her eyes, attempting to hide her bewilderment. "I'm not sure what you're referring to."

Kara's eyebrows narrowed. "I can see you don't believe me. Does this help?" She reached into an inner pocket of the beige fleece sweater she wore and withdrew a card. Kara Washington, Special Envoy, Rockville, Maryland.

"That doesn't say CIA."

"Exactly. Ever read a business card that says Central Intelligence Agency? We don't like to advertise it."

"Don't you think it's risky to have that card on you? What if Silva finds it?"

"I keep a few in the lining of my suitcase . . . for situations like this."

"OK, so you're a spook. How can you help me? I'm an American citizen who wants to find out who killed her brother. And is he really dead? If so, I want to bring the murderer to justice. If justice means I get to shoot his balls off with a .44 magnum and stick them in his mouth until he chokes to death, then you can help me."

"It's not that easy." Water splattered from the faucet, urging her farther away from the sink. "I've been working this for two years. We have a complete team behind us, and we're after more than just Silva. I can't afford for you to fuck it up."

"Then why tell me now?"

"Because I know you're here to try something. I may be the only one who suspects, but I know you're not stupid. You stay hidden for days, then leave yourself more vulnerable than a naked newborn. That doesn't fit your persona, but luckily for us, these idiots here haven't figured it out."

Reagan pondered this new information, not allowing her facial expression to betray her thoughts, but Kara said, "I see you still don't believe me. I wasn't going to tell you this, but we know all about Silva's game of death, and—"

"What do you know about my brother?"

"And we know that no one lives. He was killed and then cremated."

Reagan remained stoic, knowing her brother was dead, but not knowing how he was killed. She knew she had to show strength here, and knew Kara was testing her. "Do you know if he suffered?"

"I do not think so, Reagan. I am so sorry."

Reagan shut off the water and wiped the counter dry with a large velour bath towel.

"I'll see you at breakfast." Kara left the room.

She wasn't hungry after her late dinner, and even less so now with the news of Jaden's death. "Those are beautiful," she said, referring to an impressive arrangement of South American rain-forest birds on the wall.

"I collect them," said Silva. "My friends know this and it's a cheap present, so that's what they give me."

"Oh, cariño. You're being too sensitive. They don't give you those because they're cheap. They—"

"I know who my friends are, Kara. They aren't the ones who give me the birds. It's their way of insulting me, but my memory is long."

"But the Tunisian gentlem—"

"Kara! We have a guest. This is not to be discussed."

"Perdóname, mi cariño."

When the meal had been cleared, Silva said, "Kara tells me you're willing to cooperate with us today."

"As long as it does no harm to me or my loved ones, yes, but will I be able to go home after this?"

"That remains to be seen, but if you would like us to communicate your well-being to anyone, we would be happy to do so."

Reagan had expected this offer and was ready. "No disrespect, Mr. Silva, but until I have your trust and you have mine, I'd like you to place an ad in the *Riviera Maya Times*. I've taken the opportunity to create a draft for you." She reached in her shorts pocket and withdrew a piece of paper.

"Quite impressive. I was told not to underestimate you, but it is clear I have already done so." He pulled the paper across the table.

Need singer? Neil Sedaka is safe to hire.
He will return tomorrow mourning.

"What is this code for?" asked Silva.

"It just means I'm safe, and that I will report back tomorrow morning."

Silva's eyebrows narrowed. "How do I know this?"

"You don't."

"What if I refuse to send it?"

"You might not get the cooperation you seek."

"I can be rather persuasive."

"From what I have been able to tell from the times I have used the necklace, if—"

"You've tried it before coming here?"

"Yes, when I first discovered it. I learned that if I'm stressed, it doesn't work as well, but feel free to stress me and we can test it out."

"No need to get dramatic. Kara, be a darling and get this sent to the *Times*."

Kara rose from her chair and left. Silva lifted the necklace from around a white marble vase on the mantel and respectfully presented it to Reagan like an official handing an Olympic medal to a winner.

"Will you be using your gun again to insure I'm properly motivated?"

"If needed." His face remained expressionless.

Sitting back in her chair, she glanced at the clock on the wall. 9:17. She placed the necklace over her head and looked suspiciously from Silva to Kara, who had returned from sending her message.

Silva went through the usual dialogue of introducing and explaining the situation to Reagan.

"The British Open golf tournament is this weekend and starts today. Close your eyes and visualize the final leaderboard."

She shut her eyes.

"Tell me who is in first place. Kara, write these down."

"T. Fleetwood."

"Is this the final leaderboard?"

"Yes. It says the word *final* on the television. That's where I am seeing it."

"Now go down the list in order."

"S. Lowry, T. Finau, B. Koepka, L. Westwood, R. Mac-Intyre, R. Fowler, D. Willett, T. Hatton, P. Reed."

"OK, that's good," said Silva as he reached over and removed the necklace from around her neck.

Reagan's eyes cleared and she noted the time as four minutes later than when she started. "Well, I don't see a gun this time, but just for my edification, what did I help you with?"

"You helped me pick the winner of the British Open. We'll know Sunday how you did."

Reagan rose. "So, does this mean I'm free to go now?"

"I would love to oblige," he said dismissively, "but we need to play this out a little longer. On Sunday, if the results are as you offered, you have my word you will be free to join your family."

This is what Reagan expected, but she also knew he would never allow her to leave. She knew too much, and why would he part with a golden ticket to wealth? *I just hope this plan works. Four minutes might not be enough to give me any residual skills.* "If I must continue my stay, do I have access to the outside grounds? I need fresh air."

Kara responded, "I'll watch her, my cariño."

Silva's eyes furrowed into a unibrow. "Take Winston with you."

After he left the room, Kara glanced at Reagan, giving her the I-got-you-girl look. Reagan followed her out the door and down the hall into a room that surpassed her expansive bedroom.

There were two walls of computer monitors showing the external as well as some internal views of the villa from every angle. Winston sat at one of the consoles and watched an approaching Hummer but jerked to his right when he heard them enter.

"Kara, what is *she* doing here? Remove her immediately."

"What?" Kara asked blithely. "You didn't see us coming on one of your monitors?"

"I mean it, Kara."

"Can you spare us a few minutes? The boss says you must accompany us when we go outside. And we're just gonna take a walk around the villa."

"I'm taking care of some important business right now. I'll be out in about five minutes but get her out!"

Reagan had taken advantage of the short repartee and studied all the monitors, piecing together valuable information. They were all numbered, one to forty-eight, and she had logged away each one.

"OK, but just know we're waiting." They walked to the north side of the complex. The sky was, as usual, a cerulean blue, interrupted only by the traces of a few cirrus cloud wisps and some Bahama swallows hovering into the southern wind. The cliff's edge was only a few hundred feet from this side of the villa.

"Do you live here full time?" Reagan asked, making an earnest effort to figure Kara out. Her newfound skill for seeing into the future did nothing for reading someone's mind.

"For now, yes I do."

"How long have you been here?"

"Two years, as I said before. I also told you before that I knew you weren't stupid, so is this just a test to see if my story repeats?"

"Maybe." Reagan knew Kara couldn't be transparent right now, not knowing when Winston might show up.

Kara continued to gaze through the door glass. "Isn't it beautiful? I could live here forever." To Reagan, this sounded believable. "Reagan, how do you know someone will read your message in the *Times*?"

"After my brother disappeared, we made a decision to use the paper as a means of communication if we were cut off in some way. I don't know . . . maybe I saw myself being kidnapped when I had the necklace on, so it just made sense. I don't—"

"All right, ladies. Let's make this quick. I'll give you a short tour." Winston slid the door open with no effort and ushered them through. "The villa was purchased from a Viennese billionaire in 1943 by Mr. Silva's grandfather, using both currency and some rare paintings to finance the acquisition."

The terrain here was more uneven than Reagan expected. *They might not use the south side of the villa much.*

There were no paths, no manicured shrubs, no lovers' benches, no hummingbird feeders. Just a helipad with a red-on-gray Bell 505 named *Angelina* seated in the middle like a praying mantis waiting to take flight. Reagan took a wide swath to peer over the cliff's edge to the south. A sheltered cove toward the southeast was over 100 feet below and framed by rock walls that allowed entry from the sea on the east side. The opening was just large enough for a small boat to maneuver through. They walked by windows that showed gym equipment in an otherwise empty room.

Toward the rear of the villa, close-cut Bermuda grass was traversed by asymmetrical pathways of fine gravel that exited through forested evergreens. Palm trees punctuated the bends and turns, casting enough shade over concrete benches to allow a temporary respite from the afternoon sun. Hummingbird feeders were spread throughout the grounds.

"Mr. Silva loves his hummingbirds," Winston commented.

These energetic creatures seemed to be the only breathing lifeform for which Silva had any tolerance or appreciation. They rounded the corner to the road entering the compound with guard gates.

"It is now and has always been heavily guarded, both by a border wall and by my selection of ex-sumo wrestlers who carry Avtomat Kalashnikovas with fixed bayonets. Most of the compound circumference has a twelve-foot concrete wall topped with four feet of barbed wire. The remaining border is the cliff."

At the front of the villa, he said, "You can't see them now but under the breezeway here are three identical 2019 Mercedes AMG C 43 black sedans."

Reagan estimated maybe twenty-five inhabitants after the short tour: cooks, landscapers, and security.

"OK, you've had enough time in the sun, and I've got to get back."

"I think I'll head to my room," said Reagan, once Winston had lumbered away, "unless you want to just let me go. I can hitch a ride into town, so no need to take me."

Kara glanced at her. "I wish I could, but that would jeopardize the last two years of our operation. You must trust me. It will be OK."

Reagan half-grinned, lips unparted, said nothing, and walked to her room. In the distance, she heard Kara. "Would you like me to call in that wager, darling?"

"Yes, get Peter on the phone for me. I want a parlay on the British Open." Reagan thought his mood had improved.

"Will he do a parlay on a golf tournament?"

"He'll take any bet. He's got Vegas connections that can make this happen."

"OK, so how much do you want to put down?"

"Ten million."

"That sounds like the apostles' money that we haven't re-funded yet."

"Yes, it is," Silva said with finality. With the *Cauliflower* now gone and with it all his records, he knew that if the information in La Ostra were to get into the wrong hands, his days in the cartel would be numbered, perhaps in the single digits. He had named his large safe La Ostra or the Oyster as a pet name for something that once contained a tiny bit of grit, but through much irritation, now contained pearls of great worth.

"I was sending a crew to retrieve it, but NCIS was already there. It's obvious they knew the *Cauliflower* would be hit before it even happened, so at least I know who's responsible. I'm not very liquid right now, so I'm using the ten million to rebuild my capital. We know Ms. Prefontaine has the gift, so a parlay of the top ten winners should get the best odds available in Vegas."

CHAPTER 30

The monitors in the situation room had provided some useful information. Monitor 1 showed the hall outside Reagan's room, but none showed her room inside, unless there was one hidden somewhere. The sun was almost overhead now and through her bay window and past the javelina, the Caribbean beckoned her to explore its depths, though she knew it would be a few days before she could accept it, if at all. She envisioned what her parents were going through right now. The loss of a son and the disappearance of a daughter. *Was Sabbi treating them well? Was Rocky getting on their nerves?*

An oak bookshelf near the window held more remnants of the sea than books. There were three conch shells, some old bottles, a turtle shell, and some starfish skeletons. Book titles included *Of Mice and Men, Quo Vadis, Catcher in the Rye,* and three novels by Daniel Silva: *The English Assassin, The Messenger,* and *Moscow Rules.* She fingered through a few of them.

She lifted *Moscow Rules* from the shelf and settled in to read for a while to calm herself down.

Jeff Rodgers, Ken Mogell, and David Schwartz surfaced from exploring the *Cauliflower* that lay in eighty feet of water. They had removed six bodies the day before, wrapping them in burlap and stowing them at the stern. They would stay onboard the Riverine Command Boat (RCB) *Honeysuckle* for seven days to salvage any evidence from a hit on a yacht against the Hetacalín cartel.

They knew it could take enemy fire from the cartel, so it was heavily armed. Two universal topside mounts and a remote-operated small-arms mount (ROSAM) for mission-dependent armament would allow them to go on the offensive, if necessary. The ROSAM allowed for more safety by keeping the guys inside the boat while operating the weapon. The cockpit's construction used armor plating, protecting them as well as the engine compartment against small-arms fire and explosion fragments. This RCB had been borrowed from Squadron 8 off the east coast. It was also chosen because it had a twenty-four-inch draft for navigating the shallower waters of the Caribbean on the way to the target site. This one even came with a decompression chamber, although the boys hoped it was not needed during this trip.

"By the way, do we know if Silva's guys plan on trying to recover anything?" David asked.

They removed their gear and set up their tanks for the next dive.

"They said they would radio us if they sighted anything unusual," Jeff said, "and so far, no messages. No worries, though. If we're down there and they spot any danger, they know what to do. Either way, we should get the sub before they have a chance to. I knew the boys in the lab were working on a sub that would be propelled out of the torpedo tube, but no one told us it was already in service. This Silva must have pulled some strings. I wonder who he knows. I'm putting in a call to get a sub captain here, so we'll be ready. We're not spending twenty-four-seven on this boat for nothin'."

They placed their masks, checked their air, and backrolled into the sea.

CHAPTER 31

The knock on the door surprised Reagan. She laid the book on the bed and walked toward the door.

Kara said, "You want lunch?"

The door was unlocked from the hall and Kara's footsteps faded away.

She now possessed a complete visual of the complex's floor plan and had memorized all the monitors. She knew the guards would be on high alert since the *Cauliflower* air assault. *Why couldn't he have been on his yacht when that bomb hit? I'd love to have seen him blown to hell.*

She left her room and purposely strode to the meal room. The chef had laid out a buffet of barbacoa, lime cilantro rice, corn, salsa, guacamole, fruit salad, taquerias, tostados, and red snapper filets. "This is a feast," she commented upon entering. "Are we expecting a party?"

"Not at all," Kara said. "You're an honored guest." She wore a lavender sundress, tied with a yellow belt, her hair pulled back into a ponytail.

"May I take a fruit salad and strawberry margarita out to the garden to enjoy some of the ocean breeze?"

"I'm sure that will be fine. I think I'll join you."

They loaded their plates, chose their margaritas, and walked out onto the patio and into the enclosed garden area. They sat on a bench to eat. The buttermilk-colored brick walkway contrasted with the lush green hedges that lined the walk.

"Reagan, what do you have planned for your life?"

Reagan hadn't been asked that since her mother approached her as a junior in high school. She wasn't sure what to say then and circumstances hadn't moved her any closer to a decision. "I sound like I'm carefree and unfocused if I say I have no immediate plans, but hopefully—"

A blinding flash caused an explosion of facial and brain tissue splattered against the green shrubs in front of her. Kara's body lurched onto the walkway, head thrown sideways, revealing no more features for Reagan to recognize. Blood formed a circle around her gutted face. Reagan fought the urge to both run and vomit. Her margarita crashed on the pavement beside her and she focused on the broken glass, fearful of what would happen next.

"I trust you have seen blood before, Ms. Prefontaine." Silva's voice came from her through the hedges.

"Why . . . why did you do this?"

"The only reason she got a bullet and you're here to enjoy the show is because you gave Kara the correct names, but she switched them when she gave them to my bookie."

He really thought she was CIA. He screwed the pooch on this one. "Why would she do that?"

"I've suspected for some time that she was CIA . . . even trailed her and had her phone tapped. She was a pro at concealing it, but with this stunt, she confirmed it. At the very least, she was intent on losing my ten million. She slipped up by thinking I wouldn't check with my bookie to make sure the bet was correctly placed."

Now Reagan knew. If there was any hope before of her being released, it just vanished. Even if the plan worked perfectly, she couldn't see a way out, and with only four minutes of wearing the necklace, there wasn't enough vestigial power for her to use.

"Why don't you get yourself cleaned up," Silva said without remorse. "I'll get this mess taken care of."

Was everyone aware this was going to happen? Were they just avoiding the scene, not wanting to be a witness if it ever came up?

She spent thirty minutes in the shower, where she allowed herself some self-pity and a mini-breakdown. She had grown to like Kara, even with her misplaced efforts to convince her she was with the CIA. When the time came, if it ever did, she would mourn Kara, and of course, Jaden. She followed the shower with a hot bubble bath and found a handwritten note next to the bottle:

Dear Reagan — I hope you enjoy these bubbles as much as I have. Your new friend, Kara.

Chris arrived at Sabbi's villa shortly after Reagan's kidnapping. Shelly cried and beat him on the chest until Carlisle pulled her off. "How could you agree to this? There had to be a better way than letting her walk to her death!"

Carlisle said, "I understand her need for revenge. I've been there. But you both saw what we could do to his yacht. We could have handled this."

"You know Reagan. Do you really think I could have stopped her? You should have seen the determination in her eyes when she figured out a way to get back at him."

Carlisle and Shelly had to agree. Slowly nodding, arms around Shelly, Carlisle said, "I think we still may be able to help. Perhaps as a backup."

This Friday morning, Chris said, "Her ad showed up again!" He read from the *Times: "Neil Sedaka has been delayed but will be available again tomorrow mourning. Anxiously awaiting a second tour."*

"How do we know it was Reagan who sent that?" Carlisle asked.

"Because of the way she spelt mourning. She purposely misspelled it."

"Thank God," Carlisle said.

C-Ham had called Chris three times over the last twenty-four hours, but he let it go to voicemail each time. His voice messages showed little originality.

"Dude! Where you at? Let's parrrrrrty! C"

Chris planned to turn C-Ham over to Raul, who did not like Reagan's plan any more than her parents did, but it was in motion and there was little he could do. Sabbi was in Boston but due back tomorrow.

Rocky convalesced, enjoying his time in their new digs. He fantasized living here with naps in the hammocks, servants to bring him smoked old fashions with Bulleit rye whiskey, daily massages, and a chef begging to feed him anytime he got hungry.

Amused at Rocky's quick assimilation, Alpheus said, "You're gonna hate returning to your—wait, you blew up your pad, so what's your plan?"

"I just figured I'd bunk at your place when this piece of heaven gets yanked out from under me."

"I'd love to oblige, but my old lady would shit a brick if I brought home someone named Rocky."

"You can call me Beatrice for all I care, and I didn't know you were married."

"Who said married? This is just my current old lady. I say old because, well, she's old. This one might be a keeper, though. She's a damn fine cook, so I wouldn't want to upset the delicate balance we have."

"Well, I ain't going back to the states," Rocky said with finality. "This is where I will finish my earthly time. I'll just find another place to rent and blow up." They both chuckled, enjoying their repartee.

Sabbi called Chris. "I'm headed back tomorrow, but in case you don't see an ad tomorrow morning and decide to head there early, I wanted to run over some details." Knowing they needed information on Silva's compound, they had contacted Sabbi to see what she would be willing to offer. They were forced to reveal their plans to get the needed information. It was a risky move, but they found it necessary.

"I'm listening." He sat on the side of his bed, sun tumbling through the window.

"You have my map of the compound, right?"

He reached into a bedside drawer to withdraw a folder. "Yes."

"And I don't need to remind you how he takes care of people he wants to torture?"

"Nope."

"Do we still feel Reagan falls into that category?"

"Reagan knows the plan and she's a smart girl. She won't jeopardize this." Chris wished he knew her even better.

"Have you checked the time the British Open is over on Sunday? It's UK time, remember."

"Yes, about 1:00 our time, assuming no playoff."

"You realize the importance of that timing, right?"

"It's not good, but it does buy us some time." Chris ran through the exercise in his mind.

"Yes, but the window is more open, which means it's less predictable."

"I'll be prepared," Chris said confidently.

"Are you taking anyone with you?" Sabbi asked.

"Wish I could, but they're all quite a bit older than me, as you know, and I'm afraid they'd slow me down. I'd rather not put anyone else in danger, and I'm not telling anyone else when I'm leaving since they could try something."

"I understand. If you're gone by the time I get back, god-speed."

"Thanks, Sabbi, and thanks for all your help." He disconnected and went back downstairs where the group was spread out—Shelly and Carlisle sat by the pool, Alpheus on the couch, and Rocky at the breakfast table.

"Everything set?"

"Yes, Rocky. Well at least as much as possible."

"God, I hope we keep seeing those ads."

"No reason why we won't. Reagan's the smartest girl I've ever met. I have full confidence in her."

"I'm not worried about her," Rocky said between bites of his omelet. "I'm worried about that son-of-a-bitch holding her hostage in his castle."

CHAPTER 32

"That goddamned boat is still out there. Don't we have enough firepower to take them down?"

Winston shook his head. Bobby and Heather had joined them. "Jefe, I've told you that's a fool's errand. They have eyes in the sky that'll rain down holy hell if there's even a hint of an insult to their men. You really want to draw the attention of their cavalry? Just mess with their operation."

"I don't need your lecture again, Winston. I asked Bobby and Heather to come by so we can create a plan, and Chaz will be here later. I let you have your say. Now you listen to mine. No one scares me. Not you. Not the goddamned U.S. Navy. They're just puppets and no one's going to pull their strings until the puppetmaster gives his blessing. They don't turn on a dime because they can't. We get in and out before they flinch."

"What is the plan after you destroy their boat?" Heather's last job at the Sweaty Old Cigar was to ensure the bomb was properly armed by the jukebox. When she met Silva at the funeral of his murdered nephew who she had been dating at the time, he offered her some steady work.

"We've got enough divers to kick off from land, so we can salvage the Oyster and the sub that way. I've got some gold bars stored away that we also need to bring up."

"I suppose you're set on this," Bobby said.

"Yes. We still have the missile launchers, right?"

Winston replied, "Yes, but . . ."

"But what?"

"They have a sixty-degree trajectory. Basically, it's like a rainbow, and I could easily see their anti-artillery taking out our missiles without a problem."

"We've got some Rebikof spearguns," Heather said. "We could come in from the west side of the cove and take out their divers if they're down there. Either way, we get your Oyster and gold bars and if Giovanni is available, we can get the sub at the same time."

Silva replied, "As long as they aren't using sonar."

"That wouldn't surprise me," Winston said. "They know we might try something. They'd be idiots to think we don't care about recovering anything."

"We'll just have to take our chances. The Oyster is priority because everything about Hetacalín is in there, and I don't need any lectures. That Oyster is both gold and kryptonite."

"Do you think there's any chance they've already gotten the Oyster up?" Bobby asked.

"No," Winston said. "We've been watching them since they arrived. We would have seen them pull up something that big, and even if we missed it, we've seen nothing to indicate they're getting it picked up by authorities. They don't know what's in it, and they have no reason to try and break it open before they get back to the states."

"So, if it's not in the *Cauliflower*," Heather replied, "we'll have to find a way to get it from their boat."

Winston turned toward Silva and said, "OK, let me talk to our dive team and see if they have an underwater transportable to bring the Oyster along the ocean floor. We can't pull it straight up to the surface with their boat there. We were able to borrow one from the Dutch a few years ago when we searched for the Golden Image of Cabrakan."

Silva said, "Those Dutch bastards charged me for that."

The hatch was an aftermarket addition to the *Honeysuckle,* which sported more name changes than P Diddy. It allowed them to bring the safe up unseen.

"All we need is a storm tonight," said Ken, scanning the sky's periphery. "The *Honeysuckle* isn't made for hunkering down as it is, but I'd rather not get rained on. Maybe it'll stay to the south. I checked radar and I think we're good. Is our sub driver getting here tomorrow? We need to get that midget out and get our butts back to the base where they can get to work on the safe."

The *Honeysuckle* had launched from the Isla Mujeres Naval Base, and Jeff had since arranged for a naval yegg to be there to open the safe and get the contents airlifted to the Office of Naval Intelligence (ONI) in DC, who would then likely hand it over to the CIA.

The winds picked up, gently rocking the *Honeysuckle.* "Yeah, those bodies we pulled up smell rank, too," David said. "Are we taking them to shore before we take off or having the boys at Isla take care of them?"

Jeff gazed out at the darkening sea. "We don't know friend from foe on land here. Can't take that chance."

"Hey, they're dead," Ken said and shrugged. "Why don't we just escort them back to the *Cauliflower?*"

Light flickered through the clear hatch. "Shit! Someone's down there. Douse your lights!"

Jeff bent down to get a better surrounding view of the underwater landscape. He counted eight lanterns. "OK, boys, it's showtime. They'll soon realize we have the safe, and assuming our intel is good, they'll go to extreme measures to get it back."

"They'll need some pretty extreme measures to breach this baby," said David.

"If we stay here, we're sitting ducks," Jeff said. "They'll likely try to surround us if they get a chance. We take shifts tonight, gentlemen."

"I'll take first shift," Ken offered.

"OK, the hatch will be the post. Wake us if you see them coming up to the boat or if you see any boats approaching. I know our guys are watching our asses, but we have to be smart."

"The Oyster wasn't there, Jefe." Rather than tell his boss the news in person, Bobby elected to call. It was half past midnight, and the call didn't last long.

"Get your ass here and bring the others."

Bobby already knew what would happen and had warned Winston and Heather to be prepared. They were en route and Winston put in a call to Chaz to get eight boats prepared for an ambush, fully loaded. Bobby hoped the navy drone would not have enough time to launch the H-guided JDAMs that had been used to sink the *Cauliflower*. A surprise attack would be essential.

Winston arrived first and took the brunt of Silva's tantrum, but the boss saved some for Bobby and Heather when they arrived. They knew it would be a long night, so Bobby brought coffee for everyone, wishing he could slip some Xanax into Silva's cup. Chaz sent word that the boats were on the way, which Bobby relayed to the boss.

"Rise and shine, boys!"

"It's my shift already?" David yawned.

"No, but the lanterns went back to shore. If I had to guess, they were only after the safe."

Jeff rubbed his neck. "We can expect them to execute Plan B now. They'll know we have it, and if we weren't sold on the intel, this closed the deal."

"What if they were just hunting for their dead buddies?" David asked.

"Cartel aiming for some closure, huh?" Jeff asked sarcastically.

"And for proof they weren't searching for bodies," said Ken, "they had an underwater sled with them that wasn't meant to transport bodies. Just big enough for a safe, and they left with nothing on it."

"All right, guys," Jeff said. "That midget sub isn't worth fending off an attack. Let me cancel the sub guy and let's get the hell outta Dodge."

David agreed. "I like the plan, as long as—"

"Holy shit!" Ken said. "Here they come."

Ken and David quickly put on their body armor while Jeff started the *Honeysuckle*. David handed Jeff his vest and a handgun as gunfire erupted. Ken grabbed the remote for the unmanned weapon and returned fire. With his left hand, he deployed four four-round smoke grenades from the stern launchers, three of which found a target. David addressed the machine gun mount and littered the oncomers, shattering glass and creating havoc in the previously streamlined boat advance. Jeff gunned the *Honeysuckle* to its max speed of forty knots, quickly outdistancing the cartel boats.

"What the fuck?" Jeff exclaimed.

There were no boats ahead of them and no effort to surround them. It did not feel right. The *Honeysuckle* had sustained little damage other than a busted navigation light and some dings in the Furono navigation radar that had not been lowered quickly enough. When they felt safely away, David made an executive decision he was not allowed to make. He opened the extraction stern door and let the dead bodies slide out unimpeded. The others smiled and nodded.

A ball of fire rose into the night. David shouted, "Shit! Something done got blown up!"

"What the hell was that?" Jeff received a text over the SAT phone.

> Had to take their helicopter down. No doubt they were planning to drop a load on your Suckle. Considering the size of the explosion, it appears as if we were right.

Jeff replied.

> Much appreciated, boys. Headed back to base.

CHAPTER 33

Silva went ballistic. Winston was dead and the helicopter in ashes. Windows blew out on the south side of the villa. There was a hole shorn in one of the worker's rooms by a spinning rotor blade, killing both him and the friend sleeping over. She was split like a magician's sawed-lady act, and he was sliced in half vertically.

The sound woke Reagan, but she remained in bed, listening for sounds of trouble. She heard shouting and the sound of frenetic hustling, and she smelled smoke tinged with gasoline . . . or maybe not gasoline. She glanced over at the bay window, realizing she could shatter it with the lamp by her bed if the need arose. She did not hear gunfire.

Bobby was on the east side of the house, taking a call from Chaz. "What was that explosion?"

"Winston's dead, Chaz. Someone torched the *Angelina* when he was about to take off."

"Do you think there's someone on the inside tipping them off? A mole?"

"I doubt it. Gonzo killed Kara two days ago, so she couldn't have leaked it."

"Good god. Why'd he do that?"

"All the explanation I got was, 'She was CIA.'"

"If they had one mole, they could have another. What about the girl?"

"We've had her in our sights or locked in her room since she arrived. Unless she's got some special skills, I don't know how she could communicate."

"If she can tell the future," said Chaz, "it wouldn't surprise me."

"Let's leave her alone for now. I want to know what happened with the attack on their boat."

Chaz hesitated before responding. "I don't plan on telling the boss about this, but we had plans to surround them, then let the *Angelina* drop the incendiary, but one of our boat captains saw lights come on in their boat, panicked, and started shooting. At that point, we had to go for it."

"That fucking idiot. If Gonzo finds out, he's toast."

"He won't have a chance. I took care of that already. Had to set an example for the men, but you know he'll blame me anyway."

Bobby sighed. "You're probably right. You gonna face the music?"

"Still considering my next move. Maybe if I can out the girl, he'll forgive me."

"He's not gonna forget losing that safe, man."

"You're right. Nice knowing you, Bobby. You were always a stand-up guy."

"I'll be sure to give you a head start before telling the boss."

"How about a year?"

"I'll see what I can do."

"Bye, Bobby."

Sabbi's flight got in at 9:35 p.m., and her assistant Fiorina picked her up for the hour ride home. She rang up Raul on the way.

"In the spirit of cooperation, I am offering my help with the Prefontaine family."

"Tell me more, Ms. Chavez-Escano."

"I know we haven't had an exemplary relationship with the Policía Federal Ministerial, Inspector, but I would like to see a metabolic change. I'm hoping we can create an alliance, perhaps lightly defined, but an alliance just the same."

"What's the catalyst for this proposal?"

"My brother's missteps. I'm hoping for a new season with law enforcement and wanted to start with you. I don't use the Silva name for a reason. I believe the sins of the brother do not predict the actions of the sister."

"What fairy tale inspired that, Ms. Chavez-Escano?"

Sabbi sighed. "It's from the book of First Cartel, chapter two, verse one."

"Ah, I see. You'll have to excuse me if I'm hesitant to embrace you or your family with sincerity. Erasing the memory of the cartel killing my parents because they wouldn't sell their land is beyond my capabilities. Now if you can help put an end to the POK game, that would be a good start."

"First things first. I need to know you will not interfere for the next forty-eight hours."

"That depends on what pops up on our radar."

"Just stay away from my brother's compound."

"Not sure I can make that promise," Raul said.

"If you want me to help Reagan, you'll stay away."

"Have you heard from her?"

"No, but I'm told she's alive."

"I'll do my best, but I can't speak for the department. It's unlikely they'll move without my knowledge or approval."

"One more thing, Inspector. Put your money on Lowry to win the British Open on Sunday."

Raul was an accomplished golfer and had played on his college team. "This is the first time the Open has been played in Ireland in sixty-eight years. Lowry will choke playing in his homeland. Did you get a hot tip?"

"Let's just say I know people. Goodbye, Inspector, and I know this won't help, but I'm sorry about your parents."

After hanging up, Sabbi sent a text.

On the way to villa. Everything a go?

Yes.

Police are no problem.

Good.

CHAPTER 34

Silva had kissed away the night by drinking a full liter bottle of eighty proof mezcal, consuming the maguey worm and chasing it with two lines of coke. He was known to abstain from drugs, but last night, he had deserved a detour.

Today, he would attend the horse races in Chihuahua, watch the third round of the Open, and decide who to punish with how much pain for the loss of his safe. He refused to take any blame for having so much sensitive information on his yacht. Bobby reported Chaz's disappearance as soon as Silva awoke. He was not taking the hit for delaying the report. Better Chaz get his neck slit by a piano wire than his.

Tropical storm Belaroo brewed, expecting to make landfall in the Cancun area sometime Sunday night.

CHAPTER 35

Silva's Saturday schedule always included horse racing. He used it as a cap of the week to scrutinize and learn but never to plan the future. He rarely missed. Today he just wanted to clear his head and to reflect on the last seven days. Having lost his long-time bodyguard and closest companion Winston, the *Cauliflower*, his *Angelina*, and his lover, it had been a rough week. The best news involved his son, so today, that's what he would dwell on. "I will have grandsons," he said, knowing Bobby would understand. "Who's watching the girl?"

"I brought Forrester in from the front gate. He's a good boy. I doubt she'll try anything but can't be too careful."

"She's my salvation, Bobby. Tomorrow, I make enough to buy another yacht."

"Not the *Cauliflower Two*, right?"

"Hell no. I don't need reminders. Taking her to lands far away as well. I believe my time in Mexico has come to an end."

"Why do you say that, Jefe?"

"I don't need to tell you what losing the Oyster means."

"I understand."

The skies darkened prematurely, winds gusting to forty miles per hour. The horses struggled to walk straight as they entered their gates.

"I thought the tropical storm was hitting tomorrow," said Gonzo.

"This may be something else. Maybe a warning from God."

"Yes, a warning from God. But what is He warning us about, Bobby?" Gonzo continued looking at the sky.

Knowing he had to be careful with this answer, he said, "That we must watch out for ourselves because no one else will do that for us."

When they arrived at the villa, Bobby told Gonzo he would check on Reagan. After releasing Forrester back to the guard gate post, he knocked on her door.

"Yes?"

"It's Bobby. May I come in?"

"It's open."

Bobby turned the knob and noticed it was not locked. "Have you been out of your room?"

"Not really. I've been getting to know Forrester. Nice guy."

"I'm going to have a talk with him. He has no business in here."

"Be easy on him. You know how boring it is to sit by a door all day?"

"I've had jobs like this before myself and never complained. He knows his job."

"Did you know he's got a brother in the monastery with Silva's son?"

"No. That would've been nice to know."

"You have to talk to people, Bobby. He didn't do well with the helicopter explosion. It woke me up, but I didn't know what had happened. Did you know Forrester's a Jainist?"

"What the hell's a Jainist?"

"It's an ancient philosophy that originated in India. They practice ahisma, which is the avoidance of physical or mental harm to any living being."

"Fuck."

"Yeah, maybe a little personality test or talent alignment using some good people analytics is in order for your little organization."

"You interested in working for the Hetacalín? I think we could use your talents, and I'm sure Silva would make it worth your while."

"You flatter me, but let's see if he's still happy with me after tomorrow."

"I just checked the golf scores. The players you gave us for the top ten are still in contention and the third round is over. With two players in that group who started at five-hundred-to-one odds to win, I have no doubt he'll be happy with you."

"Bobby, let me ask you a question that's been bugging me. I'm usually a good judge of character but can't understand Silva's attraction to hummingbirds."

"Gonzo doesn't love hummingbirds. What he loves is selling their carcasses."

Reagan cringed. "Why would he do that?"

"It's illegal. That's why. They call the carcasses *chuparosas,* and people wear them as amulets for their spiritual powers. Gonzo wears one, but it's always tucked under his shirt, so you don't see it. He's the biggest supplier to the U.S. of these chuparosas, by the way."

Her eyes bored into his. "Why do you work for this guy, Bobby?"

He did not immediately answer. He had often wondered this himself and usually rationalized his way into continuing. "I don't know. He took me under his wing and made it financially worthwhile. I'm part of a family here, and I've never had that."

"I'm an excellent judge of character, Bobby. I know this isn't where you belong. You have a good heart, and you shouldn't let your past circumstances twist your character into a knot you can't untie."

He sat for a moment, not responding with words, the pain visible in his eyes.

"All I want right now is to live through this, Bobby. And I need Fleetwood to win tomorrow for that to happen. Am I reading the tea leaves correctly?"

"I'm not concerned. He's four strokes back but coming back from four happens all the time. I know it was upsetting to be with Kara when she paid for her mistake."

"This conversation has turned morbid," Reagan said, wishing to change the subject. "Tell me about your family."

"You're not doing that to me, Reagan."

"What does it hurt to know about your family? I suspect you had a part to play in my brother's death."

Bobby avoided her eyes. "Who is your brother?"

"Unimportant right now, Bobby."

"Now who's tight-lipped? Is that why you're here? Some measure of revenge? You're too intelligent to allow yourself to be kidnapped and brought here against your will."

"I wish I were that smart. You've placed me on a pedestal with too much height."

"Will you be having dinner with us tonight?"

"Not very hungry." Reagan gazed out the window. "I miss my family. Will he really let me go after the tournament tomorrow?"

"Maybe you can put on your necklace and see for yourself."

"You'd let me do that?" Reagan knew the answer already.

"No, Reagan. I have strict orders that he's present when you, or anyone else, wears it."

"So, after he lets me go, what will he do with the necklace?"

"This discussion is over, Ms. Prefontaine."

"I'll have dinner in my room tonight."

"I'll let the chef know." He left the room, closing the door. Reagan heard the lock turn and smiled.

CHAPTER 36

Chris awoke Sunday morning, anxious but exhilarated. As an athlete, he had learned to channel any challenges into manageable avenues that allowed him to feel excitement instead of angst, opportunity verses concern, and superiority in place of insecurity.

His grandpa Willett would say, "If you can do it, at a very base level, be the fox, work like a beaver, and take on the psyche of a mongoose. Use these animal characteristics that ignore negative thinking."

Chris knew this day would bring reward. He just didn't know in what form it would be. He meditated and prayed while the sun said hello from across the calm water. Waves monotoned enough for him to gather his thoughts. At 6:30 a.m., Alpheus and Rocky joined him by the pool.

"You guys shackin' up here?" Chris asked playfully.

"He's a very tender lover," Rocky deadpanned.

"Just don't tell JoJo," Alpheus said, bushy eyebrows impishly raised. "Remember. She's a keeper."

"Sure you don't need help today?" asked Rocky.

"I knew you'd want to come, dude, but you're still healing and will be for weeks. You can't tear open those wounds again, and where I'm going, that would happen."

"I've lived a good life, Christopher, but I need some excitement. I know I could help."

"Love ya, Rock, but honestly, you'd slow me down. It wouldn't matter to me, but it could endanger Reagan."

"You had to play that card. All right, I'll lay back for Reagan."

"Thanks for understanding . . . and for your bravery. I expected nothing less."

Chris excused himself and went upstairs to get ready. He put on his three millimeter dive shorty and booties, then slid his mask and fins around his neck. "I'll see you guys soon!"

As he walked toward the Tzuro in the front driveway, Shelly yelled, "We're praying for you!" She stood in Carlisle's arms as Chris drove south.

The clock said 8:23 a.m. when Reagan awoke. *Today's the day. So much riding on this and so much could happen. Concentrate, Reagan! See into the future!* Her eyes squeezed shut like a grape in a wine press, but no photos of the future came. It had been too long without the necklace around her neck.

She showered and quickly put on a robe when someone knocked at the door. Straining to hear through the bathroom door, she heard "Reagan!" The rest of the outburst was too subdued to hear.

"Just a minute! I'm coming!" She opened the door, hair still dripping down her neck.

"Get dressed," Bobby demanded. "He wants to see you immediately."

She shut the door without saying a word. *Here we go. Chris, I know you're out there. Be safe.* She hurriedly dressed in a military jumpsuit Kara had left for her and walked to the library but found no one. Noises sounded from the security room. She entered the room to an inebriated Silva spinning in a swivel chair, holding a Modelo in his left hand and a Ruger-57 in his right. He stopped with the gun aimed at Reagan. The British Open was up on all forty-eight monitors, security be damned.

"Our guest of honor has arrived!" Holding the Modelo high, he toasted her arrival.

Bobby entered just after Reagan.

"Why the fuck did you show up?" Silva asked her with slurred speech.

"I was told you wanted me here."

"True, true, my dear, but what I really need to know is why your man isn't winning."

"I have no control over that," Reagan said, folding her arms.

"Or do you?" Silva's eyebrows lifted with some effort. "I thought you could tell the future with your fucking necklace."

"As you have told me yourself, it's not my necklace. I found it in *your* sea, and I am unaware of anything that happens to me when I wear it."

"How do I know that?" He continued to point the gun at her midsection, waving it up and down.

"I don't suppose you do, and I can't prove it."

"There's two hundred and fifty million dollars riding on this. I don't think I need to tell you the ramif . . . the famir . . . the rafimi . . ."

"Ramifications, Mr. Silva? No, I'm aware. You'll hold me responsible, even though I have not wronged you."

"Oh, but you have. You've been at my whore sister's house— shit! Your guy just lost another stroke!" He rose precariously out of the swivel chair and found his way to a putter leaning into the corner of the room. Taking a full backswing, he swung the club into one of the lower monitors, shattering the screen.

Reagan could not resist. "You were a little strong with that putt, Mr. Silva."

"Sit down, bitch!"

Reagan was still positioned near the door, and she hesitated, lacking the immediacy of blind subservience, then sat slowly on one of the wooden chairs behind a plexiglass table. Silva found his seat and began spinning again. "I like you, Reagan, but business is business."

Chris parked the Tzuro on Av. Kukulcan, as close as he felt comfortable, knowing a passing car or helicopter could recognize him. He was not sure how far the compound's surveillance net was thrown, but this seemed safe when he was making his plans. He made sure it would bring no curiosity and could easily be seen from a high-rise apartment building across the street.

He observed the area without appearing to do so, then bent down, feigning to zip up his bootie, and placed the car key on the inside of the rear left tire. Rain fell, and the wind gusted to thirty-five knots. He approached two seaside villas, climbed a fence only intended to keep out very short people and iguanas, then walked to the water's edge. He shielded his eyes with his hand. He figured it was about two miles to the Silva compound. Few people were on the beach as the angry waves and rain slapped and pelted him.

This could be a stroke of luck, Chris thought as he walked through sand and shallow water. He knew there would be sections along the beach that would cause him to place fins and mask to swim around, but if he could crash through a few of those restricted areas, maybe duck under some docks, asking for forgiveness instead of permission, so much the better. His mission was more important than the consequences of raising a few hackles.

"This is private property!" one villa owner yelled as he hustled by, undeterred.

It was almost 11:00 a.m., and the compound was not in sight. The rain pelted the left side of his face as the wind barreled from the east. His mask protected his eyes and helped his vision, which proved necessary for the vigilant processing of the dangers ahead. After thirty minutes of jogging, swimming, and dodging, Silva's compound came into view.

He struggled against the powerful winds. Chairs, umbrellas, tables, and portable grills were tossed askew. He decided it would be safer to travel by water, so he put on his fins, dove headfirst, and swam against and across the waves. Now close to noon, the sky transitioned to graphite gray, and trees swayed like an afternoon drunk.

"Bobby, put her in her room. I've got some decisions to make." Reagan rose and left with Bobby. When they were close to her room, he said, "Do you have any idea how all of this happened, Reagan?"

"No, Bobby," she lied. "But I know golfers are disqualified sometimes. Maybe that could still happen."

"It would make sense to me because from third to tenth place, you were perfect, and the odds of that happening are, well, impossible."

"So, what happens to me?"

"This is Gonzo's decision. If you're a praying person, now's the time."

"I am, Bobby. I'm not worried. I'm at peace."

Bobby opened the door and encouraged her to go in. "You're a good person, Reagan." He closed the door and locked it.

Chris edged toward the rock harbor wall Silva's family had built in 1947. The walls stretched twenty feet above water level and were roughly six feet wide. This allowed guards to walk the top of the walls so they could patrol the area, but on this stormy day, no one was on sentry duty. The winds would have picked them off the wall like a ten-year-old cowboy on his first bucking bronco.

These walls extended from land, creating two bowed halves that would have intersected except for the necessary ingress and egress of cartel boats. The opening was only three meters wide, preventing larger boats from entering, but not the tide, which made the water depth inside the protected area rise and fall, influenced primarily by the moon.

This body of water terminated at a narrow beach named Silva Bay. There was a single dock extending forty feet into the water that became partially submerged near land at high tide.

It was at this dock that Silva's ritualistic killings would occur. At low tide, he would have the victim tied to the dock post, leaving them there until the tide rose enough to drown them. He was known to leave victims there until the next one, but there were more than enough dock posts to allow a body to remain until the triggerfish had eaten the meat. He called this form of torture "docking" before docking stations had been manufactured.

As Chris swam up to the wall, he became hypervigilant, not knowing if a sentry would appear. Even in this storm, they might find a way to check occasionally. His intel from Sabbi had been good so far, but there was always the element of surprise. He knew there would be an iron gate across the opening into Silva Bay that would retract vertically using a remote system in the security room.

He worked his way along the bowed wall, keeping only his head above water, wishing now for a snorkel, and eventually found the opening. There was one boat at the dock—a catamaran. No one was around, but he did not know what kind of sensors might be on the iron gate or on the walls adjacent to it. He took comfort in not seeing Reagan already docked.

He felt with his fins to see how deep the iron gate extended, stretching his leg and slightly submerging himself, but could not feel the bottom of the gate. The railing would lift no more than twenty feet from its current position. To get enough clearance for boats like the catamaran to maneuver under, the fence could extend about ten feet underwater at a maximum. He decided on a trial run, took a deep breath, then pulled himself down the ten feet using the fence bars as leverage. Feeling the bottom, plus enough clearance to swim under, he knew it would be possible. Now he could go over the variables again, playing through the scenarios.

He was used to this exercise, having done the same with baseball since he was in middle school. If the runner took off from first, there was no other runner, the batter and pitcher were left-handed, and the score was within two runs in the seventh inning or later, he would sprint to cover third base and let his shortstop cover second because the left fielder would be cheating in. There were hundreds of these variables, and he had to act on instinct.

One: I could get stuck underwater on the gate and drown. Two: There could be sensors that go off when I enter the bay. Three: I may not make it in time to save Reagan if the tide is already on her. Four: Silva might station a guard to ensure no rescue is successful. Five: This storm could pass and the guards could resume their guard duty. Six: Reagan may not be able to swim under the gate. Seven: We escape but they catch us on the way back to the car. Eight: Silva uses a completely different playbook and doesn't dock Reagan. Nine: My hypnosis doesn't work and Silva is two hundred and fifty million dollars richer. I think that's everything.

And now he waited.

CHAPTER 37

Reagan spent two hours in her room without a word from any-one. *Chris! Hang in there. I should be there soon.* At 2:30 p.m., a knock at the door startled her. *Is this it?*

Bobby opened the door and walked in, leaving the door ajar. "What do you think is going to happen to you?"

"I think he'll let me go back to my family."

"To be honest, Gonzo is confused. He realized if he had let Kara make that change, he would be two hundred and fifty million dollars richer, and she would still be alive. He's trying to figure this whole thing out."

"What am I supposed to do with that?" Reagan asked out loud, while internally she thought, *Why doesn't he just jump off the cliff and end his miserable life?*

"Nothing. Just thought you should know where his mind is at right now."

"Well that gives me great comfort. Can I go home now?"

Bobby considered the bay window. "This storm will present challenges. If I didn't know any better, I'd say it's nine o'clock at night out there."

The rain drummed on the window, and palm trees flexed like blown-up characters in a used car sales lot. "I'm shooting straight with you. Isn't that what they say in Texas?"

"Go on."

"He still thinks he can use you. The Kara thing really has him messed up."

"If he's not going to kill me, then I don't think this room is the safest during this storm. That window could implode."

"Let me take you to the security room for now. There's no windows and it's on the interior of the villa."

"Thanks, I appreciate it. Let me get a few things first." She put on some tan Nikes and grabbed *Moscow Rules*. The security room had not changed from her first visit, except Winston was gone.

"We've been interviewing for a replacement for Winston, but no luck yet. I guess that means you're the interim head of security for now." His grin belied his thoughts on leaving her here alone. "Let me know if you see anything unusual. There's an intercom right here." He opened a panel to the right of the monitors to reveal a speaker and button. "Push this and speak into it. I will get the message sent to my cell phone immediately. I know this is not in your wheelhouse, but there are rival cartels that could attempt to penetrate our compound. I'll be checking back every thirty minutes, but just send me a message and tell me which monitor number alerted you. I have the locations memorized."

"I think I can handle this, boss." Reagan was pleased with this propitious arrangement.

"I'm sure you can. It's pretty dark out there, but our monitors use thermal imaging technology to capture infrared light when the ambient light dims below 200 lux. About half of the monitors right now are using infrared viewing due to Belaroo knocking out so much sunlight." He pointed at a few that exhibited the view. "I'll be back in thirty minutes, but intercom me if you see anything I need to know about."

Within seconds of Bobby leaving, she walked close to the monitors, only seeing the bay view out of the corner of her eye. She did not discount the possibility of this being a test. There could be a camera watching her right now. *Chris, where are you? Have you made it? Are you inside or outside the bay?* She saw no movement. There was a zooming feature on each monitor, so she used it on three other monitors first: the front gate on Monitor 1, where she zoomed in on Forrester. Then she zoomed in on Monitor 6, the portico monitor, where the Mercedes were hidden below the slide-away driveway. Monitor 13 showed the back yard. She zoomed on 13 to watch a hummingbird, obviously agitated at the hiccough in her usual routine. She finally went to the Monitor 27, the bay monitor, and zoomed in to see . . . nothing. No sign of Chris.

Chris guessed that about an hour had passed while he hung in the water next to the gate. His scuba mask kept him from being miserable in the torrential wind and rain, and the waves washed over him without mercy. In the distance, he made out a light sending a Morse code signal. Dot-dot-dot-dash-dot-dash-dot-dash-dash . . . *No, it's a boat light. Someone's crazy being out in this weather.*

A voice came over the intercom. "I need the gate opened! Coming in hot!" Reagan panned back out and saw a boat approaching, fighting waves three times the height of the boat. They approached with some speed, so she knew she had little time, and if Chris was on the outside of the gate, she couldn't let the boat have any time waiting at the gate. *Where's the gate remote, Reagan? Why didn't you find that first? Should I call Bobby? No!*

She canvassed the massive room. There were very few places to hide a remote. She inspected under chairs, under the desk, and behind everything that had a behind to it. *He must have taken it!* She ran to the intercom, pressed the button, and said "Bobby! Open the bay gate! There's a boat that radioed in, and they're about to crash into it! Monitor twenty-seven!"

In a few seconds, he replied, "Opening now. Thanks." She returned to the monitor to see the gate rising and the boat within one hundred meters and closing fast. She saw it slow down enough for the gate to give them enough clearance, then watched it jet through and pull up to the dock. *That had to be close. I wish I knew where he was right now.*

As the boat approached, Chris moved farther away from the gate along the wall. He calculated the variables again. He could remove one, maybe two, by moving through the entrance after the boat went through and before the gate retracted back into the sea. On impulse, he moved to the entrance and through, just as the gate was closing. Now inside, he had more decisions to make, and the respite from the maelstrom he had just escaped allowed him to think more clearly. If he stayed put, the calmer waters could more easily expose him, but moving through the water could do the same. Currently, he was under the water with just enough airholes exposed to stay alive. This was not working well, as rain continued to fall, though with fewer ninety-degree turns.

He worked his way along the wall toward land. A jellyfish sting had made his journey up the coast even more challenging and reminded him how miserable it felt to have venom injected into your bare skin from thousands of barbed stingers. Now that his adrenaline surge from fighting storm Belaroo had abated, the venom took center stage. He knew this would subside and rationalized that staying in seawater would help to dilute the effects.

He inched closer. The speedboat had two passengers who, after tying up to the dock, walked to a hole in the cliff and disappeared. One of them had a walk that looked familiar to him, but he could not place it. He did not remember this cliff entrance from Sabbi's description but wondered if he forgot or if she was unaware of its existence.

CHAPTER 38

Sabbi came down to eat breakfast with the group, upbeat about the day. Everyone else was reserved but hopeful, and they were all curious about her positive outlook.

"Do you know something we don't?" asked Shelly.

"I have faith in Chris and Reagan. Don't you?"

"I wish I had your confidence," Carlisle said. "We know how competent Reagan is. What we don't know is how ruthless Silva and his group might be."

"No promises, but my guess is you'll be with your daughter tonight."

Carlisle and Shelly were not sure it was warranted, but Sabbi's confidence did give them some relief and a surge of hope.

After having a bagel with some decaf coffee, she announced she would be leaving and might not be back today. "Take care of my place. Hope to see you all soon." And with that, she was out the door and gone.

Reagan's eyes rarely left Monitor 27, the one showing the bay, but she made a show of looking at all forty-eight to assuage any prying eyes. She wondered if Bobby might test her by showing up in one view, waving a gun or something, just to make sure she was on task. She could see the empty gym in 34, the library in 37, even the underground sealed garage with the three black Mercedes sedans on Monitor 9, all present and accounted for. As she panned over the garage, she was surprised to see a 2019 Tesla Model S hiding behind the sedans, connected to the power supply, fully charged but not actively charging.

Monitor 9 was different. It had a pocket on the side that held a remote. *I wonder if this starts the cars.* There were several labeled buttons. She pressed Start 1, immediately seeing signs of exhaust from one of the sedans on the monitor. She pressed Start 2 and Start 3. More exhaust. *This could be fun.* She left the three running but didn't push Start Tesla. Seeing a Charge button, she pressed it to start the Tesla charging again and pocketed the remote. She had read an article on Tesla fires that could occur with overcharging batteries and with heat buildup, causing a thermal runaway. She then found a thermostat setting for the car garage set at eighteen degrees centigrade. She punched in forty-eight, the maximum allowable, then closed the display cover. She inspected broken 18 again, thinking the pool view wasn't that important during a tropical storm. Monitor 22, which showed the helipad on the south side, was puzzling.

After the explosion of Silva's *Angelina*, there were fragments strewn throughout that side of the villa and a blackened and severely damaged helipad. Now on the monitor was a red-on-gray Bell 505 in perfect condition, sitting in the middle of an undamaged helipad.

Could some of these monitors be showing old images? Why would anyone do that? Then she noticed movement. *Is someone playing an old video?* Then she compared lighting to other monitors.

The storm's effect was identical.

How can this be?

She moved back to the bay view on 27. Those in the boat had tied up at the dock and left. She zoomed in. Still no movement . . . no Chris. She pulled away to view another monitor and Bobby walked in, appearing as if he had taken a shower in his clothes.

"Any news?"

"All quiet on the homefront. Where have you been?"

His dripping blue jeans and white T-shirt clung to his chest like fresh wallpaper. "I guess I need to change. There were some hummingbird feeders that needed resurrecting."

"You're a kind man."

"Not really. Gonzo would have gone ape shit if he saw those. It's Bobby-preservation that drives me."

"Hey, who were those two in the boat?" Reagan asked nonchalantly, hoping it did not sound like she was prying.

"Unimportant. You don't know them. I'm going to change, and—"

"Wait. Before you go, look at number twenty-two. What's this all about? The helicopter's back."

Bobby stared and leaned into the monitor. "What the hell? We haven't replaced the *Angelina* . . . and the helipad . . . it's restored!" He ran out of the room without saying another word. She stared at the red bird until Bobby stood in the rain next to it. He moved closer and opened the door. Reagan zoomed in to see him removing a piece of paper from the inside of the windshield. She watched him read it, then shake his head, and stuff it inside his pocket. A sense of anxiety washed over her.

What could this be? Something isn't right.

She looked back at 27. Still nothing. Within a minute, Bobby returned.

"That *is* the Angelina. Do you know anything about this?" His demeanor had stiffened.

"I have no idea what you're talking about. How could I have done anything? You've had me in this jail since my kidnapping." He removed the piece of soggy paper and carefully unfolded it, handing it to her. The writing was smudged but readable.

> You've been fooled. Your son will never leave the monastery and Reagan switched the names for the golf bet.

"How could anyone say those things? I don't even know what I'm doing when I'm wearing the necklace."

"I'm not showing this to Gonzo," he said as he refolded the note.

"What if he finds out you hid it from him? He may have already seen it."

Bobby thought for a moment. "Why are you trying to convince me to show him? It could only hurt you."

"Instinct, I guess. Just trying to think it through," she said, hoping her reasons sounded rational.

"I think I'll dry this out and return it, but I still don't know how the *Angelina* was resurrected."

Sabbi spent the morning on the phone. She made calls to the apostles and made her last call to Ephraim. "It worked, Ephraim, but I'm sure this isn't news to you. I couldn't believe what I saw."

"The future is 4DNS, Sabbi. The future is 4DNS."

CHAPTER 39

"It's confirmed, Jefe. The CIA has possession of the documents from the safe, but we have reasonable assurance that fact has not left Mexico." Heather was elected to pass the message on to Silva but did not relish the opportunity.

"They made me the incompetent fool," a lugubrious Silva replied. "Damn Americans. I'll find a way to return the favor. I'm not done."

Cunningham nodded. "When we were coming in during the storm, it was difficult to tell, but did you replace the *Angelina* already?"

Silva jerked his head toward Cunningham. "What the hell are you talking about? You must either be seeing things or playing a very poor joke on me."

"OK, I guess I was seeing the 412, then."

"The 412 is in Mexico City. Fernando took it there yesterday to pick up a package."

"Maybe he's back already?" Cunningham asked.

"I just talked to him. He leaves Mexico City tomorrow, and unlike you, he wouldn't lie to me."

"Maybe I was just *wishing* your bird was back. The mind can do funny things in a storm like that. I swear, Jefe. I'm not trying to—"

"Let's go see it," Silva said tersely. "I need something to get my mind off your message anyway. Maria! Get these two some coffee. We'll be right back."

They walked the hall to the sliding glass door to view the helicopter pad. Silva cupped his hands on the sides of his eyes to remove glare from the hall lights. "Shit! That's my *Angelina*. What's going on here?"

Cunningham had his hands cupped as well. "Jefe. There's a piece of paper attached to the windshield. Want me to go get it?"

"Go!" Silva replied.

Cunningham slid back the door and raced to the helicopter door. When he returned, he said, "It was already a little damp, Jefe, so it must have been placed during the storm."

Silva's expression did not change while he read the note. "Where's the girl?"

"We don't know," Heather answered. "We came straight to you."

Silva pulled out his phone and called Bobby. "Yes, Jefe?"

"Where's the girl?"

Bobby paused before answering. "She's in the security room. Her room had a large window and wasn't safe during the storm."

"That's fuckin' brilliant. I don't care how safe her room is. In fact, right now, I don't want her safe at all. Is that clear?"

"Yes, Jefe. I'll get her back to her room."

Back in her room, Reagan worried about Chris. She was sure Silva currently planned her demise. She considered again what it would take to break the bedroom window. She picked up the table lamp with the pewter base, lifted it a few times to assess the weight, then set it down to explore other options. Circling her room, she opened her closet and found a compound bow and a quiver full of arrows.

Is this some kind of test? Are they trying to—

An envelope was taped to the wall behind the bow. Opening it, she read:

Since my conversion, I've been hoping for a good home for my bow. I figured you could use it —Forrester.

She picked it up and tested the draw. It had more weight than ideal for her. She liked sixty pounds, and this felt close to seventy.

The sound of gunfire erupted outside. People yelled and screamed in Spanish. She remained still for a moment, then slung the quiver over her shoulder. The cacophony lessened in intensity and frequency with just a gunshot every twenty or thirty seconds. She watched out the window for any signs of disruption, but at least on this side of the villa, detected no movement.

The gunfire stopped, and someone barked orders, followed by footsteps in the hall outside her room. She hastily put the bow and quiver back in the closet and closed it, just as someone attempted to enter her room. "Open this door!"

Not knowing if this was friend or foe, she replied, "It's been locked from the outside to keep me in here! I have no way of opening the door!"

"Stand back!" the voice ordered.

Reagan was already standing back but she backed up farther. A loud gunshot sent a bullet through the locking mechanism, projecting its contents to the opposite wall and creating a hole previously occupied by the door handle. The door swung open from the force and standing in the doorway was someone dressed in camouflaged combat gear, including a ballistic vest, a Phoenix programmable transmitter, grenades, a night vision device, and a .204 Ruger with six magazines. He wore army green boots that had experienced the muddy landscape Belaroo had painted. "Come with me."

She obeyed and walked toward the front door, encouraged by the periodic tapping of her back with the Ruger. "You need to see this," her escort said, as they approached the foyer. The front door opened into the portico and she was horrified to see a large wooden cross, fifteen feet high and nine feet across, and Silva hanging upside down, feet nailed to the top, arms nailed to the crossbeam, and a twelve-inch nail driven through his temple. As the Ruger prodded her to move closer, she was able to read the message hanging from the nail like an unfurled scroll.

From your 12 apostles

A large crimson pool formed under his body, his eyes fixed open, scar blending with the blood trails crossing his face. The atrium and halls were strewn with bodies lying in various positions, none moving. Maria's crumpled body lay ten feet away, a bullet hole in her forehead. "What's going on?" she asked, not expecting an answer.

"I was only asked to show you this. No questions," the soldier responded.

The sound of footsteps approaching revealed three men, two outfitted like her escort, and Chris in between them, sporting a newly bloodied nose and scratched face.

"Chris!" she blurted.

"I'm OK," he said as the two men holding his arms gripped

them tighter. "I think we were set up—" That comment drew a vicious kick to Chris' left knee. He buckled, wincing in pain.

"No more words out of you," ordered her escort.

Sabbi strode in, smiling broadly. "My dear Reagan," she said, her tone reminding Reagan of Cruella Deville. "What are we going to do with this nice young man?"

"Sabbi, what are you doing?"

"A new sheriff's in town, Reagan, but we have some plans for you."

"I'll cooperate if you let Chris go."

"Now, now, sweetie. What should we do with a young man who knows all our dirty little secrets? No, I think you'll cooperate regardless of what we do with him, and to carry on my dearly departed brother's tradition, I've decided to dock him." Turning toward the three men, she said, "Take him to the bay."

"Nooooo!" Reagan pleaded, struggling to free herself from the tight grip of her escort.

Sabbi walked over, leaning into her face for emphasis. "And *this* time, you won't have Mr. Baseball to hypnotize you. It was very clever of you to have your mind manipulated into seeing my nephew with a family, and fixing that bet was the coup de gras. I sincerely appreciate the effort *and* the outcome, but you won't have that luxury this time. By the way, I have a partner who would very much like to meet you." To her escort, she said, "Take her back to her room."

Approaching her door, Reagan said, "Well you ruined my door, big guy. How are you going to keep me in here?" That was the last thing she remembered before she woke up two hours later with a knot on the back of her head screaming for relief. She checked the cabinets. No medicine stocked. She went to the door to check the status of the lock, only to find a new door had been installed.

She struggled but managed to move the javelina enough to get a good swing at the window glass. Using her rowing muscles, she swung the Fisher lamp back, then slammed it against the window. Crack lines spidered in the glass from the impact. She was unaware a silent alarm flashed in the security room without a security officer. Sabbi's appropriation committee had decided manning the room was unnecessary, since their seizure constituted an intrusion the security failed to prevent.

She swung again, aiming for a different area to create propagation and to connect the impact zones. After a dozen swings, the window finally surrendered. Rain was now coming into her room with a healthy dose of Belaroo's attitude. Her arms were fatigued, but she grabbed the bow and quiver and maneuvered through the opening.

On hitting ground, she crouched to get her bearings, thankful that her study of the monitors had provided a detailed map of the compound. There was no movement at the guard gate. She worked her way along the wall, using shrubs for extra protection from the storm and wandering eyes. She was fully soaked within minutes of leaving through the window, and she hoped no one would check her room anytime soon.

She came to a pony wall close to a heavily pitched slope of the roof. Laying the bow and quiver on top, she jumped, and holding herself up with her forearms, she lifted herself up and onto the wall. From there, she had a good sightline of the roof. Three feet above her was the edge. She tossed the bow and quiver ahead of her, then jumped enough to get her upper body flat on the wooden shingles, pulling one leg up, then the other, rolling onto the roof. The wind complicated her journey, but she crouched low, navigated her way across the roof, around some parapet walls and turrets, and to the side facing the bay.

She peered over the edge to the dock below. Chris held his head above the water, tied to a dock post with rope that appeared to be—

Wait a minute. This bow has a 2X lens on it.

She held the bow in position and saw five rope strands around the post.

If I can get just one of those, it should release all of them.

She knew the tide would soon overtake him, so she had to work quickly.

If this wind and rain weren't so bad, this shot would be easy, but I have no idea what it will do to the trajectory. It could just as easily hit him as the rope, but he's going to die if I don't try.

She figured the shot to be close to seventy yards, and the arrow would not have enough force to negate the wind. Holding the bow steady would be one more challenge. On her left was a parapet wall that could give her some stability. It would add about five yards to the shot, but it was a good tradeoff. She ran to get into position. Since the wind came from her left, she calculated a sixteen-inch deflection.

She wiped the water from the lens, drew the string back, and let the arrow fly. Continuing to look through the 2X lens, she saw it bury into the water just to the right of the pole. Chris whipped his head to the left but did not attempt to find her. She wondered if he knew. Drawing back the second arrow, she felt strange having to aim at Chris to account for the added deflection she needed. Thirty inches. The water lapped his face now, submerging it and then receding with the tidal flow. She let the arrow fly, hearing a scream from Chris before she realized what had happened. Blood mixed with the water, but Chris still struggled for air. He angled his head toward her, although she was not sure he could see her. She let another arrow fly, correcting her deflection to twenty-two inches, seeing it hit wood. Straining to see through her lens, she saw one rope strand missing, but the others stayed.

OK, I think I have time for maybe one more shot before it's too late.

As she drew the string back, the ropes collapsed into the water and Chris climbed the post to get a breath of air. He gave her a thumbs up with his left hand and swam with his left arm only toward the gate.

He's free!

She ran to the edge of the roof she had scaled earlier, threw the bow and quiver to the ground, slid down onto the pony wall, then jumped to the ground.

Her time on the roof had allowed the rain to wash away most of the mud she had accumulated after leaving through the window, but she was now back into it. Seeing enough movies growing up, she knew to smear some mud on her face for camouflage.

She edged around the villa toward the room eviscerated by the helicopter rotor blade. The storm had forced everyone inside so she could finish her task, but now she needed to be inside herself to raise the gate for Chris.

The room was full of debris from Belaroo. Wading through the mess, she came to the door and pulled it open against the mud and branches. When she had it open enough to see inside, Bobby sat against the wall with three bullet holes through his torso and another through his neck. Blood and spittle oozed out of the right side of his mouth, and for a moment, Reagan thought he might be alive until he slumped forward and fell to his side.

Poor Bobby . . . but you had something to do with Jaden's death. Not going to grieve for you.

She rifled through his pockets and located the remote for the gate, shoving it quickly into her shorts pocket.

She headed for the security room, bow loaded. She heard

conversations through the walls of the conference room. She opened the door of the security room, where one of the guys who had held Chris dropped his radio and reached for his gun. He never got to it as an arrow pierced his neck and pinned him to the wall by the monitors.

She ran to Monitor 27, where Chris hung by one arm to the wall by the entrance gate. Removing the remote from her pocket, she realized there were six different speed options for opening or closing the gate. She pressed the lowest speed to let him know it would be rising, then the fastest speed that raised it within three seconds. He awkwardly swam through the entrance and she collapsed into the chair from relief but knew this was not over.

The boat Cunningham had brought in was being started by one of Sabbi's men, and he headed for the gate entrance. She started the gate retraction at the slowest speed and watched him keep the same course. He could see it closing but was unconcerned. When he was within fifteen feet, she hit the fastest speed, timing it well enough to split the boat in half, throwing the man against the closed gate. He fell into the water and she saw him floating, face down.

CHAPTER 40

"Where's the bitch?" Sabbi yelled at the man who had come to report Reagan's escape.

"We're hunting for her. She can't have gone far."

"Do we know she left?"

"Why wouldn't she? There's lot of trees and she could hide for a while. If I were her, I'd be headed back to safety."

"Well you're not her," Sabbi fumed. "You're hunting in the wrong place, you fool. She's right here in the compound!"

"Yes ma'am." And he was off.

Reagan had her bow ready and edged out of the security room and into the hall. She still heard voices in the conference room, so she went toward the library, walking slowly and quietly but with purpose. She heard voices around the corner and ducked into a hall closet, closing the door carefully. As the voices passed, she heard them mentioning her. They headed to the security room, so she knew she would not have much time once they discovered the impaled soldier.

After they passed, she slipped out and continued to the library. Poking her head around the corner, she quickly entered, walked to the mantel, and reached behind a buddha to find the necklace. She grabbed it and stuffed it inside her shorts. *Now to get out of here.* She moved down the hall and stepped over the slumped body of Bobby to exit the building.

Feeling more exposed, she laid down in the muck and crawled, holding the bow in her right hand with the quiver slung over her left shoulder. She crawled slowly to the guard gate and found Forrester, lying in a pool of blood. She placed the bow and quiver on him, kissed him on the cheek, and ran to the trees lining the long approaching road to take her north toward her family and Chris. She hoped to meet him at the car he was going to leave on Av. Kukulcan. Standing by a white oak, partially shielding her from the rain, she removed the remote for the three Mercedes and found the "Start 4" button.

"It's been fun," she said aloud, and as she pressed the button, the ground exploded underneath the compound and within ten seconds, the entire compound had collapsed into a heap of metal, wood, and rock. In the midst of the wettest storms Quintana Roo had witnessed, flames licked at the wreckage to extinguish any remnant of evil. Reagan smiled.

She searched for Chris's car and heard a helicopter on the other side of the wreckage. It lifted up like the dragoon queen out of the ashes and took a southern cant, then looped back toward her. She hid behind a tree trunk. Sabbi was at the controls.

That lucky bitch.

One hundred yards past her, it exploded in a ball of fire and crashed into the woods.

CHAPTER 41

Raul sat in Sabbi's living room. "We know a lot more about the deceased Sabrina Chavez-Escano now that we have interviewed her business partner and financier, an Ephraim Ben-David. When she returned from Boston this last time, she met with her board here, along with Ben-David. They have been using satellite technology to create past images of an object. You know when you use Google Earth to see your house?"

"You can do that?" asked Rocky, lifting his eyebrows to show his sincerity.

"Yes. You usually see a past image, not the current one, so they have been using this technology to see an object that has been destroyed or damaged in some way and were able to see the object before it was damaged. Is this clear so far?"

"I'm good," said Reagan, although she was the only one.

"So, they had harnessed a new 4D imaging system developed by Goolldwatzen, Inc. that could reproduce the destroyed item using new 4D printing with incredible speed. It could print objects as much as seventy times faster than any other system. In 2016, they crushed a thimble and printed an exact replica in eighty-nine seconds. Their initiatives have grown over the last three years, although not without failures, notably the recreation of human organs. A flip-flop took about three minutes, a lounge chair forty-five minutes, and a wave runner just a little over an hour. The *Angelina*? That took about six hours.

"Sabbi miscalculated in functionality. Yes, you can recreate a flip-flop, but will it withstand miles of walking? You can reproduce a lounge chair, but will it hold anyone over fifty pounds? The *Angelina looked* the same but didn't function the same."

"Was there anything left of her after the crash?" asked Reagan.

"Nothing we could identify. We're taking your word that it was her at the controls. Most of their work over the last twelve months has involved 4D stitching," Raul continued. "Repair, rather than reproduction, had proven to be more of a challenge, but with the first repair of a broken coffee mug, they christened their new technology 4DNS, as it added the time dimension to the process. They used magnetic fields as the stimulus and a patent-pending ink that allowed the seamless stitching. It was into this environment that Ms. Chavez-Escano had stepped, having access to capital from the apostles, which was unknown to her brother."

"So, is that how the windows Alpheus shot out at the villa were replaced during the night?" Rocky asked.

"Exactly. It was her villa and they had plenty of images saved from before it was shattered. Same when the villa's landscaping out back was destroyed by the tropical storm. They had been experimenting with this villa for the last few months. It was just more practice."

"But the dead body . . . "

"She also had cleaners. Every project involved these professionals when needed. Of course, they were paid handsomely, and you know the side trips to Boston to see her wife? Just a ruse. She was going to Boston to deflect attention away from her. She rightfully assumed we wouldn't pay close attention to her when she was out of the country. Ben-David would meet her there. They hatched a plan to spirit Reagan away and use her to help foretell the future of their new technology, but after further questioning and to gain a measure of immunity, he told us they wanted to also use Reagan on Wall Street so they would no longer have to depend on the twelve."

"I'm just glad this is over," Reagan said. "I'm anxious to get away from Mexico, sad to say."

"After Reagan told me about Kara," said Carlisle, "I had the guys run every piece of cartel undercover data they could, and we have no one who was either named Kara Wilder or used it as a pseudonym."

"But why did she switch the name of the British Open winner if she wasn't CIA?" Chris asked.

"Women can be complicated," Raul said. Carlisle snorted and Shelly frowned at him. "From my interviews of survivors, which were sparse, considering Sabbi's elimination of the Silva clan and then Reagan's clean up, opinions have varied. There were some boat captains, folks in town, and I even talked to Alpheus over there who helped fill in some blanks for me. I also spoke with some FBI agents who were called in to sort things out. Some say she knew Lowry would win, and she was trying to make sure the bet was placed correctly for him to win. Others say they had a lover's quarrel, and she was trying to get back at him. Still others say she felt like he was going to take the two hundred and fifty million in winnings and leave her. This makes the most sense to me, but I suppose we'll never know." No one knew about the tip Sabbi gave him for the golf tournament. He had put ten thousand on Lowry to win and was now considering retirement.

"Inspector!" said Rocky. "Since you told us Sabbi has no heirs, we have a saying in the U.S. Finders keepers, losers' weepers. Let's just say I've found this house and there's no losers to weep. What'ya say?"

Raul smiled. "I'll try to make that happen." Raul asked Reagan, "Have you put the necklace on again?"

"Once. I wanted to see if Chris was in my future."

"And?" asked Rocky.

"That will have to be my secret."

"What are you plans now?" Raul asked.

Carlisle and Shelly waited anxiously for a reply.

"Well, when Chris' shoulder heals—"

"By the way, why didn't you shoot me in my left shoulder anyway? *You know* I bat and throw right-handed."

Reagan smirked. "Anyway, when he heals, we're taking a trip to Fiji. I have some unfinished business."

EPILOGUE

"It's the most magical place in the universe," Reagan had told Chris in preparation for their trip to Fiji. "It takes almost an hour by boat to get there, and you have to time it right to be there at four o'clock. It's called Grand Central Station because that's when the tide's coming in—"

"Hey, let's not mention tide coming in." He bristled.

"Oh, good grief. Anyway, at four o'clock, hundreds of schools of fish line up, ready for dinner. It's like someone rang the dinner bell and they all showed up. They're arranged in schools. Jacks, barracudas, snappers, triggerfish, wrasse, butterflies, anthias, fusiliers, surgeonfish, trevally, and even sharks, and the best view isn't even deep. The ledge where they wait for dinner is at about twenty-five feet, so the lighting is amazing. The tide nutrients bounce off the ledge into the shallow water where they wait. They're so engaged in mealtime that they totally ignore you. It's magnificent."

Chris's shoulder had healed, and he was anxious to spend some time alone with Reagan. They were now in the water and he was ready to witness this most magnificent place in the universe Reagan had soliloquized. She and Jaden used to say this place was what heaven must be like. As they approached the ledge, the schools began to form. She had not exaggerated about the colors . . . beautiful hues of blues, greens, and silvers, with silver flashes as the schools frenetically moved from one strategic position to another. They were like race cars jockeying for position as they entered the final five laps.

They had convinced the dive operator to allow a private trip for them. Reagan might have mentioned she was a travel reporter for Condé Nast. When dinner was over and the schools departed with the waning light, Reagan motioned for Chris to come over to the part of the ledge that had a large piece of brain coral. Behind it were some staghorn coral and a small ledge that formed a recessed area out of sight.

She removed the necklace from her BCD pocket and carefully placed it under the overhang. Then she took a small vase from under her weight belt, removed the top, and sprinkled Jaden's ashes over the necklace. She had negotiated with her parents. Half of his ashes would be sprinkled on the high school baseball diamond back in Argyle, and she would deliver the other half to their favorite dive spot in the world. They hovered there for a few minutes, then bid adieu to Grand Central Station, her brother and best friend, and to a necklace that made the summer of 2019 unforgettable.

ABOUT THE AUTHOR

Kent Smith has authored many scientific papers, but with the debut of his first novel, *The Unfortunate Gift*, he has transitioned from a medical writer to a fictional author. For 40 years, Kent and his wife, Diana, have dived together. Diving is a family affair, with all four of their daughters certified scuba divers and their eldest granddaughter catching the diving bug. Inspired by the Mayan influence in Tulum, *The Unfortunate Gift* combines Kent's passion for and experience in diving with his love of storytelling. You can learn more about Kent and his books at www.ksmithbooks.com or find him on Instagram or Facebook.